The

The Houseshare

PAT O'BRIEN

Black Lace novels are sexual fantasies.
In real life, make sure you practise safe sex.

First published in 1996 by
Black Lace
332 Ladbroke Grove
London W10 5AH

Typeset by CentraCet Limited, Cambridge
Printed and bound by Mackays of Chatham PLC

ISBN 0 352 33094 5

Chapter One

*T*ine had loved John. She had worshipped his talent, admired his brilliance, and cared for the hurt child in him. The months of mourning with their painful dawns and aching loneliness persisted and, until now, she had thought she would never rise to another happy day.

John had been an artist. His work was a unique blend of delicate, Japanese-style images and surrealistic caricature, planned and designed on a computer, then transferred by hand onto canvas. Their home was hung with them, each room like a shrine. He had been a bear-like man with the talent of an angel and the causticity of the truly disillusioned; and he had loathed his public. The discerning had clamoured to buy his pictures. Every year his price would rise and he would snort contemptuously at the bank statement, then sit before his computer and dash off another blueprint. He had been a cynical man who created achingly beautiful works to what he called his 'hackneyed formula'.

Grief had left Tine during the night; a fickle, restless lover. She knew of its departure when, for the first night in eight months, she had slept through the panic hours and woke to bright-gold fingers fussing at dust motes through the bedroom curtains. A feeling of well-being

1

crept over her, an awareness of life and relief like waking after a bad dream.

Ten years of marriage had left John and Tine childless, comfortable and cranky. The large Edwardian townhouse, since John's death the previous winter, allowed isolation. Each day Tine had risen and toured the house, pausing before his art, his favourite chair and bookshelves crammed with much-read books. This new day saw her regular circuit. Perhaps her pauses were a little longer, but it was in farewell to John. The rooms chided at her neglect and, despite the summer's heat, were musky, dust-laden and dim, their drapes not drawn for months.

'This is the first day of the rest of my life,' she murmured, and suddenly felt overwhelmed with pleasure at the idea.

In the heat she had slept naked and now, hugging herself tightly she felt discomfort, the perspiration sticky on her back and her breasts crushed and sore. She deliberately relaxed her folded arms, eased her shoulders downwards and shook her hands loosely at her sides. A sense of ease, the tension flowing from her, strengthened a growing resolve. She would start afresh, clean this house, and live again.

Tine moved into the lounge, daylight barred by heavy curtains. She sank into a cushioned seat, thrilling to the embrace of the chocolate-coloured velvet. She had loved to view John sprawled in this chair, watching the large man with muscular thighs and hands which appeared more suited to the local butcher than to an artist. With the curtains opened wide to the busy day and main street he would watch life; perceiving pedestrians as outlines shifting in front of a bright, swifter-moving background of cars, then superimposing the combination of movements against the backdrop of still trees, lending colour with their load of pastel blooms, dark pods and rampant greens. His art had often reflected his abstraction of these moments.

Tine tried to picture herself as another would see her.

2

At forty, she was attractive; petite with hips still smooth. Her chestnut hair hung, shining like a seal's coat over her shoulders. Her breasts were small and refused to droop, her areolae brown tears.

Now, as she recalled the past, she found her hand had strayed. She was wet, her fingers gently stroking between her parted thighs. She took her clitoris between taut fingers and pinched softly and repeatedly. Soon her palm settled hard on her mound and she pressed herself to sudden orgasm. It was mute but, as she had not thought of intimacy at all in the last months, it was a warm and alive gift. The velvet seat seemed to hug her kindly.

She sat thinking until thirst drove her from her nest. She had decided what she was going to do. A parade of options had marched before her. Most had been spurned, such as selling the house or finding employment. John's estate left her well provided for and had supported her eight-month hermitage, with the same comfort in view for some time. It would not last indefinitely, however, and needed a supplement.

The decision was simple. Tine would share the large house; thus finding companionship or at least filling silent places. She would secure an income and resume her life. Her abiding passion, prior to John's death, rested quietly in her study. She went there, cup in hand and, leaning on the frame of the open door, gazed into the room. It was a mess. She had not entered it in six months and the room seemed silently accusing, the computer screen blankly reserved. When John worked in his office downstairs, Tine had played here, exploring the Internet.

She had spent endless hours on Internet Relay Chat, known to its users as IRC, engaging in typed conversations with like-minded people all over the world. She never lost her awe of the way that the group came together like a tide, from all over Europe, Australia, America, and Africa. It was an international cocktail party, at first frightening, then familiar. She had shared their everyday recital of hopes, habits and experiences.

They had been her best friends and, in some cases, her lovers.

During her mourning, Tine's rare forays from home had led her to supermarkets, the bank and post office. The lawyers came to her, as did John's friends. Like her, he had few, and it dawned on her how insular their life together had been. Perhaps they had thought they would be together forever and no other person need pierce their lives. Now she looked forward to re-establishing her friendships in far-flung places, sharing care and laughter. There would also be people in the house; tenants who would mount the stairs noisily, play unfamiliar music and set the volume on their televisions too loud. She would hear them in the kitchen, meet them in the hallway and on the landing, exchange smiles and pleasantries. Perhaps on warm evenings they would share a bottle of wine with her on the patio.

Tine's resolve was warm while she showered and dressed. She stood before the large bathroom mirror for some time, critically examining herself. Her hair was unkempt but strangely luxurious, its chestnut fall a sensual cascade to her mid-back. She had lost weight and looked waif-like, her face too thin and eyes too large. In the shower she felt her ribs, the sharpness of her pelvic bone, circled a thin wrist with her fingers. She would fill out again, she determined as she dressed.

Time had become a remote thing but, with her new awareness, she slipped a watch onto her wrist. As she had not worn one for so long, the unaccustomed weight felt intrusive, and she had to telephone the speaking clock to set it. When she exited her room, she knew it was midday. The afternoon was a flurry. She posted advertisements in the local morning and evening newspapers, looking for housesharers.

Professional person to share large, detached town house. All rooms with *en suite* bathrooms. All mod

4

cons, convenient to the city. Shared kitchen and laundry facilities.

It would appear on Friday and Saturday, which would allow her a day to restore the house to cleanliness; prepare for sharing. Tine had never lodged anywhere, or shared a house with strangers and it never occurred to her that, as a widow alone, she was vulnerable. The first intimation had come from the telephone sales girl at the newspaper when she phoned in the advertisement. Tine, in designing the advertisement, had written that prospective housesharers should call her, giving her name. The girl advised that she should not do that, since cranks might pick up on it and harass her. She advised Tine to just give a telephone number. Tine felt absurdly grateful.

She went first to the misnamed 'attic room'. In truth it crouched comfortably in the eaves, brightness flooding through sloping windows, and comprised a generous lounge, double bedroom and large *en suite* bathroom with a small seat-tub, shower, bidet and basin. In pale yellow, the room was cheery. It led through to the French-blue pile of the bedroom carpet; John's sketches adorning white walls braced with dark beams. The lounge walls were covered in a flowery, Liberty-print style wallpaper, the furniture sculptured from pale cane and the floors clad with light, highly-polished board. There was an old mahogany desk, huge and heavy, with carved feet, deep drawers and secret cubby-holes. Before her study was complete Tine had worked at this desk, the massive space easily accommodating the computer, in front of which she had spent hours curled in the creaking leather seat.

These rooms were dear to Tine and she had considered them her private space. It was a place for pondering, leisurely afternoons spent reading and enjoying music. The sound system spread throughout the house. On music days Prokofiev or Shostakovich, Mozart and Tchaikovsky would seep through all the rooms, rising fantastically up the stairwells and lifting her heart. Remembering this, she raced downstairs, inserted Prokofiev's *Love of Three Oranges* into the CD player and dashed up to the attic amid the soaring score.

She cleaned the attic first, leaving it smelling of lemon and pine, with gleaming tiles and boards. She worked her way down the stairs, with their mahogany banisters, maroon carpets and pale walls. Two other rooms were cleaned and polished. The one on the rear of the first floor, facing west, Tine thought of as a fun room with whimsical violet and patchwork decor, black ash furniture and wrought-iron bedstead. The *en suite* shower-room was adequate. She had named it the 'purple room'. The other room was massively wooden; teak and bright greens, etched glass. This 'green room' did not have an adjoining shower-room but was conveniently adjacent to the bathroom.

The bathroom itself was huge and lofty, the porcelain bath on claws and pedestal, the toilet ornate with an old-fashioned chain-and-tassel pull. John's best picture was in this room, an abstract representing a day they had made love in the chair downstairs. He had unveiled it, tugging a silk shroud from it with a string, as they sat in the huge bath, drinking champagne from thin crystal flutes.

The wall beside the huge tub was entirely covered in amber mirror glass. The room's light could be dimmed and love-making was reflected in warm, gold tones. That night, she had perched on the wide rim of the bath, her thighs wide, feet balancing on the bath sides. His mouth had quested, at first gentle then firm and demanding, until she shuddered and spilled her warm juices. He doused his nose, cheeks and forehead with her sweet liquor which she then lapped, cleaning his face like an eager puppy. Then, while he knelt, she eased down and took him in her mouth, working his sac in gentle hands and seeking his anal pucker with a curious, penetrating finger. He had come with force, shooting his bitter-sweet fluid in her throat as she gulped greedily. These memories worked with her as she scrubbed and wiped, with a small smile of tribute to John.

Tine polished John's office last. She had completed the lounge, the elegant dining-room and kitchen, the larder and laundry. The office had already been cleared of his papers. The large computer screen was dark and silent. She knew that much of his unfinished work remained on the machine's hard disk, but she had not backed-up the computer's data nor used it in the last months. Each time she sat in John's chair she felt his presence; his large enfolding arms. Sometimes she had watched him, his back stiff with concentration, his face creased intently as his fingers flew across the keyboard, manoeuvred the mouse, or latterly, the pen. She would massage the tension from his neck.

Now she sat determinedly in his place, switched on the console and pressed the button to fire up the mini-computer. While not wholly comfortable with the power-ful UNIX operating system, Tine knew enough to administer the system at a competent level. Her own machine was linked to John's, the cable which bridged their computers providing their cord while she played in the study and he created his shining art below.

The screen came alive, reeling through file listings and checks; then, pronouncing all in order, the cursor blinked lazily on the command line, awaiting her instructions. She immediately logged on as 'root' so she had total command and could see all the computer's files, including hidden ones or those not created by her. She trawled through John's files and felt no sense of intrusion until she reached deep into his personal directories. These files would ordinarily be hidden from prying eyes but, with the special password, Tine could now see them all.

One directory was labelled 'j_piks', with other sub-directories leading from it, and she felt excited, believing that she had found her late husband's works-in-progress. She could tell from their names that the huge files were all pictures and she started the viewer program, selecting 'janine1.jpg' at random. It unfolded slowly to reveal a tall blonde, tanned to mahogany, sat with wide-apart, elegant legs. Thin to the point of skeletal, she leaned back on straight arms. It was a beach scene. Almost a duplicate, another blonde girl leaned to her, her face buried between her legs. The picture was taken from the rear of the crouching girl. There was a clear view of her muff, and the gleam of a clitoral ring. Pale sand clung to her bum-cheeks and laced her wispy pubic curls.

Tine reeled through more pictures. They were similar, mostly lesbian, and depicted lean, tanned blondes. She felt no repugnance or shock. John had not told her of these pictures or shared them with her, but she realised that he had perhaps needed this space entirely for himself.

She found more photographs in a sub-directory. They were amateur, labelled 'sally1.gif' to 'sally10.gif'. The girl was no more than sixteen, waifishly pretty and shy. She was alone in her various poses, showing her pink labia with a coy smile. It came to Tine slowly that the pictures all displayed backgrounds which were familiar to her. Leafing through more, she recognised the deep, dark velvet sofa in the lounge, the scrubbed wooden butcher's block which commanded centre position in the huge kitchen, and the soft, satin-clad duvet on the water-bed in the master bedroom.

It was obvious John had taken these photographs. This much was revealed in the bathroom pictures. Sally leaned against the mirror, one foot balanced daintily on the bath edge, her fingers easing apart her young, outer lips. John's muted reflection showed in the glass, the camera awkwardly held in one hand. He was naked and sported a huge erection which he held with the other hand, in frozen stroke.

Tine felt no more than curiosity. That night she had, after months of mourning and obsession, genuinely let go of her husband's memories and was determined to remember him with affection. She knew her gentle giant of a man had kept secrets, and she hoped he had felt no remorse but had enjoyed his special young women, and they him.

In another directory she discovered Sheena. Again young but this time dark-skinned, the girl's springing black hair haloed a mischievous grin as she abandoned all pretence of modesty. The young siren cavorted for the camera in an amazing display of splayed limbs, and ingenious employment of an alarmingly large dildo.

There were more: Denise sullen, with flaming red hair (a true redhead); Angela, gypsy-like; and Toronto, hale and athletic. It was only when Tine found Demmy that she felt a sense of shock. The girl was known to her and had been a constant visitor during John's last summer. She was tiny, looking younger than her professed seventeen years. She was an art student and had begged to assist John in any way in order to profit from the experience of working with him. Towards Tine she was shy and respectful, but she had worshipped John, and no more so was this evident than in these pictures. One revealed Demmy's jet curls pulled back into a rough ponytail by John's large hand. The photograph, taken from above, showed the girl's watery blue eyes, as her lips prepared to surround his glans. A glistening drop of pre-cum oozed to her small pink tongue as it touched the flange of skin beneath his bulb. A startlingly clever series of other pictures revealed the prelude to his bursting over her face.

Tine stared. She sat now where John had sat while Demmy had worshipped his cock. He had planned and carefully handled the camera to capture these exquisite moments, observing while he was pleasured by the slavish young woman. Where had Tine been? That summer she had barely been away from home, just visits to the supermarket, the stores in the city, and the bank. The normal humdrum of domestic life. Long sojourns at her computer. Had John risked her discovery to gain these jewels? What truly amazed Tine was not the fact of his lusts and secrets but her reaction. Far from appalled she was violently aroused. She shuddered,

9

closing the viewer, then carefully slid a data-tape into the drive and, selecting the 'j_piks' directory and all its sub-directories, she set the back-up going and went to make herself a cup of tea and a snack.

Effectively the house was ready. It was past midnight and Tine was exhausted, but her mind raced with images of the young girls. She fantasised, while eating, that tiny noises issued from the office. Were she to investigate she would discover her husband, his cock being consumed by the worshipping Demmy. Scenes whipped through her mind at fast-forward until she imagined herself buried between the young girl's thighs, supping eagerly. Her thoughts left her feeling restless and uncomfortably aroused. She had abandoned her snack while her mind strayed. It now seemed unappetising, insufficient to sate her hunger; which was still enormous, but no longer for food.

Tine returned to the computer, slipped the tape from the machine and methodically deleted all the secret pictures from the hard disk. She slotted the tape amongst the many already abandoned on the desk, labelling it 'Work In Progress', then headed to her study where she switched on her own computer and, with a strange excitement, watched the familiar start-up routine until the cursor sat, blinking, at the command line. She started up the graphical user interface, selected her Internet group from the icons displayed, and clicked to connect. She listened with pleasure to the trill and gruff exchange of the modem as her machine linked to the outside world and she entered the electronic chat world.

'Astyr', one of Tine's assumed names when using IRC, was the one she used when she felt naughty, and had been known to only three users. They had been her virtual lovers, with whom she had shared verbal sex across the miles, in whom she had confided and with whom she had fought, wept and laughed. They had been as close to her as any men she had experienced in the flesh. Now, eight months later, she felt they would have

10

grown away and Astyr would be only a fond memory for them. She thought for a moment, then as the machine prompted her for an alias, swiftly typed in 'Astyr'.

She peeked around the well-attended IRC channels, each housing groups of chatting people, then with some trepidation joined what had been her regular group, channel '#midlife'. Tine's chosen nickname in this group had always been 'Leeter', and as 'Astyr' she would be effectively anonymous. It did not matter because she recognised none of the users, and the conversation, once intelligent and caring, now reflected bickering and disenchantment. Formerly a place where she talked with animation to like-minded people, the channel had changed a great deal. There was no reasonable exchange or tolerance and Tine left the channel sadly.

She sat quietly in limbo, staring at her still screen, and missed the 'whispering' she used to enjoy before her long absence. Suddenly words interrupted her nostalgia.

Dickens> hello :-) I hope you don't mind me just whispering to you but you have a lovely name. I am in California, where are you?

Normally Tine would have ignored or rejected this approach, which usually implied a prelude to being sexually harassed. She envisaged an eighteen year-old Californian youth seated at a computer in his university laboratory. Around him would be the clicking of many keyboards. Another lad would be peering over his shoulder, reading his screen. However, the image made up from the colon, dash and close-bracket represented a sideways, smiling face and implied friendliness, with no insult intended. Now, with the strange, tantalising day tugging her libido, she smiled gently and typed back:

Astyr> Hi! Thank you, it is not my real name though ... just a nickname (please keep it that way). I am in UK. What do you do in Calif?

11

Dickens>   Thank you for replying. People have been so rude ... I guess it does sound like I am hitting on you. I am working for a computer company, just a contract.

Astyr>   Aha ... a clever bunny then?

Dickens>   *laugh* ... they think so! May I ask how old you are, what you look like?

Astyr>   Hmmm ... so you are hitting on me then?

Dickens>   I am sorry. It is true, just that I have the place to myself, it is going to be a long night and unless there is an emergency I am at a loss. You have been kind so please tell me to go away if I am bothering you.

Was this true penitence or another game?

Astyr>   Happens I am lonely too, and I have had an arousing day.

Tine wanted to test the waters before committing herself to raunchy conversation in case her new friend turned out to be a damp squib, so she tried to sound available but phrased her words cautiously.

Dickens>   I am at work. It is late and very hot despite the air-conditioning, so I have opened my shirt and loosened my shorts. I am just under six foot, sort of thin and have long, dark hair.

Astyr>   How long?

Dickens>   I can sit on it :)

Astyr>   Oh wow *gasps*. Now I would _love_ to see that flowing over my thighs on a warm Californian night!

Dickens>   You mean while I bury my face in your love hole?

Almost a turn-off but Tine allowed for overseas banality and giggled instead, then found herself imagining

12

her thighs wide-spread with his hair across them in a soft, shifting sweep. Her 'love hole' stirred gently. Keeping to her personal code of honesty she returned:

Astyr> Look, I think it is only fair to tell you I am forty-one. I am petite, long chestnut hair, small breasts ... brown eyes. Some say I am pretty ... whatever that means.

Dickens> Oh fuck! I *love* older women! I am twenty-five. Please, please don't leave me. You sound soooo good. I mean it.

Better. Tine was sure he meant it. She shifted slightly and felt her jeans tug at her crotch. It tingled pleasantly. Prepared by her fantasy, her mind leaped precociously into sensual mode. She decided to go for broke and ease her aching needs, deciding to be candid.

Astyr> Dickens ... I have to tell you that I have been fantasising. I am very aroused and want to enjoy you, but I don't want you to feel depersonalised so please tell me if you feel abused.

Dickens> Oh no – I am thrilled. But you may not want me if you saw me, I am no oil painting although they say I am nicely built and have great buns!

Astyr> I think I would like to kiss those buns <ponders>. Look, would you like to join me privately? I shall make a channel and invite you.

Dickens> Hold me back Elijah!!! Would I? *YES*!

Tine smiled. She brushed her hand over a nipple, pleased to find it perking and sensitive. With a few keystrokes she created her own channel, naming it #glade' and quickly making it secret from prying eyes, then invited Dickens to join. He leapt in swiftly, writing:

13

*Dickens looks deeply into your eyes and smiles broadly.

Dickens> Damn, I am happy to be here! Um, would you tell me what your fantasy was? I would love to know what turns you on!

Tine did, weaving text to portray strong images. Her fingers flew over the keys as her mind raced excitedly. Dickens remained quiet and she imagined his eyes widening as he read his screen, his hands stroking, then drawing more tightly over his proud cock. Perhaps he would lose control and shoot come over his keyboard. As the words flashed on her own screen Tine felt the story come alive and reach into her. She completed her monologue burning and swollen, thighs clenching hard together.

Astyr> I drew Demmy's bum towards me and spread her cheeks. Her pink pudenda were furiously swollen and she moaned ... a stifled sound around John's cock, as I sunk my tongue into her gleaming hole. She came almost immediately. As John spouted he pulled from her and burst gloriously over both her and me. We licked each other clean.

As soon as she finished typing Tine slipped her hand under her waistband, slid forward on her seat and forced her fingers down as far as possible, until they reached her hungry cave. As with the mythical Demmy, she came almost immediately. She heard her own moan, signalling relief and pleasure as her orgasm bore down and around her fingertips. She sat limply for a moment, eased her hand free and then typed once more, her fingers sticky on the keys:

Astyr> I am finished ... in every way :-)
Dickens> Astyr, you are exciting me more than I have ever been before! I never had a woman talk

to me like this. I want to be really with you
– would you be like this if I was?

Astyr>   Yes, I would.

Tine realised she had told the truth. Now, as she sat in
the wane of her excitement she wanted a man with her,
a man sated, with his arms enfolding and the smell of
fresh sweat and after-sex filling her senses. She felt guilty
that she had taken a stranger and perhaps used him, not
asked him any real questions, and laid her rampant
libido bare. Perhaps he felt abused.

Astyr>   Dickens . . . I am sorry.
Dickens> What on earth for?? Look, I have to confess
          that I was wanking as you typed. Hell, I
          could *see* your fantasy! I came.
Astyr>   You are a nice guy, Dickens. *hugs*
Dickens> And you, Astyr, are a profound lady who I
          am proud to know.

They talked late into Dickens's night, which was early
into Tine's day. With the dawn she realised that her
typing dragged and her head was fuzzy with tiredness.
Friday, as it now bloomed into heat, would be demanding. As she made her farewells and logged off, she
determined not to go to sleep; instead she would go
early to the supermarket, then settle in a comfy chair by
the telephone and doze. She felt kindly towards Dickens
and had little doubt that she had made a new friend
who later, at his pace, would become an IRC lover.
Strangely she felt very awake, and presumed that she
had got some kind of sexual second wind.

Her five-year-old Citroen started immediately and
purred happily into action while the car radio informed
her that the blistering heat over the past two weeks was
the hottest since the Second World War. The sky, clear
with the promise of another long, hot day, seemed
brighter than before but she reasoned that she had not

15

bothered to notice for some time. Young girls paraded down the pavement, their slim legs naked, clad in tank-tops and minute shorts. Tine thought of John and the innocent allure of the girls in the pictures.

It gradually dawned on Tine that Demmy's worship of John must have made her terribly vulnerable and open to manipulation. In recompense, she would see if she could trace the girl on the pretext of sorting John's work-in-progress files. She would promise that Demmy could judge the output, and perhaps discover if any of the art was in a saleable state. Meanwhile, Tine could carefully watch the girl to judge her state of mind. These thoughts absorbed her as she parked the car, collected a trolley with wayward wheels and entered the cool of the supermarket.

It was busy. Shoppers in colourful cotton clothes hustled each other for aisle space. There were many students, loud with youthful exuberance, wishing to make their presence felt. Tine found her eyes drawn to the jostling cheeks of the young women's bottoms and the bulges of the men's groins. Her attentions paid off at the wine section where she turned into the aisle just as a heavy-breasted girl, rising from a lower shelf with a bottle of Frascati, drew her hand softly over her companion's already bulging crotch. He took advantage by cupping her breast to help her rise. They stood close together in wicked laughter before they noticed Tine and then did not draw apart. Honouring their moment, she did not stare, simply smiled into the wine-racks to show she thought their actions fun.

Tine bought all the luxury food the supermarket could offer. Smoked salmon, caviar, fillet steaks, and exotic fruit and cheeses. She pulled bottles of Chablis and Chardonnay from the racks, then five bottles of Piper Heidsieck champagne. With the latter she could welcome the new tenants in style.

It felt good to function. To notice people, light, senses and feel the familiar stretch of muscles as she loaded her purchases into her car. Even though she was tired after

16

her night's vigil at the computer, Tine felt the rush of blood at the new stimulation of her senses, to breathe the scents of car fuel, mingle with the bustling shoppers and hear the shouts of youths as they greeted their friends in the street. She tingled at the thought of their limbs moving easily under the scanty clothing, the bold bulge of the young man at the wine-racks and the taut nipple of his generously endowed girlfriend. She wondered about Dickens, imagining him striding, laughing in the car-park; his long, dark hair loose and wind-played.

The house was cool and welcoming, full of cleaning scents, with the kitchen surfaces glistening in the bright day as she stored her booty. She sat at the breakfast bar eating cereal and peering, appalled, at the rear garden. Plants, weeds and grass were rampant. She vaguely recalled opening the door to a young man who claimed to do gardening maintenance. Only two weeks earlier he had pushed a flyer into her hand which she had consigned to a drawer of the tallboy in the hall, along with all her unopened junk mail. She sought and found the advertisement among the heaps of envelopes and, with a sigh, resolved to deal with the pile during the next week.

Jerry the Gardener answered to her first ring and promised to call to view the garden within the next few minutes. This showed Tine two things: he could not be terribly busy; and secondly, he lived close by. Sure enough, he arrived within ten minutes, sporting tousled, sun-bleached hair and creased dungarees. He was deeply tanned, lean under the baggy clothing, his arms wiry.

Tine led him down the alley and into the garden through a wrought-iron gate. The garden looked worse close-up, and she saw him grin with delight. After agreeing terms, he made it clear he wanted to launch straight into work. It seemed that he was able to communicate better with plants than people, as he responded to Tine in monosyllables, yet muttered happily to himself

17

as he examined the garden tools in the garage. The air was shortly filled with the first cough of the lawnmower and then the drone as long grass was tamed by the blades.

Tine watched Jerry's progress from her vantage point at the breakfast bar in the kitchen. He had shed his overalls and now sported a pair of abbreviated shorts. His arms bunched with the effort of moving the mower over the neglected lawn and his back ran with sweat. She imagined taking him a glass of cold water. While he drank, she would lick along his spine, sipping from the small, salty rivers. So powerful was this thought that she had found a glass and opened the refrigerator door before she was saved by the strident demand of the telephone. She jumped, almost dropping the glass, and felt relieved. She might be feeling alarmingly rampant, but she simply could not race into embarrassing rejections by young men.

Only two people phoned in response to the advertisement that day, but both arranged to visit and view the accommodation. The first introduced herself as Sharon, a customer liaison officer with National Telecommunications. Her accent was home-counties and refined, and Tine found herself cynically applying the adjective 'Sloane'. She would arrive straight from work at six o'clock. As she replaced the receiver Tine felt a little awed. Sharon sounded decidedly confident, a go-getting manager type, who was no doubt thoroughly proficient and bossy. It was the second caller who intrigued and annoyed her. Offering no preliminary greeting, the rich Australian accent blasted down the line, causing Tine to hold the receiver an inch from her ear:

'You've a room advertised.'

What could she say? This was a statement of fact, not a question. She paused for a moment, but he continued:

'When can I see it?' Ah, that was safer. She affected an exaggerated politeness as she gave the address, then asked:

18

'When is convenient for you?'

'Tonight at eight o'clock.' He banged down his receiver. The rich, lazy vowels rang in her ear for some seconds.

She felt sorry she had not rejected him, he sounded curt and unlikeable. Nor had he left a name or bothered to ask about the accommodation. He also sounded young. She had advertised for professionals, imagining suit-clad thirty-somethings, not youths with no manners. She stamped into the kitchen, encountering Jerry who had completed his ministrations. The garden looked fresh-shaven, brown and forlorn.

'It needs serious watering – hot, you know,' he muttered. 'That's four hours.'

'Did you fetch a drink?' Tine felt aghast. Jerry had laboured, sweating for four hours without liquid.

'Nope.'

She wondered how she encountered the abrupt men as she raced to get him a glass of cold spring water. He downed it and poured himself another, which disappeared as swiftly.

'Good, that!' He surprised her with a wide grin.

'Help yourself to drinks in future, okay?' She resented having to sound like his mother. 'Keep the garage key to get to the equipment – it's a spare. When are you coming again?'

'I'm not finished yet – I'm going to water now. I'll do that each day until there's a hose-pipe ban, then I'll use a bucket. I'll be back tomorrow. You need stuff like lawn-feed, although it's a bit late in the season to do that. I can get it for you; it'll only cost about £30.00 for everything because I get it cheap. You owe me £20.00 so far. Thanks for the drink.'

Tine gazed mutely at him during this sudden deluge of words. He stood almost naked before her, glazed with sweat. His stomach fluttered as he punctuated his words with quick breaths. He was rangy, long-legged and smelled of fresh, hard labour. His pale blue eyes, surrounded with sun-lines, fixed on her breasts as he spoke,

19

and she felt her nipples harden under his stare. He shifted in appreciation to study her zipper. She suspected he was not even really aware of her and felt relieved not to have attempted her cold-water fantasy.

'A cheque will do,' he added.

He watched her bottom as she leaned to write the cheque. Time would show if he was ripping her off but, after his massive effort so far, it seemed he was genuinely involved with his work. She gave an unnecessary wiggle to entertain him, and deliberately pushed her small breasts forward as she rose to hand him the slip of paper. He rewarded her with a slight widening of his eyes and quick glance at her face. Tine kept her expression neutral although she smiled politely. Then he was gone. She peeked out the window and, with satisfaction, noted that one hand was clasped absently to his genitals whilst the other held the gushing hose.

Tine moved the telephone set to a socket in the lounge and stretched the long cord so it would lie beside the sofa. The labour of the previous afternoon, her reawakened sensuality and the night's excitement with Dickens finally buried her in sleep. It was evening when the door-chimes penetrated her senses then drew her, alarmed, to her feet in sudden waking. She was tousled and disoriented as she opened the door to face her first housesharer.

Chapter Two

A car was parked at the far end of the gravelled yard in front of the house, two hundred feet from the door. A silver Porsche, its strange lines softened in the overhang of a heavy-blossomed pink floribunda. There was no one in it. The evening heat, although abating, was still intense and Tine felt the cool of the house leaking around her in the open doorway. Still sleepy after her afternoon nap, she stepped reluctantly onto the porch and peered around the columns, disconcerted that the owner of such flashy metal would desert it in a stranger's driveway. The main road which fronted the property was alive with traffic, office workers and students ending their day of endeavour and rushing home in bad-tempered acceleration. Its noise was intrusive after the lofty silence within the triple-glazed house. When a cultured voice rose above it, Tine's puzzlement changed to alarm as she registered that its owner stood behind her, inside the house.

'It's not mine, you know.'

The two women faced each other. Tine, ruffled from sleep, anger replacing the shock of the intrusion, registered bare impressions. The slim stranger, taller than her, stood calmly under her scrutiny. Her hair was dark blonde and carefully drawn back to expose a high forehead etched with fine, arching eyebrows. Her eyes were startling, violet-blue slants outlined with fine lashes. They held Tine's gaze steadily, returning the appraisal.

'The back door is open. I was looking around because the door wasn't answered.'

'I was sleeping.' Tine transferred her annoyance to Jerry, realising that anyone could have entered while she slept. The door to the kitchen was not at the back of the house, but a side door from the drive. When she was in the rear garden Tine made a point of ensuring it was locked because she could not see it from the patio.

'There's a guy watering your back garden. He did not see me.'

'He's still there?' It struck Tine that in the absence of a response from the front door, the woman would have surely approached the gardener rather than intrude. The feeling was uncomfortable. 'He has been doing that for an hour!' She suspected she should investigate but was strangely reluctant to pass the woman in the hallway.

'I am sorry, I didn't mean to startle you. I am Sharon; I phoned earlier.' The woman moved aside as if suddenly aware she had transgressed and, now supplicatory, conceded the space for Tine to pass.

Sharon had presence. Her white linen suit, tailored to severity, emphasised broad, swimmer's shoulders tapering to mannish hips although her breasts seemed generous. Her slim calves were sculpted, muscles taut to cope with high-heeled court shoes. Tine felt disadvantaged by comparison, with her crumpled oversized T-shirt, and leggings. Her bare feet caused her to stand at least six inches shorter than Sharon and she felt like a pure slob. She cautioned herself to be wary of first impressions and indicated that Sharon should precede her down the hall and into the kitchen, which lay directly ahead.

'Coffee,' she muttered absently, watching the minute sway of Sharon's hips, the buttocks barely pushing at the skirt. The woman seemed severely repressed when compared with the students at the supermarket. A little stand-offish, beautiful, but with a 'keep your distance' demeanour which repulsed Tine. She was disappointed, and suddenly had a flash of a parade of likely house-sharers to be interviewed before the house settled into companionability. She felt dispirited as she poured freshly brewed coffee from the jug into large, colourful mugs. Jerry was visible through the window. He appeared to be doing something complicated with chicken wire and grass; making a bowl. Two finished articles lay nearby which Tine recognised as the basics of hanging baskets. Still slightly annoyed, she wished he would realise the time and go home.

Sipping her coffee, Sharon was aware that she had transgressed. Unlike Tine she had formed a favourable opinion, drawn to the sleepy-child appearance of the older woman, and wished to appease the natural annoyance which shone in those honest brown eyes. Tine could not know how important this meeting was to her, and it was crucial for the younger woman to make peace. Sharon felt sure that they would be friends, whatever their contrasts, and the brief glimpse of the house assured her that this houseshare would not simply be a new berth in a long line of short accommodations. There was a sense of home-feeling in the house which attracted her.

She decided to be honest. Although small, Tine struck Sharon as having a powerful presence, if only because her instincts seemed alert and it showed in her intelligent face. Whilst musing, Sharon had absently removed her shoes and slid onto a stool by the breakfast bar, her legs straight, feet resting on the parquet. The cool seeped from the polished floor into her stockinged feet. She longed to discard her jacket. The day had been a hot rush of customer frenzy and, while outwardly calm, she felt a damp irritation under the fabric. She envied Tine in her loose, crumpled comfort.

As if clairvoyant, Tine said, 'Make yourself comfortable.'

This, accompanied by a small smile, delighted Sharon who relaxed with a grin.

'I usually change straight after work.' She didn't add that this was exactly the reason her current landlady was evicting her, as she set about divesting herself of garments. Tine watched, initially with equanimity then with growing surprise.

Sharon tugged the clasps from her hair which, loosed from restraint, cascaded thickly like fresh buttermilk to her shoulders, resettling in soft waves at a swift toss of her head. She groaned with pleasure as she massaged the back of her neck, then rolled her shoulders, leaning back to expose a length of swan-like neck. Far from simply freeing her hair, Sharon appeared to be dropping a persona. She glowed with pleasure, her eyes shut softly and her wide mouth lifted at the corners as she sighed. When she looked back at Tine, a friendliness shone through. This was the first intimation Tine received that Sharon's work was what restrained her, not the woman's own barriers. She took time to admire Sharon. It did not feel intimate, rather more objective, as if she were peering through other, male, eyes.

'That is the nicest thing that happens every day!' Sharon laughed.

Tine averted her head, sipping at the coffee, and tried to imagine sharing many cups with Sharon. She found it difficult and decided the other woman would feel more comfortable with men. Tine felt oddly lonely. When she looked up Sharon was peeling her stockings from her calves and urging them over her ankles. They fell in a silky, silent drift to join her discarded shoes.

With a swift, clever manoeuvre she slipped her fingers beneath the waistband of her skirt, tugged slightly and produced a lacy suspender belt which she unclasped and dropped unceremoniously on the pile on the floor. Her jacket was similarly despatched and she stretched luxuriously, rising from the stool to release her skirt. It flowed smoothly over her hips and legs to crumple in a puddle of cloth around her feet. The only garments which remained were a silky, lace-edged camisole top and French knickers. It was apparent that she wore no other undergarment; her areolae were mute stains under the fabric and a relief of lacy, pale hair embossed the vee of the crotch.

There was no suggestion of seduction in Sharon's manner, simply a sense of relaxation. She had taken Tine very literally and made herself comfortable. Now she sat on the stool, hooked an ankle under her thigh and leaned happily to her cup. The action seemed so terribly normal that it took an effort for Tine to appreciate that a perfect stranger now sat in her kitchen wearing merely wisps of undergarments and some understated jewellery. She credited Sharon, now looking more like a model in a mail-order catalogue, with a naturalness she envied. The woman was transformed, her eyes now more blue than violet as she peered at Tine in friendly interrogation.

'I expect you want to know about me,' Sharon said. 'At the moment I have a bed-sit in a house ten minutes from here, but I have to leave.'

Tine learned that Sharon had come into conflict with her current landlady, their philosophical differences were unresolvable, and her propensity for discarding her work-clothes in heaps had created mountainous problems. She hinted that the husband of the house wished for far more than a peek at her unfolding curves and had allegedly been caught with his nose buried deep in the crumpled silk of Sharon's discarded stockings.

'He was a sniffer!'

Sharon's exclamation made Tine chuckle. It implied there was no complicity on Sharon's part, and the fault lay with a man with a fetish unacceptable to his jealous wife. In response to the laughter, Sharon smiled apologetically. Tine decided in that moment that Sharon was the most beautiful and probably the most naughty woman she had ever met. The image of the husband with his face buried in Sharon's stockings, breathing

25

deeply to capture her day's scents of exertion, was deliciously disturbing.

'The Porsche belongs to a friend. He is away for a while and lets me use it,' Sharon mentioned.

A rich friend, thought Tine, and a close one. She conjured an image of a film star look-alike tossing the car-keys negligently at the almost-naked Sharon. 'Use it,' he would smile and set off on great adventures, returning months later with a deep tan and a sated, slightly dangerous expression. Their reunion would be steamy and full of new experiences.

Tine recognised the danger of her dreamworld, especially as her eyes met those of Sharon. A message passed in a moment of caught breaths. We know each other! Tine's thoughts raced on. There was a fundamental sense of recognition, despite the differences between them. It seemed a scorching moment of certainty, leading to the realisation that, whatever happened from that moment on, they need not fear ill-judgement. She anticipated that they would perhaps be uneasy conspirators at first, but definitely friends. A small silence preceded her words:

'Would you like to see the house?'

In that query, and Sharon's eager assent, lay the host of permissions each needed to continue. Tine had invited Sharon into her space and her home; the latter accepted unconditionally.

Tine led Sharon to the green room, the one which had no *en suite* bathroom. With its curtains open to the bright evening, the room gently glowed. Sharon's reflection was caught in the etched glass of the full-length mirror opposite the bed. She thought she had become jaded to simple feelings, her life in constant combat, but the joy of feeling at home once more seeped through, with a promise of starting again. She saw herself, her feet bare and buried in the thick, dark pile of the carpet and, recognising the delight in her expression, murmured:

'I don't need to see the other bedrooms. This is my room.'

It did not escape Sharon's notice that Tine swiftly averted her eyes in inner exploration; she was tuned to observe. While some seemed shocked by the overtness of Sharon's sensuality, she sensed, in the blush of Tine's thoughts, an empathy. There was an excitement in her which led to the hope that the next few months would yield the pleasure of complicity. This house would become her sanctuary, and Tine a friend and confidante.

She felt slightly uncomfortable with imaginings, being given to a far more practical nature, but something felt inescapably right and she caught Tine in a swift, friendly hug.

'This is going to be great.' Her laughter rang free and Tine smiled delightedly with the sound and its echo through the long-quiet house.

Sharon was silent when introduced to the bathroom. It was sheer magic to her, heightened by the fact that she would not be sharing it with the other tenants. The heat of summer was still extreme and the thought of a long, cool soak in the oversized tub was entrancing. She perched on the edge of the bath and gazed at John's painting without comment.

Although it seemed intrusive, they sat in there and discussed practicalities, reaching agreement on rent, keys and sharing the facilities of the kitchen. Sharon could move in the next day and would be settled before the start of her next working week. One question remained, which she felt was academic.

'What's your view on men?'

'Is that a philosophical question?' Tine was teasing, then contrite. 'This is your home, to use as you wish.' She paused, then added with a smile, 'I insist on it!'

The last barrier breached, the women linked arms companionably and descended to the kitchen. Jerry sat at the breakfast bar, drinking water, a silk stocking

27

twisted loosely in his appreciative fingers. He dropped it, embarrassed, under Sharon's mock-stern glare.

Jerry raked Sharon with narrowed, pale intensity. It was clear from his expression he was dumbfounded, and Tine surmised that he had little prior closeness to such beauty. He did not hold up well, but Sharon transformed. She eased forward, bent over slowly and lifted her clothes from the floor at Jerry's feet. As she rose, her hair stayed curved over one planed cheek. She remained just a couple of feet from the spellbound man, her sultry eyes direct, lips pouting as she murmured, 'It is so hot!' She placed the garments on the surface of the breakfast bar.

Tine was as fascinated as Jerry, watching wide-eyed at the sudden predator in Sharon. She leaned softly against the sink, feeling the cool metal press into her waist. The other woman turned gently and winked at Tine, almost imperceptibly signalling her to stay. Tine realised a game was afoot, but this was outside her experience. She was happy to remain and, in fact, was rooted to the spot. Jerry stared much as, Tine imagined, a frightened rabbit caught in the glare of oncoming headlights would. His eyes followed Sharon as she sashayed across the kitchen to the sink. He watched her hand rest on Tine's hip and gently push her to the side, then turn the faucet and scoop the cold water to her neck.

It soaked through Sharon's camisole top which immediately moulded itself wetly to her breasts, making the material transparent. As she turned back to face Jerry, her nipples were hard buttons. His eyes held fast to them and did not veer even when Sharon plucked the wet fabric loose. Some of the water had splashed onto her knickers and she flicked her palm over them, brushing the worst from the material and drawing his stare to her flat stomach. She left her hand lying softly against her thigh.

It seemed that Jerry could not take in all the sights. His gaze focused swiftly on Tine, glossed over the discarded clothes on the bar, returned to Sharon and swept down her to her bare feet. His head swivelled almost comically but Sharon's expression remained deadpan. It dawned on Tine that the woman was serious. A sudden devilish urge leapt in her, and she placed her fingers gently in the small of Sharon's back to urge her from the sink.

If Sharon was startled she did not show it, but she was immediately aware of Tine's complicity. She read in the action the willingness to see her carry through the scene she had provoked. Whether Tine knew it or not, Sharon now understood that the petite woman at her side wanted to watch, whatever might happen. She heard Tine's breath quicken and felt the gentle insistence of the fingers trying to press her forward. They exchanged a look, brown eyes wide to the slanted, violet irises. With that glance they both relaxed, recognising that Tine's voyeurism was a perfect foil for Sharon's exhibitionism. It was enough. With exquisite skill Sharon eased the atmosphere and, walking lightly back to Jerry, perched on the stool facing him, to start a soft conversation.

That he was the gardener delighted her, as it meant he would not be in constant attendance in the house. She could enjoy him on a part-time basis and still feel free to revel in her own space. His eyes told her he would be hers in any way she wished, even though he attempted bravado with a practised leer. That he was cute and uncouth was a bonus but the only thing that really mattered to the scene would be Tine, and she had quietly volunteered.

It was almost a relief when the doorbell claimed Tine's attention. She had remained silent and watchful, if frustrated, beside the sink while she forced herself to control her breathing. The two players in front of her conversed, and she watched them lean towards each other. Jerry's hands were nervous in his lap. Sharon started to discard her jewellery, gracefully easing pearl globes from her earlobes, bracelets from her wrists, shedding neckchains and rings. All were consigned to

29

the surface of the bar, and she gently massaged her swollen lobes between soothing fingers under Jerry's entranced gaze.

Tine was flustered when she opened the front door, more so as she stared at the man who stood impatiently on the welcome mat.

Chapter Three

*O*ver the years Tine had been given cause to alter her appreciation of men many times. In maturity she had eased into the understanding that looks were not nearly so important as other attributes. At forty-one, she had decided all that really mattered was between a man's ears; the rest would fall in place favourably or not. It was one thing to fancy a well-turned bottom, another to fondle it. As men watched beautiful women, Tine watched beautiful men, with appreciation and inner enjoyment. When pressed by women friends to describe her ideal man, she floundered.

The person who stood in the doorway was as close to her ideal man as she could hope. His mouth was perfect, although unsmiling. A thin top lip in a straight line, with the merest hint of a cupid's bow, stood atop a generous bottom lip. The flanks of it had been pursed into a curve of disapproval, each side in agreement with the other. Set in the landscape of a square chin with a dimple, Tine found it intensely desirable. With the after-image of Sharon and Jerry in her mind, she found the temptation to run her finger over that mouth very nearly irresistible.

He was tall. Tine, who had been peering upwards to study his mouth, eased her eyes down. He wore a top that must have been a T-shirt at one time but now, its sleeves torn out and edges frayed, it lay over his chest. Its neck was stretched to a degree which allowed dark curls to escape to public view. It sported a faded motto: 'Programmers do it with a dongle', which Tine had to squint to decipher.

The shirt's hem hung loose to the top of cut-off jeans, denim greyed with time and wear, ripped and fraying at the knee. Their owner's legs were muscled, matted and finished at the foot with stained, sockless tennis shoes. Tracing upwards, Tine saw he had crossed his arms over his chest. Strong hands and, she noted with approval, a peculiarly grazed knuckle; the sort sported by fellow nerds accustomed to digging around the sharp edges of computer innards.

When she finally met his eyes, it was with the words:

'You're in computers.'

'Not hard to work that out when it's written on the vest.' He sounded scornful.

'The knuckle.' Tine peered at him. 'You grazed it on the hard drive?'

He seemed taken aback, and paused to study her intently. His eyes were disconcerting: jade green and careful, almost oval and fringed heavily with long, black lashes. On a woman Tine would have suspected too much mascara, on him they merely seemed incongruous. Their effect on her was startling; she felt like wishing to pet a cat although, no matter how enticing the animal, she knew in advance she would be scratched. His hair was looped back in a loose ponytail, the almost-black tendrils escaping untidily around the stubble on his chin.

'Who are you?' she asked.

'Rupe.' The accent was exaggerated with long, lazy vowels. 'I phoned about the room.'

'Rooms,' corrected Tine, 'but one has gone already.'

Behind him she saw a battered van, the paintwork a dull, pitted red. The driver's door still sported grey metal primer. The licence plate betrayed it as eight years old but it looked much more world-weary. Parked as it was, she was able to see through the front windscreen, and the pile of boxes and baggage warned her that he had brought his belongings with him. She guessed he was in his mid-twenties and she felt terribly uncertain, despite his allure, that she wanted him to live with them. As with Sharon, she wanted to know more before she offered him the rooms. It struck her that she was glad to have people already in the house; if she had been alone she would have felt considerably more vulnerable inviting the large man inside the house.

She led Rupe to the kitchen, hoping madly that she would not face an embarrassing scene between Jerry and Sharon. Happily, Jerry had left. Sharon sat sipping coffee, legs crossed demurely, with a studied, innocent expression on her face. Her eyes narrowed as Rupe entered.

'Sharon this is Rupe. He's come about the houseshare. Rupe, Sharon lives here.' Tine enjoyed saying that.

'I see.' Unlike her reaction to Jerry, Sharon's response to Rupe was cool. Rupe glanced dismissively at the beautiful, almost-naked woman and peered at Tine.

'I need to find somewhere to live fast, right?'

It emerged that Rupe had driven from London that afternoon to continue a contract, installing a networked, software-customised system at premises nearby and had to be close for emergencies. He could do most of the programming and software transfer remotely, using his own computers at home. Therefore he needed somewhere that would give him privacy, but not bother him with household demands. The company was paying the bill, and a houseshare seemed to suit his needs better than a flat. He would need the place for six months.

Tine explained that what he needed was a hotel. Meals here were not laid on, the rooms were not serviced and each housesharer would be responsible for their own supplies and expected to look after themselves or any guests they introduced. However, she continued, if he needed privacy then the attic room was perfect, and it already had an extra telephone line installed, which she had used for a modem in the past. She continued to explain the rules of the house, ending up by pointing at, then opening, the refrigerator door. The shelves were empty but for two stocked with her own supplies.

The refrigerator was an American import. Three times the size of most British fridges, it had three doors; two covering freezer shelves and the last, much larger, hiding the cool shelves. There were also cold water and ice dispensers. In the heat of the kitchen Tine stayed in front of the open refrigerator doors, delighting in the cold flow of air. She paused, relieved not to hear her own voice continue rattling out its schoolmarm-like recital of rules.

Tine searched Sharon's face for a clue as to how the other woman felt. She suspected that the blonde woman had not taken to Rupe, and a responsive grimace bore this out. Tine wondered if Sharon was unimpressed by Rupe's lack of attention to her, but decided that it was more likely, in view of Jerry, that he was simply not her type. As Tine looked at him she felt undecided. It was tempting to let the attic to him simply for the security of having it occupied. If he was as solitary as he had indicated, it would not affect the other housesharers much.

A part of her, still admiring his physique, definitely wanted him to stay. If nothing else, he was worth looking at. As they had been talking he had pulled a worn, knotted string from his long hair and now it fell in wayward curls around his shoulders. Clearly not expecting to be served, he had poured himself a mug of coffee and was regarding Tine neutrally over its brim, his green eyes peering from beneath heavy lashes, his hair a dark tumble over his cheeks. Her hands twitched with the urge to brush the hair back from his face. Horrified even as the images rose, she pictured herself gathering the hair tightly, forcing his head back and planting her lips hard on his as she mounted his lap. She felt the crispness of his chest hair on her naked breasts as she swayed against him, the hard mound of him rising to meet her.

Sharon watched Tine with alarm. It was clear to her

that the older woman did not appreciate how much showed in her face, and even clearer that she found the arrogant git attractive. Bearing out Sharon's first negative impression of him, Rupe had proved himself to be a nerd, a breed which she thought of as social misfits with a tendency to undeserved self-worship. The man tinkered with machines for heaven's sake, she thought. It took skill but not godliness. She held the firm opinion that most men were drawn to computers in the first place simply because they didn't know how to interact with real people. She glanced at Rupe and was horrified to note that he was aware of Tine's ill-concealed interest, a small, conceited smirk playing across his mouth. Sharon felt angry and protective but unable to intercede. It was up to Tine to act out her own drama.

As she watched, Tine licked her lips, which were unmistakably swollen, in a gesture that seemed to encourage Rupe's interest. The sensation seemed to reach through to her consciousness and she gave a quick start. To Sharon's delight she came down to earth with a blush.

'I'll . . . ' she rasped, then cleared her throat. 'I'll show you the attic.'

Tine was aware she had given away too much and that Rupe was amused by her interest, but in a condescending way. Was it her age? It hurt to think the young man, now mounting the stairs behind her, had the impression of a lusting landlady. She envisaged a cheap, stereotyped character from a seaside resort, over-rouged, unsuccessfully attempting to lure young men into her parlour. For a moment she did not admire herself much, and determined to keep her distance.

It was three flights of stairs to the attic, two landings and an eternity. She kept her hips as still as climbing would allow, refusing to let Rupe think she would resort to cavorting before him. By the time they reached the upper rooms she realised she need not have bothered. As he poked around the plugs and corners in the lounge, admired the desk and tried the leather swivel chair, there was nothing in his manner to suggest that he even recalled the incident. Their discussion of rent and Rupe's acceptance of Tine's terms were conducted in a distant, almost businesslike tone.

Sharon had crept up the stairs behind them and stood silently in the doorway, approaching only when she was sure Tine had noticed her. She laid a comradely arm across Tine's shoulders, with a quick hug for comfort. Tine was almost teary with gratitude. For the first time in many months she yearned for the warmth of human contact, and now only because she feared she had made herself appear an utter fool. She moved into the shade of Sharon's support like an humiliated adolescent. They left Rupe counting power-sockets and went to Sharon's room.

'I have to go.' Sharon looked at Tine. She had drawn her to sit on the bed and had taken hold of her hands comfortingly. They had been sitting like that and talking for some time.

'I am a fool!'

Sharon laughed merrily and agreed. She seemed so irrepressible that Tine was forced to join in. Female-bonding was new to Tine. They shared a few final bitchy remarks about nerds, and then Tine walked with Sharon to the front door after watching her dress in the kitchen. Her stockings were missing.

'I shall be here early tomorrow,' Sharon promised and lightly kissed Tine's cheek, turned and left with a smile. Tine closed and leaned against the door until she heard the Porsche start. She peered up the stairwell, aware of the strange man pottering around her attic space. For some reason she felt lonely, deciding that at times she was more alone amongst people than on her own.

It was only nine o'clock and the sky would still be light for another hour, although evening was sucking the unbearable heat from the day. She quickly made two sandwiches and opened a bottle of Chablis, pouring two glasses, then lifted the receiver of the house's internal phone system and dialled through to the attic. It was answered immediately and, without pausing for a response, she informed Rupe that a sandwich and glass of wine were on the kitchen table should he want a meal.

The dining-room faced west. Sunshine, now soft with slanting shadows, poured through the glass of the patio doors. Tine unlocked the doors, slid one open on silent casters and carried her snack, the glass and the bottle of wine to perch on the edge of the terrace. The quarried slabs were cool through her leggings and the wine was crisp, the first sip biting sweetly at her throat. It was not long before she refilled and relaxed, the alcohol a buffer to the strangeness of the day.

Jerry had done remarkably well for one day's work. Was it only one day, Tine asked herself with surprise. She brought to mind a clear image of him slightly bent as he pushed the mower, then his wide-eyed expression as he was caught in Sharon's brightness. It seemed that a lifetime had passed. She felt her own smile as she thought of Sharon, accompanied by a small thrill of anticipation. The woman had entered Tine's life only three hours ago, provocative and laughing, yet full of comfort and strange ways. Tine was slightly afraid of the swiftness of all the feelings and impressions in her imagination. She sobered slightly with the thought of Rupe, resolving to learn to reserve her fantasies for private times. She felt exasperated by her own crassness and annoyed that she could not interact with Sharon's ease.

The traffic had faded to a low hum in the distance. At rush hour the rear garden could be noisy but now Tine could hear the birds squabbling in the house's eaves. A cat passed proudly through a distant flower bed, sniffing with nonchalance at a message from a fellow traveller. Tine felt tempted to get a cat herself; she liked their feline humour, the soft vibration of a purr beneath her fingertips and the small solid warmth snuggled against her in the night. As if to thwart her romancing the cat scrabbled at Jerry's fresh-dug earth and squatted with an amused stare, gave a delicate sniff and buried the product.

Rupe walked onto the patio to find Tine chuckling as the cat flounced away, having made its point. She had vaguely noted the sounds of the front door, and his trips up and down the stairwell with baggage from the van. Now he approached quietly to join Tine on the cold stone. He had brought his sandwich and wine and they sat silently, enjoying the cool of the late evening and gazing at the garden.

The roses were a bright cerise splash surrounded by variegated green shrubbery. Elsewhere in the garden the cascading colours almost jarred. Tine was aware it was no showpiece and everything was planted higgledy-piggledy, but that was her choice. She had planted only flowering shrubs, loving the extent of earth they left uncovered. With the generous watering that afternoon, the darkened soil smelled dank and thrilling.

'Thanks.' Rupe's rich tone broke the silence though not the peace. He gestured to the now-empty plate but kept his head averted, sipping his wine.

Tine refilled his glass and her own, realising this was her third. She felt like unravelling her day and decided on a soak in the tub, then she would log onto the Internet and seek Dickens on IRC.

Rupe rose to his feet and shifted self-consciously, his body-language obviously questioning.

'What is it?' Tine felt comfortable in her Chablis-glow and was inclined to be generously minded, but she avoided looking at Rupe directly and settled for continued perusal of the garden.

'Can I pay my deposit now? I want to spend the next couple of hours setting up my stuff. There's someone I have to connect with on the Internet.'

Later on, Tine would congratulate herself that she did not blurt out their mutual interest. She merely nodded and asked which on-line service provider he used. Rupe seemed unsurprised, naming a company more geared to technical than social services. It was not the same one she used and she felt relieved. Subscribers tended to recognise each other's email addresses if they searched, and she preferred to remain anonymous. She decided she would connect at about the same time as Rupe that night, and felt a definite advantage in having more information than he. Unlikely as it seemed, it was possible he would join IRC. Should he so do, she would find him.

They re-entered the house together, Tine pulling the door closed with regret. Rupe produced a battered roll of fifty-pound notes and passed a wad to Tine, which covered a deposit and a month's rent. She would invoice his company in future and they would pay the funds direct to her bank. She made a mental note that she also had to implement a direct debit system for Sharon. It was pleasing that her new companions seemed not to have budget problems.

There was a pile of equipment in the hall. Tine bent in examination and recognised a powerful personal computer and a UNIX workstation. Again she kept quiet and let Rupe believe her impressed but incompetent. She felt this knowledge could work to her advantage at some future stage and, in any event, he was likely to be far more proficient than her. It never served, in her experience, to display computing expertise to a strange nerd, especially if you were female. For some reason it caused angst. She did look with regret at a laptop she would have liked to examine, and a box seemingly full of hand-held computers. Tine simply smiled, stepped over a jumble of strewn cables, and bid Rupe goodnight.

The huge tub in the bathroom was far too long for Tine but she had, from experience, devised a method which let her stretch out fully without the risk of drowning. Leaning back against a bath cushion, she would loop one arm over the rim. This left her other arm free to hold a wine glass, read a book or simply scoop bubbles over her glistening breasts.

She had added essential oils to the water: frankincense,

bergamot and ylang-ylang, along with a generous pour of pine-scented foam-bath. The pungent steam was heady, especially combined with the effects of the wine. She felt detached and sensual, images from the day rising pleasantly in her mind.

She turned to lie on her stomach, feeling the water eddy around her. Gentle currents slipped over her breasts and traced softly between her thighs. She encouraged them by sliding slowly, using her elbows for purchase, her chin cupped in her palms. Now safe, alone in the locked bathroom, she allowed her mind to reach out for Rupe, acknowledging, despite her earlier humiliation, that she craved him. He was not sophisticated. She imagined him sweaty, untangling a myriad of computer cables, lugging a terminal to the mahogany desk and lying underneath it to reach the sockets. Perhaps he would have stripped off his T-shirt and be seated before a console, its glow ghost-like on his naked flesh. The thought of sliding her hand across his chest, pressing against him, aroused her and she cursed her imagination before succumbing to its allure.

Of course, she mused, he would need to wash off the sweat from the long drive and the exertion of lifting the equipment up three flights of stairs. Like her, perhaps he yearned to soak away the day, to mull over the last hours and put scenes in perspective. Tine gave him a sensitivity she was uncertain he possessed, but it suited the purpose of her fantasy. She drifted into the scene, her limbs lethargic and heavy, buoyed up by the warm, fragrant water.

She imagined . . .

Rupe entered the bathroom unprepared for the scene before him. The light was dim, the mirror a dull bronze, reflecting the flame of an aromatic candle. The deep bath, full of glittering bubbles, nearly hid Tine's soft-toned flesh. She lay on her tummy, her chin propped in her palms, eyes closed. Her hair floated with burnished highlights, a silken veil hugging the soft curve of her shoulders. She was moving gently, her hips rising so her bum-cheeks surfaced, globes shining. Her parted thighs allowed the current to trace along her cleft, chasing the bubbles clear. As she lowered herself, the suds closed secretly until her next emergence.

It was apparent to Rupe that Tine was lost in sensation. Her lips moved soundlessly in sweet request, then she whispered as her arousal increased. Rupe fancied she shaped his name and, when he crept closer, was sure of it. The surface rippled softly as her hips once more rose and, unable to resist, Rupe dipped his fingers into the water and traced along the small of Tine's back. She stilled, her bottom a pale island in the suds. He drew his palm over one globe, then trailed his fingers between the cheeks, which parted soapily to allow entrance. Her flesh quivered, which excited him and made him aware of his erection which surged in its denim prison, but he dismissed his own discomfort and reached between Tine's thighs, his fingertips meeting the soft surround of her folds. She was hungry under his hand, whimpering her need and his name. He urged a finger along her cleft, then pressed on the small hood of skin which slid back to reveal her most sensitive nub. He rubbed it softly, and her answering groan undid his resolve. Breathing heavily, he took off his cut-offs with one hand and slid into the bath.

He covered her from the rear, gently forcing her thighs wide and easing between them. His penis throbbed almost painfully as it met Tine's wide demand. Her fluids, diluted with bathwater, failed to lubricate his entry as he pierced through the petals of her flesh. A slight burn thrilled her as he forced past them then stopped, aware of her body's small resistance. He paused, intensely aware of their shared breathing, then focused on his shaft and savoured the anticipation. Tine clenched tightly, her thighs holding him until she pushed back, closing around him with agonising slowness. They both groaned as he inched into her tight cave.

Rupe fucked slowly, fighting his instinct to plunge, and resisted Tine's now wild, almost angry, demand.

His arms were muscular rods supporting his weight above her as his eyes feasted on her glistening movements. She bucked to his teasing rod and he watched himself disappear in her, his shaft burying in her sex; first his tip, then his length expanding in her heat.

Agile, and surprising Rupe with her strength, Tine rose to her knees until he was forced to kneel. The position bent his penis to a painful, downward angle and, to relieve it, he slid his hands under her pelvis and lifted her. She quickly clasped her legs around his waist and stretched forward to grasp the rim of the bath with her hands so that she formed a bridge. Their movement was now totally under his control. He eased back on his heels and stared at their conjunction. The sight was startlingly explicit, his rod half submerged, her starry anal pucker coyly tight. Rupe released her hips, unable to resist tracing its tiny ridges. He pressed for access with his little finger, the exploration drawing small pleas from Tine. His hand curved loosely to brush his shaft.

There was an excited wonder in him, the thrill of being absorbed. He fluttered his fingers against his half-exposed penis to discriminate his own sensation, then with his little finger caught deep in her tight rear passage, he eased its neighbour to lie inside her along his buried shaft. With the space between anus and vagina trapped, he felt the pull on the web between his digits; his surrogate small penis lying inside her along his true length.

Tine kept very still, concentrating on the stretch of her arms, the strength of his thighs bearing hers up, and the tight, hot, multiple invasion. She felt caught, pinioned, and at that moment she wished for more, that another would enter to imprison her nipples; whose prick she could work with her yearning lips.

Rupe slid his other hand from Tine's hip and under her lower belly. His fingers sought and caught her clit. Trapping it between two iron fingers, he cupped his palm over the swollen flesh of her mound and pressed it rhythmically. The insistent knead on her trapped clitoris

42

and the mounting throb of her flesh caused Tine to shudder. Her cave felt fuller as his erection burgeoned in her, rewoken by her movement. He pushed into her, his thumb and forefinger sliding against his root. The pressure on his little finger was intense and the slight pain increased his excitement. He watched its stiff penetration as it rode her arse, and revelled in stroking himself whilst rooted in her.

Three separate sensations rolled with Tine; the sharp external demand on her clitoris almost thwarted by the hard palming of her mound, the yearning of her rear for a more massive impalement, and the relentless double sliding within her corridor. She also sensed Rupe fingering himself. His knuckles pressed into her vulva as he thrust, then rode back when he withdrew. She could feel him building to climax, entering with extra force, and she held her breath for the ride to her own release.

He took longer than she anticipated, although she felt her own roil begin, her legs shoot with thrills and her vaginal walls clench in preparation. Now starving for oxygen, Tine's senses heightened and she felt Rupe bunch before release.

The water erupted around them as Rupe lifted her hips clear of it in the throes of his coming. Her hard-clenching sex-muscles grabbed at him as he gouted inside her and he threw his head back to roar his release. Tine's head expanded in an explosion of light as she fainted, overwhelmed with sensation.

She came to, choking and coughing, and felt dazed as she recognised the ache between her thighs lessening in orgasm. Lost in her fantasy, she had slipped beneath the water and swallowed some. Her throat felt raw, the taste in her mouth unpleasant, soapy and oily. She rolled onto her back and, leaning on the bath cushion, struggled to breath normally. She was alone but caught in the physical sensation of being with someone, feeling the imprint of arms holding her and the heat of a body pressing against her. The door remained securely locked. Her confusion increased as she failed to recall how she had achieved such bliss alone; how intense the reality of her own imaginings had been.

She was rigid with conflict. The certainty of the afterglow of her powerful climax fought against a fearsome hunger, which brought before her the image of Rupe's jade eyes narrowed in glazed lust, and his lips, swollen and pressed together firmly before his release. Tine was thrilled and horrified. She realised that she could not relax until she had conquered Rupe. Her need was paramount and her tool for seduction would be the Internet. No matter how long it took, he would come to her, as wild with want as she.

Tine climbed, shivering, from the tepid water and mopped the floor with towels before drying herself absently. She felt slightly sore and knew she had been rough with herself, but it was not an unpleasant sensation. She was still roused and felt that she could easily come again. In her predatory determination she held onto her arousal; it would be useful to maintain her state of mind as she approached IRC.

Wrapped in a towel sarong she crossed the landing to her study, half-hoping that Rupe would appear on the stairwell. She wondered how loud she had been in her ecstasy, then dismissed it with a shrug. The house, properly built in the late nineteenth century, was well insulated against noise. A small devil in her also whispered that it would be no harm if he had heard her yell with passion, and perhaps it might strike some chord.

Tine slumped before her computer, brought it to life, and connected to IRC as Astyr. Almost at once her screen flashed words at her:

Dickens> There you are! *multiple hugs*
Astyr>   Oho ... have you been hanging around
          waiting for me?
Dickens> Too damn right! :-) Although I confess that I
          also have a prior date with another – are you
          jealous?

Astyr>   Not if you share her! Otherwise yes, I want
             you all for myself :-)
Dickens>   It's a him, actually. Can we meet on #glade?
             I have already created it.

'#glade' was the channel on which Dickens and Astyr
had exchanged confidences the previous night, and it
warmed Tine to think he wanted to make that space
their own. Before joining Dickens there, Tine quickly
asked the computer to identify any users currently
logged onto IRC who were using the on-line provider
which Rupe had named. She did not know what nickname he might use, but none of the dozen responses
seemed likely so she joined #glade.

Dickens>   Took your time :-) That's right, tease me!
Astyr>   It may be worth the wait, honey.
Dickens>   Okay. I have some news: I might be coming
             to the UK! I may be doing a site-check for an
             English subsidiary, and I am trying to get
             extra time for a vacation.
Astyr>   That would be wonderful ... and of course
             'here' is where you will be. Mind you, you
             had better move fast before this house fills
             up completely.

Tine spent the next half-hour briefing Dickens on the
new housesharers. Dickens was charmed by her descrip-
tion of Sharon and demanded great detail. Tine was
careful when describing Rupe. She did not mention his
name, but confessed her yearning for him. Dickens fell
silent for a moment, then:

Dickens>   What is this guy to you, Astyr?
Astyr>   To be honest, I do not really know.
Dickens>   I reckon there is a lot between the lines there,
             sweetie. I wish it was me, but my advice is
             go for it. And, hey, I want ALL the gory

45

	details! I won't get jealous if you share it with me.
Astyr>	Oh I hoped you would say that. You see, he is about your age, and I really need your help with this!
Dickens>	The man is mad if he thinks about age. Does he have a name?
Astyr>	Rupe. He's Australian. I know he uses the Internet but I don't know yet about IRC. I hope he does because I can touch him via this medium, I just know it. I just don't want him to know who I am here ... I mean that I am me in Real Life. Oh, you know what I mean!
Dickens>	And you say he just moved into your house for six months? He's in *your* house and you're gonna seduce him over the Internet???
Astyr>	Yes.

Tine's screen went quiet, no new words appearing. She wondered if Dickens was upset. Previous relationships formed on the Internet had shown her that users shared very real feelings, living the spoken word. She herself had been wounded in electronic love.

She queried Dickens' activity and discovered that he was whispering to another user, person-to-person, just not talking to her.

| Astyr> | You are whispering. |
| | *Astyr sings a little song to herself while waiting. |

Tine again searched the list of IRC users. This time to her shock it yielded to her query, producing a user called 'Rupe' on the provider he had named. She could glean no more unless she interrogated his machine directly, but then he would know she was looking.

Dickens>   Someone wants to join this channel. It is the
            guy I mentioned earlier – I have been talking
            tech with him. I think he may surprise you.
            Just be careful, okay? I think you should
            know I know him well.

Rupe joined the #glade channel. Tine sat shocked. She
had known with sick certainty that the Rupe on IRC had
to be the same Rupe who now sat in her attic, but the
sheer coincidence of his friendship with Dickens seemed
surreal. She found she could not take in the words
appearing on the screen, and something akin to panic
caused the letters to jumble before her. She forced herself
to breathe calmly as Dickens greeted Rupe and introduced Tine as a new friend. Rupe greeted her in turn,
and then launched into a highly technical conversation
with Dickens. She was uncertain how long she had
remained silent, and decided to pretend that she left her
computer for a moment.

            *Astyr is BACK, and reads to see what she
            missed.
Astyr>   Oh! Hi Rupe.
Dickens>   Rehi Astyr. We are just solving AI problems
            here (I think!)
Rupe>   Hi Astyr. Dickens has been telling me what
            a wonderful lady you are.
Astyr>   Why thank you, but I do prefer 'woman'.
Rupe>   *grin* The gender preference or the term? :-)
Astyr>   *groan*! I forgot the ambiguity. I have been
            away from this medium way too long.
            *Astyr slaps Rupe with a Wet Fish[tm]
            *Rupe retaliates with a green jello bomb[not
            tm]

Tine read the screen, amazed at the typical, juvenile
IRC nonsense they were sharing. She began to wonder if
this was really the right Rupe.

Astyr>	Hey wait a minute ... that is not a legitimate bomb, it had no trademark!
	*Rupe looks sheepish
	*Dickens looks stunned
Dickens>	This is not a side of Rupe I have seen before!
	*Rupe grins foolishly ... he is a closet SPOD
Dickens>	What is a SPOD?
Rupe>	Someone who lives their sorry life on this medium. Well, let's just say I've been around :-)
Astyr>	Oh? Tell me more.
Rupe>	Not, young lady – er ... woman – until I know you a helluva lot better!
Astyr>	Less of the young! I am a wrinkly.
Dickens>	*laughs* In all the right places too!
	*Dickens has to go save a 'puter, back in 5!

Dickens left IRC. Tine felt sure that he had not contrived his departure and would be back soon. Rupe seemed relaxed and inclined to chat, and Tine needed the time to establish his real identity. Before she had time to start, Rupe had resumed the traditional IRC banter.

Rupe>	Just us chickens, huh?
Astyr>	Don't call my squirrel a chicken!
Rupe>	Now _that_ can be read in many ways.
	*Astyr blushes
Astyr>	I can see I am going to have to watch myself very carefully around you.
Rupe>	Nah ... I shall do the watching, you just relax on this sofa.
	*Rupe conjures a black leather sofa.
	*Astyr throws herself on the soft cushions and arranges herself elegantly, in order to be watched.
	*Rupe squeezes in at her feet, slips off her shoe and begins a soft massage.
Rupe>	Are you in England, Astyr?

Astyr>	Yes, are you?
Rupe>	Sure. I have just moved into a new house-share. Nice place.

Tine proceeded with caution. She desperately needed to avoid being questioned, as she would feel obliged to answer honestly. Fortunately she was a good listener in real life and had carried her talent into this written environment, and she felt certain she could remain mysterious while she learned a great deal about him.

Astyr>	Are there many of you in the house?
Rupe>	Not so far. Looks like a new thing. Just the landlady, an oddball and me.
Astyr>	An oddball? *grin*
Rupe>	Yup. I walk in and there is this female sat in her knickers in the kitchen. She hasn't even moved in yet and has already tossed her clothes!
Astyr>	Sounds promising, perhaps she'll keep your life SPOD-free.
Rupe>	Not my type ... she would eat me up and spit me out for breakfast. The landlady is strange.
Astyr>	How so?
Rupe>	Well, she is old. No, perhaps mid-thirties, not old ... just older than Oddball and me. But she has this way of looking that makes you feel undressed.
Astyr>	Well it worked on Oddball, didn't it? *grin* Sounds like reverse-roles to me. Guess you must be sexy, huh?
Rupe>	*laugh* ... NO WAY
Astyr>	Perhaps the landlady thinks so ... What is she like?

Tine held her breath. She figured that if you eavesdrop you hear ill of yourself, and this deception felt to her like eavesdropping.

Rupe>	Strange. She looks older but seems young. I mean, she is sort of sexy. I thought about this earlier. She stuck in my mind.
Astyr>	Why not just forget about age? How old are you?
Rupe>	24. It is sort of hard regarding age you know ... she could be older than thirties, I never can judge. She could be old enough to be my mum.
Astyr>	Yeah *evil grin* but she is not. Has she got kids?
Rupe>	Haven't seen any. Perhaps she keeps them in the cellar with the rest of the fish!
Astyr>	Haha! So she is old and sexy :-) What about you?
Rupe>	Not much to tell <glances in mirror>. Long messy hair, I have been told I am built like a brick outhouse ... a slob. Girly green eyes.
Astyr>	Uh-huh. So you are tall and well-built, with dark(?) long curly hair, and have beautiful green eyes?
Rupe>	Hey, you been talking with my mum?
Astyr>	Ah well, Dickens will confirm that I have this 'thing' about long hair on men.
Rupe>	Oh yeah? Tell me about this 'thing'. *Astyr reluctantly pulls her foot from Rupe's massaging hands, kneels on the sofa and leans towards him. She gathers his hair in her hands and plunges her face amongst the curls with a small, delighted groan.
Astyr>	That sort of thing :-)
Rupe>	Oh. How about if I tell you I am very hairy all over?
Astyr>	How about I warn you that talk like that makes me *very* irresponsible? *Rupe gets serious

There was a pause, during which Tine wondered at the direction the conversation had taken. This chatter

50

did not confirm the impression she had received of the dour Rupe upstairs. This one was fun, sexy and friendly. She felt slightly bemused and realised that she liked him. It failed to take the edge from her lust for him, but she realised she did not merely want to provoke an IRC affair; that would depersonalise him, and she did not want that to happen. She also rued her deception. Even after this short time she believed he would be angry when he found out. It was a case of either being honest before things went further, or of never revealing herself.

Dickens jumped back into the channel as Rupe's next words appeared on the screen.

Rupe>   Look, Dickens did tell me about you. I
          reckoned you were some IRC bimbo wan-
          nabe. My swift apology for that. He likes
          you a lot, and he is my mate.
Dickens> Oho!
Rupe>   Oh you bastard! Next time warn me, cobber!
          *Dickens laughs
Dickens> Sorry mate :-) Hey, I'm real pleased you two
          have hit it off! Not bad for a sheila, huh?
          *Astyr glares
Astyr>   When you two have quite finished male-
          bonding . . .
          *Astyr brings out the ropes and handcuffs,
          not to mention The Whip[tm]
Dickens> It was him!
Astyr>   Joking :-) I wouldn't know what to do with
          them. Mind you, I am open to instruction
          grin.
Rupe>   Not that I am a coward or anything but I
          gotta get some work done. I *really* don't
          want to go!
          *Astyr looks indignant and points at her
          other, unmassaged foot.
Dickens> Know the feeling . . . the work, not the foot
          :-) I just deserted a sick T500 to check up on

51

	you two. Astyr, sweetperson ... come to California! *hugs*
Astyr>	What? And leave this reprobate alone to terrorise the UK?
Rupe>	*laugh* I wish! Astyr, it was great meeting you ... soon again.
Astyr>	Bye, guys ... I just _knew_ I had been away too long!

Tine closed the connection. She realised that Rupe was seated at the heavy desk directly above her workstation. She felt like a character in one of those cross-section house illustrations where every resident is visible in their own room, doing their own, disparate thing.

She stretched, hands clasped behind her head, shivering as the damp towel slipped from her. She felt cold and was already exhausted, having had little sleep over the past forty-eight hours. It was not yet midnight but she decided to hug her discoveries in sleep.

In her room, she threw off the towel and pulled on an oversized T-shirt. She brushed her teeth awkwardly because she could not stop grinning. So she was sexy, huh? She recalled Rupe's words: 'She stuck in my mind.' Tine believed she should feel despondent. After all, she had failed to be honest when she could, and now she may have wrecked her chances of seducing Rupe in the real world.

Tine slipped under the satin duvet feeling the gentle rock of the waterbed lull her as she reached to turn off the light. Oddball, she thought with a smile. Sharon's face rose before her, one eye slowly dipping in a lascivious, conspiratorial wink.

Chapter Four

*T*he strident ring of the telephone shattered Tine's dreams early on Saturday morning. She scrambled to reach the receiver on the bedside cabinet, lifting it just as the call was taken by Rupe. She glanced at the bedside clock, which smugly blinked seven o'clock, and cursed Rupe for having anti-social friends.

The elation of the previous night had worn off, and her dreams had left her with a feeling of despair. She struggled to recall the details and remembered a shining, white crescent of beach across which a blurred but unmistakably Rupe-like figure strode. Over the crashing of waves she heard his angry accusation: 'You lied!' She was helpless in the turbulent water, fighting to cross the surf, with her efforts growing more feeble. Without the aid of the man on the shore she would drown and, enraged, he would not help.

Tine was alarmed to feel her eyes blur with tears. The sense of desperation from the dream was still with her. She realised she had to reveal her deception, if only to clear her conscience, but facing Rupe with the truth seemed foolish. He was larger in her imagination than in real life. Still a stranger in her house, he would find a sudden confession alarming. At best he would consider her hysterical.

In the true spirit of denial, she shoved the problem aside for later consideration, and made her way downstairs to collect the milk and orange juice from the front doorstep. As she stooped to gather the bottles a movement crossed her peripheral vision. Tine was reassured by the sight of a jogger passing her front hedge. It was not unusual for joggers to be about early. The air was not yet polluted by the morning traffic and the road, long and straight, was an excellent sprinting mile.

She was, however, surprised when the jogger paused, running on the spot, to peer into the yard. Tall, clad in colourful lycra running shorts and a brief stretch vest, the woman stared for a moment, then ran into the yard. Her skin reminded Tine of roast coffee beans. It shone, partly from a slight sheen of perspiration catching the early sun and also because, Tine realised, the runner's legs were oiled. She resisted the urge to race into the house and slam the door, supposing that the woman might simply want a drink. The day already promised to deliver the now-expected high temperatures of the last two weeks. Jogging, she thought, was synonymous with masochism in this heat. She offered the pint of fresh juice to the jogger with a sympathetic grimace.

The woman accepted the offering with a nod of thanks, eased back the foil cap and tipped the bottle to her lips. She drank deeply, her head thrown back and her dark throat working smoothly in appreciation. Once sated, she wiped her mouth with her hand.

'Well, that puts the kibosh on further running.' Her accent reminded Tine of Rupe, the vowels lazy, but there was a deeper, earthier suggestion. 'Sorry I took so long to get here, but I did run harder when I realised it was further than I thought.'

Tine was totally nonplussed until Rupe's richer vowels issued from the hallway:

'This is Stevie. She phoned about the house.'

Tine turned to find the Australian propping a large box against the radiator in the hall. There was something slightly shamefaced in his expression and his eyes refused to meet hers. Having no time for analysis, Tine returned her attention to the woman on the doorstep, giving her a wry grin.

'Sorry, Stevie. Come in.'

Rupe hefted the box and struggled to the kitchen, followed by the women. Once there he slid it gratefully onto the butcher's block, opened the refrigerator door and started packing its contents on the two top shelves. An array of limp vegetables, fruit and meat passed before Tine's gaze as she set the coffee-maker bubbling.

'Stuff from my previous digs,' explained Rupe, still not looking at Tine. 'I should have unpacked it last night.'

Tine examined Rupe closely. She could not understand his manner, willing to believe that he had somehow traced her identity and realised she had misled him the previous evening on IRC. Had it not been for the presence of Stevie, who stood shaking her limbs to ease her muscles, Tine would have presented Rupe with the truth. She was prepared to be honest rather than to suffer embarrassed avoidance on his part.

Rupe felt guilty. He had come down the stairs shortly after Tine, his progress slowed by the awkwardness of the box he was carrying. As she bent to collect the milk bottles, her T-shirt had risen to display her naked bottom. Her cheeks parted to reveal her quim, its sleepy pink corolla fringed with chestnut-gold curls. Surprised by Stevie, Tine had peered up but not immediately risen and Rupe had drawn closer, shocked and aroused at her involuntary exhibition. His fingers twitched, wishing to trace the cleft between Tine's globes, to draw softly through her ruff and sink into the soft flesh.

At twenty-four, Rupe considered himself woefully inexperienced. He blamed his inability to interact with women on his almost obsessive involvement with computers. Never before had he been granted such an explicit view, except for pornographic magazines which had not prepared him for the reality of the vision, nor for his alarming reaction. He felt his penis rise and shift hungrily. Wearing only the pants of a tracksuit, the loose material tented in betrayal.

Then Tine had moved and her T-shirt once more covered her, depriving his voracious gaze. He felt ashamed and guilty, a peeping Tom. He was relieved that neither of the women seemed to have noted his stare, but that did not ease his embarrassment. He was glad of the box which shielded his erection, and the fact his voice emerged steady, but he could not look Tine in the eye. Though Rupe knew she was ignorant of his voyeurism, he felt he had offended her.

Unfortunately for Rupe, it seemed that Stevie had noticed the wane of his erection and, as charmed as Rupe by Tine's early-morning muss, had misunderstood the situation, presuming an intimacy between the two. Her words betrayed her misunderstanding:

'I am sorry to have disturbed you two.'

Tine swung in sharp surprise to meet Rupe's furious blush. She had noted Rupe's bare chest and the invitation of its mass of thick, dark curls which petered out towards his broad shoulders. From the rear, as she had followed him to the kitchen, she had seen the dark pelt mirrored, though not as enthusiastically, across his back. The unbrushed, thick curls crowning his head was a prelude to the short silk below and the effect startled her senses. She wondered if that of his stomach and groin was as luxurious and the need to know consumed her. His unease, and her presumption of guilt on her part, served merely to keep her off-balance. It had not dented her desire.

Stevie's assumption had exposed their mutual insecurities and, in the shocked, shared look immediately after it, each had perceived but not understood the guilt of the other. Both Rupe and Tine failed to interpret the truth, riddled as they were with misconceptions. Neither had seen the other's culpability or desire.

As Rupe swiftly exited the kitchen in embarrassment,

Tine admired the muscle-play across his back, feeling a sense of loss.

Stevie would have preferred more orange juice to the steaming coffee mug proffered by Tine but nonetheless accepted, feeling her refusal would simply complicate the situation. She watched Tine think, and decided to wait it out. The petite woman seemed distracted by far more than Stevie had witnessed. One thing was obvious to her; both Tine and Rupe were fighting hard to deny their mutual attraction. What confused her was their failure to recognise it in each other. Somehow Stevie's innocent presumption of an existing involvement had triggered a massive over-reaction. She felt it would be intrusive to try to enlighten Tine. Besides, she felt strangely reluctant to intervene, since she recognised her own attraction to the dishevelled woman.

Tine failed to recognise her own allure. She sat with her elbows propped on the bar, her hands gingerly cupped around the hot mug, and stared almost blindly at Stevie. She was attempting to gather her concentration. Her oversized T-shirt gaped at the neck and Stevie caught a brief glimpse of the pale rise of her breasts. An untidy fall of tangled chestnut hair cloaked her shoulders and, when Tine leaned forward, covered the view.

Stevie let out an expressive sigh of disappointment, which brought Tine back to earth with a startled, 'Oh, sorry!' She dragged herself from her musing and cocked an eyebrow at Stevie, signifying her invitation to talk.

'I work at the health club.'

'Surprise me!'

They both laughed: Stevie's sculptured fitness was hard to miss. Tine recalled that the luxury hotel a mile from the house had advertised the opening of the club the previous year. Though tempted, she had resisted the urge to join. She wondered if, with Stevie's presence, she would be more inclined to get fit. The example would be before her every day.

'Where are you from, Stevie? Your accent is familiar, but strange.'

'Zimbabwe. I came here to study physiotherapy. Now I want to work here before returning home. I am hoping the experience will stand me in good stead there. To be honest, I love Britain. I am gay, and there's a good community here.'

'Oh yeah? Sharon, who is moving in today, asked me my stance on men. Are you going to ask the same question about women?' Tine laughed.

'Yes.' Stevie's voice was soft. She seemed pleased with Tine's easy response to her statement. 'Actually, not so much your stance on women as your stance towards lesbians. I do not have a partner at present. I did, but when we finished our course, she returned to London. We decided to end things there.'

'I am sorry.' Tine's eyes were deep with sympathy. 'It is hard when you lose someone you love.' She paused for a moment, thinking hard. 'I don't think I have a stance on homosexuality. It's never occurred to me that I should. I guess my general idea is that people must be what feels right for them. It's just too easy for outsiders to be judgemental.'

Tine stopped, yet the dark woman seemed to be waiting for more.

'I don't know what you want me to say, Stevie. You are welcome here, as are any guests you introduce. I am not going to make any issue, take up any causes, or try to fight any of your battles. This is simply a shared house and, as far as I am concerned, we are just a group of people who, I hope, will enjoy living together.'

There was a silence, and the two women regarded each other for a moment. Tine waited silently under the gaze of the woman's almost black eyes, feeling it was up to Stevie to decide. Far from being artless with her words, she had chosen them carefully. She hoped that Stevie would understand her and, if she did, she would be welcome to take the room. That would signify her acceptance of Tine's right to be herself, otherwise she should not move in.

Stevie, who had faced many prejudices and the disapprobation of the intolerant, was finely tuned to people's attitudes. Mentally, she ran through her list of potential guests. Many of them would take exception to Tine simply because she would not empathise with their causes. Unfair it might be, but her friends would consider their emergence from oppression as a common battle. Whether the cause was sexism or homophobia, Tine did share a fundamental fighting base; her stance would be considered a cop-out. But as Tine had said, it was easy to be judgemental.

Stevie felt uncertain of this housesharing arrangement. The house she was leaving had been her home during her time at college and its residents were close friends. Her current work demanded long hours and her recreation was mainly outdoors, which would make her remote from the other occupants. She did not want to get too heavily involved, but she was attracted to Tine and, despite her reticence regarding involvement, was eager to pursue a deeper discussion. She saw wisdom and warmth in the older woman's eyes and a peace that could have been reached only with pain and experience.

She also felt physically drawn to Tine, who sat unselfconsciously in her incongruous top. Tine had tossed her head as she spoke to urge her thick, shining hair from her face, and now it fell in a luscious wave over one shoulder. Her ear was small and elegant, and Stevie felt an urge to touch it, trace its small contours with her fingers and her tongue. As she stared, Tine licked her lips, an innocent gesture which moistened the rosy cupid's bow.

Stevie felt certain Tine's skin would be soft and pliable. She could tell that Tine needed to exercise more or her tone would be totally lost. Her muscles already betrayed the signs of a sedentary lifestyle. Stevie longed to massage the pale flesh and feel it give under her ministration.

'May I see the room?' she asked

'Sure.'

Neither woman smiled as Tine slipped from her stool, beckoning Stevie to follow. As she mounted the stairs Stevie watched the movement of Tine's buttocks. The ride of the T-shirt betrayed the lack of underwear. She suppressed the urge to slip her hand up to cup between Tine's thighs. Stevie felt conscious of the discomfort of the lycra rubbing her thighs and the fact her nipples had hardened. She felt uneasy yet was compelled to stay; something important was happening. She had not been drawn to a woman since her relationship had ended a few months earlier and she needed to see this through, although she was aware that her intention to explore Tine more intimately would most likely fail. Perhaps a different sort of relationship would develop which could be as valuable, even if chaste. She did not attempt to deny the obvious difficulty of surmounting the attraction between Rupe and Tine. That would play out its own course, in spite of her.

She was charmed by the 'purple room' with its view over the rear garden. The room was large, allowing space for the small weights she was inclined to lift to start the day, before her run.

Stevie moved with grace around the room as Tine leaned against the radiator under the window and watched. Against the massing violet shades of the room Stevie looked good, her brown flesh aesthetic.

Stevie peered into the *en suite* bathroom with muttered approval, entered and, hooking her thumbs into the waistband, peeled her shorts swiftly down. She dropped with a sigh of relief to the toilet seat almost as soon as the golden pour began. The lavatory was positioned so that, with the door wide open, Tine's view was unrestricted. She stared, fascinated by Stevie's natural move to seek relief. Stevie's stomach was a hard-muscled plane, giving gently to a softer, hairless mound. Her outer labia were tight lobes, between which the honeyed gush slowed to a pale drizzle. Stevie busied her hands with the toilet roll, tore off soft squares and crumpled them in one palm. She dipped between her thighs to pat herself dry and let the damp tissue fall into the bowl as she rose, tugging on the shorts until they once more hugged her like a second skin.

Tine felt amazed. Even as she wrestled with the idea that Stevie's sports bent would make such a display natural, Tine's experience had never included open-plan female locker rooms. Mutual peeing had been restricted to intimate play between her and John, based on watching each other rather than anything else. The memory of the dark curve of Stevie's vulva excited her and she wondered what it would feel like to cup the warm flesh and feel the hot liquid interlace her fingers. She shivered as she imaged sliding her thighs wide and slipping onto Stevie's lap to spill her own wet product over the other woman's mound, watching her pale offering mingle with the richer flow. She groaned inwardly as she recognised the sneaky intrusion of her imagination, making itself public once more, and clamped it firmly down to prevent a further liberty.

Stevie, unaware of Tine's turmoil, slid open the doors of the fitted cupboard, pulling and peering into the generous trays and drawers, and at last turned to face Tine, looking pleased.

'Can I move in Tuesday?'

'Sure.' Tine smiled. The day had started crazily and that promised to increase but, given continuity, even 'crazy' could become the norm. She had been unsettled by Rupe, further distracted by Stevie and anticipated the shock of Sharon, who would undoubtedly arrive soon.

A growing sense of excitement overrode her reservations. She decided that this houseshare, with its plethora of new-offered sensations and the diverse array of its residents, would be an adventure. At least it would be interesting. Aware of Stevie's lack of transport, she offered to drive her home but her suggestion was declined.

* * *

The Porsche drew through the gates as Tine and Stevie parted at the door, the latter promising to return and settle the deposit the next day. The dark girl strode firmly past the car, cocking her head and whistling softly in admiration as Sharon uncurled from the low seat. Tine was not certain if the whistle was directed at the blonde woman or the Porsche. Both warranted the admiration.

Sharon wore a strappy chamois leather bodice, loosely laced, and PVC shorts cut high on the leg. Her breasts were barely hidden through the soft leather as they bulged against the lacing. She was barefoot, and a delicate slave bracelet glinted at her ankle. Her hair was loose, the colour of wild buttermilk glistening in the sun. As she leaned into the car to retrieve a bag, her shorts outlined her tight cheeks to create black, shining spheres.

'I just need to wash and dress, then I'll come and help,' Tine called.

Sharon waved her fingers to signify she had heard and drew a tapestry Gladstone bag from the car, placing it on the bonnet before bending to retrieve further baggage.

Tine took longer than she had expected. She turned the shower pressure to full and leaned her head to rest her forehead on the tiles of the stall, letting the sharp needles of water massage her neck and back. She stayed like that for what seemed a long time, clearing her mind of everything but the sensation of the pummelling water; the dampness soaking through her hair. When she emerged the room was steamy, a pale sheen coating the mirrored glass. She wiped a palm across it to clear a path and peered critically at the reflection of the fine lines surrounding her eyes as she brushed her teeth. I'm forty-one, she thought at last, I am allowed wrinkles. She firmly shut the door on age, refusing to be dismayed that youth no longer touched her. She felt a sense of relief that the uneasy, unsettled days of youth were past; age lent her strength and the ability to interact unselfishly with the world. She was at ease with herself, experiencing a sense of inner being rather than borrowing her identity from those around her. She hoped she would grow into one of those women who backpack around India at the age of eighty.

With the image of the scantily clad Sharon fresh in her mind, Tine tugged on a pair of denim shorts and a cut-off vest, which left her midriff bare. With the weight she had lost, the shorts were loose and she threaded a silk scarf through the loops to hold them up. She slipped on some deck shoes and raced downstairs to find Sharon.

A pile of baggage and clothes strewn loosely to form a soft, cloth mountain lay in the hallway. A hastily scribbled note lay on top. It told her that Sharon had gone for 'another load'. Unwilling to mess with the other woman's belongings, Tine went to have breakfast and found Rupe slouched over the breakfast bar, intently reading a computer magazine.

'Hi,' Tine ventured to test his reaction, expecting rejection. She was uncomfortable to think only one day had passed and already her vision of a friendly shared house was falling apart.

'Hi.' Rupe smiled, raising his eyes to glance at Tine.

Tine felt relieved and offered him breakfast, which he accepted with a promise he would be going to the supermarket to stock up that morning. They crunched their way, in silent companionship, through mounds of muesli and brown toast with strawberry jam. Rupe read his magazine and Tine retrieved a novel from the office. Eventually the return of the Porsche broke their peace and Rupe, raising his eyebrows in comical regret, muttered that he would disappear to buy provisions. He grinned as he made his way past Sharon in the doorway, blinking at her breasts in astonishment. As he went through the door she said:

'Cute buns, Rupe!'

He pretended not to hear but both women giggled as his walk became stilted and he swiftly climbed into his van, which coughed into life and struggled out of the gate. Sharon linked arms with Tine and dragged her into the kitchen.

'What's with the black girl?' she demanded

'She lives here from Tuesday.'

'Oh la. She'll have you doing push-ups at dawn, hon.'

Tine pinched the sparse flesh of her midriff. 'I hope so.'

They toiled for the next half-hour, carrying Sharon's belongings to her room. Then Tine sat cross-legged on the bed, watching the clothes and toiletries as they were brought under control. Sharon had a mass of electrical goods and some small items of furniture still to collect, and she resolved to commandeer Rupe and his van for the purpose later that day. She chattered incessantly as she moved and Tine let the noise wash comfortably around her. She felt very happy.

'The silly cow hugged me as I left, she was that relieved!'

Tine laughed. She had missed most of the one-sided conversation but it did not seem to matter. She yawned comfortably and felt she could easily fall asleep, lulled by Sharon's elegant-toned monologue.

She woke hours later, curled on Sharon's bed and covered with a large, crocheted shawl. She was alone. She paused a moment to rue the wasted hours, then wandered to the kitchen, seeking a drink. The refrigerator was stocked, labels on the middle shelves stating 'Touch and you die!' in what Tine recognised as Sharon's flamboyant script.

Rupe sat at the bar, his back to the window, eating a microwaved lasagne from its original packet and drinking lager from a bottle. He felt impelled to mutter:

'It saves on the washing up.'

He seemed uncomfortable and, peering through the window, Tine saw why. Sharon was in the garden, wearing a scarlet, silk scarf. She had looped it, drawn the ends up between her legs and knotted them at the waist, then twisted the material to thin ropes which she had brought to tie through the loop. It formed a thong, back and front, the sheer material forced to spread over her mound. Her breasts bounced, happily naked; firm, small melons tipped with cheeky pink nipples. She was bending to scratch behind the ears of a cat, the same one that had amused Tine the previous evening. It crouched in slit-eyed approval, purring loudly, then rolled shamelessly to reveal its tummy for attention.

Tine leaned her stomach against the rim of the sink and watched, enjoying the pantomiming of the cat in its demand.

Jerry chose that moment to round the corner of the house, and froze. Sharon presented him with a wonderful rear view, her long legs slightly apart. She was leaning forward from the waist and, with the movement of rubbing the cat, her body swayed slightly, allowing a brief glimpse of her unfettered breasts as the scarf outlined her pudenda. The effect on Jerry was startling. He rubbed his eyes and stared, took a step back, then forward, then leaned against the house as if his legs would no longer support him.

Tine knew that Sharon had become aware of Jerry's presence when her body language became more sultry. She dipped her hips and parted her feet further, then straightened her back and raised one hand to lift her hair from her neck. She turned slowly and pouted, as if surprised to see the agitated man. Managing to slant a glance at the kitchen to ensure she had an audience, she said something to Jerry, who disappeared swiftly then returned, unravelling the garden hose. He quickly adjusted the nozzle to produce a misty spray.

Sharon stood in the centre of the lawn, arms stretched above her head, as Jerry played the hose around her, carefully circling her to ensure she enjoyed the cool water all over. Her areolae puckered in objection and she shrieked happily as he increased the pressure of the jet to play between her thighs. The silk thong, sodden and transparent, clung revealingly to her mons and Sharon stilled. She lifted her face to the waning afternoon sky, her hips thrust forward as Jerry rounded her to concentrate the flow over the scarlet fabric.

Tine was too far away to see the expression on

Sharon's face, but the blonde's body was rigid with delight. She brought her hands to rest on Jerry's shoulders and stared into his face before pulling him towards her and urging him to his knees. She endeavoured to face the kitchen window and spread her legs wider as the gardener reset the hose nozzle to a fine spray, holding it with one hand to run his other up the inside of her thigh. His fingers quickly slid the material aside and parted her labia, aiming the water at her now exposed clit.

Sharon gripped Jerry's tousled curls for balance. The nozzle crept closer until it almost touched her. Despite the light setting of the spray Tine assumed that the pressure would nonetheless be intense. She clenched her thighs in aroused sympathy, sending dull delight through her swollen labia. She was so caught up with the scene that she had not until then realised the extent of her own involvement, and found herself pressed hard against the sink, her hands gripping the rim. Her breathing had quickened and she was frantically aware of Rupe. She risked a quick glance backwards to find, with relief, that the Australian remained seated, his back to her. She dismissed him and concentrated on the couple on the lawn.

Jerry urged the nozzle further along Sharon's cleft, keeping the cold metal an inch from the blushing flesh. His free hand assisted a clear passage and obscured Tine's view, but she could tell when the water intruded. Sharon arched, her mouth moving in urgent demand. Jerry responded by withdrawing the soft jet, then reclosing the gap several times. The last time his fingers crept up the nozzle and tightened it to stop the water. He eased the slim metal tip into Sharon, shielding its edges with his fingers. Sharon shuddered, bending to take more, which he refused. He bent his head to her; his mouth wide. Now Tine could see little, and she was left to imagine the working of his lips and tongue among the blonde curls and the thrust of the metal in Sharon's cave.

She heard Sharon's cry of release, muted by the glass.

The woman's body froze, her muscles taut, and then softened and she staggered slightly. Jerry swiftly rose and dropped the hose to catch her, one arm tight around her waist. Sharon's head dropped to his shoulder, her mouth still whispering. He lifted her and carried her into the garage where he sat her gently on the edge of the workbench and almost tore off his shorts. His penis sprung free and he guided it urgently between her surrounding thighs and plunged into her, riding swiftly to orgasm. She laughed triumphantly, urging him on while she stared over his shoulder at Tine.

Tine felt rigid with demand, her vagina clenching jealously and her breath caught, as she watched the muscles of Jerry's bum-cheeks smoothly bunch and release. When he came his body arched into a taut bow, his hips thrust hard forward. The pair leaned into each other and Tine envied their stillness as her arousal churned in her. An almost sick disappointment invaded and she turned from the sink. Rupe was staring at her, his eyes dark and penetrating, his mouth a hard line.

Chapter Five

*R*upe broke the connection first, his eyes snapping shut. He had turned to discard the remnants of his snack and caught sight of Tine at the sink. That was not surprising in itself, but something in her stance stilled him, and he peered into the garden where Jerry crouched before the rampant Sharon.

Rupe was less interested in the behaviour of the pair than that of Tine. The muscles of her legs were tense with the effort of pressing against the sink, her knuckles white as her hands clenched the rim. Despite the looseness of her shorts he could see the clench of her buttocks. Her excitement radiated from her, and he realised the exhibition in the garden had aroused her. She seemed not to breathe, then moaned softly, seemingly oblivious of his presence. Rupe thought Sharon's display was shameless but the helplessness of Tine's voyeurism reached deep within him, accompanied by a precise memory of the sight of her vulnerable muff.

He felt a longing wash through him and yearned to slip his arms around her, bury his face in her neck and cup her breasts in his hands. A very real sensation of her hard nipples imprinting his palms made him twitch. He could almost taste the salty sweat beneath the fall of her chestnut hair. His penis shifted, hardening, as his eyes took in the contour of her hip and the tightness of her bottom under the fabric.

Rupe felt displaced, the rational side of him warring against his craving. His mouth felt dry and the muscles of his neck were tense, his throat tight. The lines of the kitchen seemed to sharpen and its colours grew brighter. The garden blurred as he focused intently on Tine.

She had risen slowly to her toes, seeking the hard edge of the sink with her mound, and now rode slowly against it. Outside, Jerry had lifted Sharon, and Rupe watched him carry her out of view, giving the watchers, as he swung her into his arms, a view of her glistening pudenda.

Rupe imagined Tine with her shorts loosed and trapping her ankles, and her bottom thrusting at him as he slid unerringly into her eager wetness. His erection became insistent and he was thankful for the loose pants, which avoided it being painfully bound. He felt slightly faint, the blood pounding in his head, as if he was actually fucking Tine. An amazed empathy rose, a sympathy with her aching need, and the means he had to ease it. It seemed, for an instant, terribly simple. He should cross to her and provide relief for the need which consumed them both. Yet he could not cross that distance. It was far greater than the mere distance across a short expanse of parquet floor. It was the chasm separating the intent and the act, the gulf between two minds. He lacked the experience to bridge that gap.

His frustration, far more than physical, changed to anger at his own futility as Tine turned to face him. Her eyes widened in shock and his bore into hers. Her lips were a bruised, swollen rouge, slightly parted with the quickness of her shallow breathing. Her breasts, constrained by the small top, rose and fell in agitation, her bare midriff fluttering. In that moment Rupe could have crossed the chasm, reached out and into her. Her need was so palpable. He felt bunched and sprung, a bright tender lust sweeping over him; but her shock changed to fear, her pupils swiftly reducing to pinpricks.

With swift insight Rupe recognised how Tine must see his stance, his aggressive pose on the stool. For the second time that day he raced from the kitchen, leapt up the stairwell and stopped only when he leaned, his breathing ragged, inside the slammed door of the attic lounge. He felt horrified that he had frightened Tine, and his mind cast furiously for a means of easing the situation. He needed advice, he was not yet capable of understanding the strange interplay of this house. He suddenly felt young and very vulnerable. Rupe recognised he needed Tine and it was up to him to find the bridge to reach her. Without further thought he logged onto IRC, in search of Astyr.

Tine could not help her fear. Roused as she was, wanting and hungry for Rupe, his muscled mass shocked her. He could not know of her months of celibacy. She had noticed the urgency of his erection riding against the fabric of his tracksuit pants, the flush rising up his neck. She heard the slam of his door reverberate down the stairwell and felt weak. Oh, this is a tragedy of errors, she thought miserably.

Her arousal had disappeared, leaving her feeling churning and empty, and she felt a desperate need for a friend with broad, comforting shoulders. With this in mind she dragged herself to her study and, dropping into the chair, logged onto IRC to find Dickens. She was stunned when words flashed to her screen:

Rupe>   I need to talk with you . . . please!

Tine wanted to avoid Rupe. She felt overburdened, and leapt to the conclusion that he simply wished to rail against her, to exercise his anger and angst with a stranger on IRC; just as she sought to exorcise her unhappiness. Breathing carefully, she forced herself to regain her calm. The scene in the garden had unsettled her. She could have changed rooms, or perhaps gone upstairs to view from Stevie's window. Instead she had let her libido loose without giving a damn for the presence of Rupe. It was not his fault and if she was aroused so was he, except he was the innocent bystander. She owed him some of her time and, for the deception, much more.

```
Astyr>      You sound upset. What is the matter?
Rupe>       I need advice. Oh, I don't know. You are
            older, I need to know things.
Astyr>      Making #glade . . .
```

Tine reassessed the situation. In a way this was worse than what she had foreseen. It had happened before on IRC; a young man seeking her advice simply because she, supposedly, had the advantage of age. She wavered, tempted between revealing herself or continuing the pretence in order to offer the help he needed. Again, she betrayed him. She created the channel and held her peace as he leapt in.

```
Rupe>       Thanks
Astyr>      De nada. You look like you could use a
            *hug*! What happened?
Rupe>       Look, I know how this is going to sound, but
            I gotta talk about it.
Astyr>      Oh piffle and poffle! Just tell it like it is . . . I
            shall decide how it sounds.
Rupe>       Oddball and the gardener had a root in the
            garden and Tine watched, and I watched
            Tine.
```

However Rupe might feel that sounded, it would have read very oddly to a stranger who was unaware of the scene. Tine decided to let him get away with it this time, but wanted him to start thinking before he wrote, rather than ranting.

71

Astyr>   Ah ... that means they fucked in the garden
          while Tine (the landlady you mentioned last
          night?) voyed, and you spied on her?
Rupe>   Yes ... but she got roused and I became
          excited and terrorised her. Now I cannot face
          her.
Astyr>   How did you scare her?

Tine knew very well, but she wanted to see the scene
through Rupe's eyes.

Rupe>   I am big. I guess I just looked animal.
Astyr>   You wanted her?
Rupe>   Oh yes, but I did not know how to do it
          though!
Astyr>   Do what? Rupe, are you a virgin?
Rupe>   Near as dammit :-(I have never gotten on
          with women. I guess I just get scared. It
          wasn't that though, I know how to 'fuck',
          just not how to get across.
Astyr>   Tell me ... do you think she wanted you?
Rupe>   I don't know about me. I just know she
          wanted and I was there. I thought I could
          help us both.
Astyr>   You were willing to be _used_???
Rupe>   Yes, but you see it would be for me too. I
          want her.
Astyr>   So, forgive my bluntness ... you wanted to
          ease her need, and she wanted to have it
          eased, whether it was you or the postman
          sat there?
Rupe>   Yes. Although it did not seem that harsh!
Astyr>   You have only known this lady two days
          and you want her. You have no time for
          Oddball, who you think is a bimbo, and yet
          'Tine' is aroused by Oddball. Rupe, what if
          Tine is shallow, or is a deceiver? How can
          you know?

Tine watched her words denigrating herself on screen. She thought of sackcloth and ashes, and cursed herself. Perhaps it was time for her to try to strengthen, rather than destroy, the fragile thread which existed between them. She, however, had to get Rupe to think hard; he seemed far too nice, far too gullible. At the risk of causing him to look at her more warily, he needed to treat her as more than a china doll.

Rupe>   I don't know. I just know she is not like
          Oddball, and I know what I want.

Well, thought Tine, that certainly puts me in my place! She liked him all the more for his refusal to be patronised, and cursed herself for treating him like a child. She could have supposed he was adult enough to know his own mind even if he was unaware of hers. Her own appreciation of the last two days was at best dodgy, and she had more exposure to Sharon and Jerry's minds than to his. She was also on home ground and presumed to have a reasonable knowledge of herself. Rupe's position was far more out on a limb and yet he had not acted irresponsibly.

Astyr>   And you want Tine. And you really need to
          know if Tine wants you? You are not gonna
          do something stupid like fall in love are
          you?
Rupe>   Yes I do want her, yes I need to know if she
          wants me and, as for falling in love – how
          should I know?
Astyr>   Dismiss the first yes, ask her ... and you
          should know better!
Rupe>   ASK her?!
Astyr>   Yes.
Rupe>   No.
Astyr>   Well then, start to look to see how she reacts
          to you. As far as I remember, you said she
          looks at you as if you are naked, and then

73

	she would have jumped you today had you not been a large animal!
Rupe>	*laugh*!
Astyr>	That genuine?
Rupe>	Yup. You were supposed to give me loads of advice, not just cheer me up, you know?
Astyr>	You don't need advice, Rupe. You were just shaken up and needed to think :-)

As did I, thought Tine, as did I.

Rupe>	What about you Astyr? You seem so calm, do you ever get shaken?
Astyr>	Uh huh ... all the time ... sometimes stirred too!
Rupe>	Oh that is _weak_!
Astyr>	Oh yeah? I can get a whole lot weaker than that!
Rupe>	You know, it is you I should be after, not Tine. I feel a lot more comfortable with you.
Astyr>	Oh wow ... what a compliment! Maybe if I was there you would feel as uncomfortable with me. This is a very safe environment.
Rupe>	You are in the UK, why can't we meet and find out?
Astyr>	That is the lousiest idea I have heard in a long time! Why muck up something good? We can talk here, make each other laugh; it doesn't mean we do not care or feel ... just that we cannot touch.
Rupe>	When you say it like that it makes sense. I just have a feeling I want to touch you.
Astyr>	Oh? I would ask you where *evil grin* but I reckon we should leave it for another time. I have to go!
Rupe>	Thanks for being here for me, Astyr, it is important.
Astyr>	For me too. *hugs and bye*

Tine logged off and rested her head in her hands for some time. When she at last looked up she had made a decision. Rupe never need know her deception. He could have his Astyr on IRC and his Tine in real life. He had said he wanted her. She refused to feel guilty any more and reminded herself of the reasons she had opened her house to strangers; for companionship, laughter and adventure. Tine yearned for Rupe, and believed she would care for him as a dear friend, but she refused to accept any deeper, restricting, emotional involvement.

Tine felt hungry. All she had eaten that day was breakfast. She also felt extremely weary, though not sleepy. Dusk draped looming shadows and gloom over the garden. It was still hot and the combined scents of the heavily burdened shrubbery created an oppressive, pungent pot-pourri of aromas.

Tine felt relieved when she failed to encounter Sharon or Rupe on her way downstairs. She retrieved her portable CD player from the lounge, slipped Rachmaninov's *Vespers* into it and waited, eyes closed, until the sweet, massed voices of the Croydon Singers rose to flood her senses through the earphones. With the player clipped to her waistband, she made her way to the garage and retrieved the garden furniture, carrying the small white wrought-iron table and the four matching chairs carefully across the flagstone to a place near the French doors. Neglected since the previous summer, the colourful waterproof cushions were covered with thin spots of white mould; easily wiped clean. The patio looked more complete and inviting now.

In the kitchen she fixed a Greek salad, seared prawns in roast sesame oil, fresh pressed garlic and lemon juice. She added a bottle of sparkling spring water and carried her supper to the patio on a tray.

The cat came to beg elegantly, drawn by the aroma of the prawns, and, having been treated, waited for Tine to settle at the table before leaping companionably into a chair. It settled sphinx-like to enjoy the evening, with a small sigh.

'I am going to have to call you something.' Tine peered at the animal.

It glanced at her and chirruped its assent.

'I expect you have a name?'

She received a silent, green-eyed stare. She assumed the cat had a home. Its long grey hair gleamed with care and it appeared well-fed and comfortable around people.

'Oh well.' Tine offered it another prawn, which it accepted gently from her fingers.

She discovered during the shared consumption of her supper that feta cheese was also acceptable to the feline palate. Eventually she pushed the empty plate from her and settled back to enjoy the choristers. Perceiving her dinner was complete, the cat slipped onto her lap, purring as she absently scratched its chin.

The garden was peaceful and still in the half-light. Jerry had found time in his busy schedule to water it, and the wet-earth smell lingered. Dreamy and appreciative, Tine felt a slight moment's annoyance when panes of light fell on the lawn, betraying the use of the kitchen. She did not feel inclined to be sociable. Seemingly this desire was reciprocated, as the light vanished after a few minutes. She closed her eyes, letting the music take over, and opened them again when more light from the dining room washed over the patio. Removing the plugs from her ears, she turned to find Rupe framed, his bearing apologetic, by the patio doors.

'I am sorry, I did not realise you were here.' His voice was soft.

Tine gestured at a seat. 'Feel free.'

She was surprised to notice he had prepared himself a competent supper: a green-leaf salad with a seared salmon steak and nutty brown bread. Perceiving her glance, he smiled.

'I cook.'

'Marry me!' Tine had intended humour, but there was an uncomfortable silence. She was glad that Rupe failed to see her blush as he busied himself in arranging his meal on the table. A glass of water joined the plates. He sat and peered at the food before looking at Tine. Caught in the full light from the dining room, his eyes appeared a deep emerald. He swallowed, then cleared his throat softly.

'About earlier. I'm sorry.'

Tine felt humble. Rupe had taken a huge risk, not merely in acknowledging the earlier situation but also in setting himself up for rejection. Almost unaware, she reached her hand across the table. It lay in soft invitation, palm up, her fingers slightly curled. She looked at it as if it were a foreign intrusion, not a part of herself. A moment passed while he stared, like her, transfixed at the pale offering, then he brought his palm to cover hers. His hand engulfed hers, his fingers curled and held tightly, betraying his tension. They sat, stupidly staring at the clasp until she broke the spell.

'I am sorry too.'

He nodded, noisily expelled his pent-up breath, laughed wryly, and loosened his grip.

Tine withdrew her hand with reluctance. It stayed warm with the memory of his envelopment and she held it to her midriff, as if to imprint him there. She forced herself to be silent and watched him tuck into his meal. He ate without inhibition and, once replete, closed his eyes for a moment as if in pleasure and thanks.

'And I won't marry you,' he said after a moment, 'but I will cook for you tomorrow night.'

'Deal.' They exchanged smiles. 'In fact Stevie moves in on Tuesday, so I would like to do a house dinner later in the week, perhaps on Friday evening.'

'All of us?' He raised his eyebrows.

Tine nodded. She felt a little uncertain as she added, 'I thought I'd invite Jerry too, because of Sharon.'

'Yeah, good idea, it'll keep her occupied.' Again they smiled.

Things seemed easier now the situation was in the open. Friendship in complicity, Tine thought with pleasure. They chatted until the garden disappeared into real night and they could view only the perimeter of the spill of light from the dining room. Rupe listened to the Rachmaninov on Tine's player and confessed a similar taste. They shared their interest in books, then skirted computers, travel, food and drink. Tine found in him a wry, self-deprecating humour and gentle sarcasm.

The cat had deserted her in favour of Rupe's larger lap, responding with good humour to his far rougher treatment, and risked a tussle which left Rupe's wrists scored by claws. When it departed, presumably home-bound to anxious owners, Tine and Rupe cleared the dishes to the kitchen, washing and drying amicably.

Over coffee, supplied by Rupe, they bickered about the Internet. She avoided mention of IRC as, surprisingly, did he, choosing instead to talk about the media's contentious allegations of rampant pornography. Both had sought, and failed to find, anything more revealing than pictures of naked adults, sometimes conjoined in pairs or groups, and sexy stories. Rupe admitted that he knew of rather more perverted sites, but had learned of them via a circuitous route, and they required registration. He maintained that a more naive user would not stand much of a chance of seeing anything more serious than could be obtained from a naughty shop in Soho.

Lulled by camaraderie, he also confessed to 'netsex' by electronic mail and on IRC. Tine managed to indicate knowledge of the subject without inviting in-depth examination of her experience of the chat arena. She learned that Rupe had been very involved in, and frustrated by, a liaison he had developed via IRC. Previously remote from the shenanigans between the sexes, he had been charmed by a women in New York. Proving herself technically expert in the first on-line meetings, she had also showed herself to be articulate, fun and sensual. It had been his first encounter with sex on the medium and he had been enraptured, his feelings following hard on the heels of his libido. He was so caught up that he pursued a contract in America in order to be with her. His disillusionment, when he was informed 'she' was in fact a 'he', was intense and bitter.

Tine was sympathetic but she could not reveal her own encounters for fear of exposure. She simply spoke of similar experiences via electronic mail and he seemed satisfied. With the increasing depth of conversation an intimacy was emerging which, to Tine, felt slightly uncomfortable. She was aware that, if she did not call a halt, they could not avoid personalising the issue more than she was prepared after the fraught day.

It was Sharon's entrance which saved them. She arched her eyebrows at the pair who sat comfortably, side by side, on stools at the breakfast bar.

'Not disturbing anything, am I?' She winked at them.

Rupe snorted and rose. He made a far more gracious exit from the room than earlier, bidding a smiling farewell to Tine and casting a mock glare at Sharon.

'I always send him scurrying!' Sharon seemed penitent and grimaced an apology at Tine. 'I can't help it.'

Tine watched Sharon, who was preparing a hot drink to take to bed. It seemed she loved Horlicks, to Tine's amusement. The blonde made no reference to her scene with Jerry and Tine understood that, as voyeur, she was supposed not to mention it. In fact it seemed a long time ago. She sighed, thinking that she would have to become accustomed to the fast lane. Living is easy, she decided, it is people who complicate things. She did not fail to recognise her own culpability in that.

The two women chatted, and Tine learned that while she had slept Sharon had persuaded Rupe to help her collect her remaining goods. He was good-natured but impervious to her charms as they drove to her previous lodging, rejecting her politely when she had attempted a more direct approach. Ignoring a mild stab of jealousy, Tine felt pleased. Her observation of Sharon's methods gave her sympathy for Rupe. What would work for Jerry failed with the Australian.

Sharon perched on the stool vacated by Rupe and nudged Tine with her shoulder.

'Besides, I know you have the hots for him.' She blew softly to cool the Horlicks before sipping, grinning at Tine's surprise. 'In fact, I figure the only one who doesn't know is Rupe.'

She placed her cup on the surface and turned to face Tine, her violet eyes friendly.

'Do you know that he has the same hots for you?'

Tine nodded.

'Well then.' Sharon shrugged and rose, retrieving her drink. 'It is going to be a wham-dinger when you two make it!' She dropped a kiss on Tine's forehead and pranced from the room. At the door she turned and frowned back: 'And tomorrow, another damned week at the mill.'

Tine could not be offended by Sharon, although she felt relieved that the sexual tension she radiated would be absent during the weekdays. At least this might allow the houseshare to gather strength to survive the weekends. She hesitated to think of the nights in between. She grabbed a bottle of spring water from the refrigerator, chiding herself for consuming so much coffee, and went to her study. She logged onto IRC and, almost immediately, her screen flashed.

Rupe>   *snuggle* Join #glade?

The channel held only Rupe and Astyr. Immediately creating an imaginary sofa with a few words, he brought her up to date about his hand-holding with Tine, how good he felt about it, and his growing sureness that she wanted him too. They snuggled companionably on the virtual sofa, while she demanded a virtual foot massage. Rupe seemed intent and sensual, his descriptions concentrating graphically on her foot, then working his way up her calf.

Astyr>   Is this what you would like to do to Tine?
Rupe>   This and more!

Astyr>   Show me. I can tell you then if it will work
            evil wink

Rupe was articulate and Tine found herself drawn into
his vivid fantasy, growing limp in her chair. He seemed
happy with a monologue, describing his actions and
feelings, without accrediting her a response. As his
words appeared on the screen, Tine rose and shed her
clothes, except for her tiny bikini pants. She pulled the
crotch aside, softly massaged her vulva, then slipped her
finger into the crease and rubbed her hooded clitoris
gently. She wanted to hold back, to experience Rupe's
words and sink into his imagery.

In the text on the screen, Rupe urged Astyr to the
floor. He created a Persian rug and rolled her gently to
lie on her back, her arms loose at her sides, her legs
slightly parted and relaxed. He had planned a massage
but, unable to delay, tossed aside the oils and applied
his lips instead. He started with her feet, taking each toe
in his warm mouth, his tongue working between, then
eased his way up her calves and the sensitive inner skin
of her thighs. Soon his tongue was working amongst the
petals of her flesh. He described his task eloquently, the
tastes and sensations, with intense and graphic imagery;
the feel of her beneath his lips, the thrill of sinking his
tongue into her. Tine realised he was very wrapped up
in his words, in the way she had become accustomed,
when she acted out her fantasies on IRC. In Rupe she
found a similar imagination, the ability to slide from
reality into a different, equally accentuated experience.

When his words faltered she took over, describing her
thrilled response. She changed positions, urging him to
the floor and taking his prick into her nurturing mouth,
licking and easing him deep into her throat, riding him
with her muscles until she fought for breath; until he
came. She swallowed most, but kept some of his cream
in her mouth, so they could exchange each other's
precious spill in a kiss. When she finished there was a
still moment. Pleasantly aroused but with no feeling of

urgency, Tine's fingers resumed their soft circling of her mound. The light pressure created a delicate pleasure, a feeling that this foreplay could continue indefinitely and reaching orgasm was not important.

Eventually Rupe asked her if she liked cunnilingus. She described his ministration as one of the most delightful she had ever received, meaning it. If he was as adept in real life he would be one of those rare, wonderful men who every women should, at least once, experience. He confessed he had never done it in real life but it was one act he yearned to perform. Nor had he been taken in someone's mouth, another pleasure he craved. Their conversation increased in daring, covering a plethora of sexual adventures.

It emerged that Rupe wanted to try just about everything, from the missionary position to mutual masturbation, anal and oral, golden showers and bondage. He wanted to experience pain but not cause it and he was comfortable with the idea of making love with another man. He was not a fetishist, eschewing 'campness', crossdressing or nappies, and would not even think about more radical perversions. He was not sure about shoes, saying there was a possibility that could be fun.

He added that he had not considered the range of his wants in such depth before, but confessed that during the past two nights he had lain in frustrated wakefulness, imagining performing his fantasies with Tine.

She had difficulty keeping calm, knowing Rupe was a mere stairwell away. Tine could mount the stairs to the attic and approach him, open and naked, to enjoy the reality of him. However, she could not deny the pure pleasure of learning about him and she felt an immediate approach would deny them both the enrichment promised later. There was a growing anticipation replacing her frustration. Rupe's sheer enthusiasm, his lust for her, and her experience would carry them through the 'wham-dinger' predicted by Sharon.

Chapter Six

Tine woke the next morning with the immediate conviction that she should attempt to contact Demmy. She felt unrefreshed from sleep and recalled dropping into bed earlier having neither washed nor changed. She still wore her panties and her bed smelled, not unpleasantly, of a mixture of the musk of her own arousal and slightly stale perspiration.

Shaking off her lethargy, she raced through a shower and tugged on jeans and a vest, remembering, as she sped downstairs, that Rupe had promised her a home-cooked meal that evening. The thought caused her to slow down, feeling a pleased anticipation. Never mind that she fancied Rupe, the idea of having a meal cooked and placed before her was a real treat. She resolved that they would lock themselves away from the madding crowd and explore the pleasure of a shared repast.

Minutes later she sat munching toast in the office, while firing John's computer to search his address database for Demmy's telephone number. She found it easily, and moments later relaxed, wiping the crumbs from her jeans, as the burr of an unanswered ring sounded in her ear. Just as she was about to give up, a voice answered. It was unmistakably Demmy. Tine had forgotten her breathy, little-girl lisp.

'Hello Demmy.'

'Who is this?' Demmy was puzzled.

'It's Tine. John's wife.' She paused, then amended herself: 'Widow.'

A silence followed, and she felt sympathy for the girl. She had little dealing with her but, knowing her attachment, believed she would be upset to be reminded John was dead. She had not bargained for Demmy's next words.

'What do you want?' The girl sounded slightly hostile and defensive.

Tine had anticipated the normal condolences or an expression of mutual sadness, but not the harsh-seeming response she received. She began to regret that she had attempted this approach, but resolved to continue. She explained her wish to recover any work-in-progress that might exist on John's computer, and Demmy, who had worked so closely with him the last summer, seemed the ideal person to undertake the task. She kept her tone friendly and a little formal.

Tine added that she was pleased to find Demmy at home, as she had anticipated she would be working or might have left to join a wider creative community in London. Demmy seemed to thaw a little. She had decided to stay at university, changing her course to computing and concentrating on graphics. She had found a mentor in John, and his encouragement had spurred her on. She was in the middle of the university break, restarting in September and would be free until then.

Something arrogant in her tone caused Tine to reassess. She understood that Demmy felt Tine to be at a disadvantage. As the cuckolded women, Tine had apparently earned Demmy's contempt. The girl was lording over her.

Tine felt surprised that she had not anticipated Demmy's attitude. Her kinder and more liberal approach to her husband's young mistress was challenged by her determination that the girl should not presume that Tine's request was supplicatory. Tine had no doubt that

Demmy would benefit from the exercise of revealing John's unpublished work. As the finder of a library of unseen art, her name and reputation would be established. She took pains to point this out to the girl, resolving inwardly that if she received a precocious response she would withdraw the offer.

Demmy again surprised her by asking how much she would be paid to do the search, adding that, should she have to complete any of the work, she would expect a share of the sale.

'You will be paid nothing! Nor will you be allowed to touch any unfinished works, if you should find some. If you cannot see the opportunity in discovering John's unpublished work, from which your career is bound to benefit, then I think I've made a substantial mistake in contacting you at all.'

Tine ended the call, annoyed. She sat in the silent office feeling guilty but unrepentant. Demmy was eighteen and an adult; her attitude was cavalier and unacceptable. She mourned that the young woman's attachment to John seemed shallow and materialistic, even allowing for the fact that Demmy had been a penniless student.

Tine sat frozen, a horrified, unwelcome realisation dawning. Demmy had been paid. John had paid Demmy for her ministrations. He had taken advantage of her lack of finances and had offered her the means to greater comforts, so securing the youthful attention that he craved.

Tine hastily revised her opinion and, abandoning the romantic notions she had assumed for his liaisons, she now recognised the selfish commerce of his indulgence. Her imagination ran wild, wondering if, during his absences, he had scoured the English city streets for more girls. She thought of the runaways, the young prostitutes, the homeless waifs who could have tendered their graft. Tine also thought of the risks he had taken, bringing his promiscuous service home to the girls featured in his pictures; and to her.

His pictures. She raced to the lounge where his last, finished work was hanging, and searched the print for its meaning; at last staring in disbelief as she associated the seemingly enigmatic lines. The picture was a surrealist rendition of the final shot of the 'demmy.jpg' series of photographs, in which John's creamy pouring spattered the girl's uplifted face. They had hung it with a celebratory drink, John, Tine and Demmy. He had caught the young woman in a laughing hug, dropping a small kiss on Tine's cheek as they stood back to admire the work.

All John had done was take his photographs, scan them into his computer and apply cleverly designed filters to achieve his works of art. All over the world, in expensive collections, his prints hung as renditions of his illicit affairs. No wonder he was cynical. Of course Demmy could finish his work. It was not the works-in-progress she needed to locate, only the system of filters he used. She could simply run his program, perhaps tinker a little with the hue and tone, and produce the same elegant effect.

Tine knew that at least one art dealer had made his fortune on the back of John's work. Exposing the nature of the art would most likely enhance the value, titillating rather than disturbing the majority of owners. John would be the king of boudoir art. She was not concerned about the likelihood of fingers pointed at her; the betrayed wife. Many artists were forgiven their libidinous transgressions on the basis that it was part of their creative flow. He would simply be considered an unrestrained, hedonistic genius, instead of merely unrestrained, and value would add to value. She could not care less what people would think of her.

Tine slowly walked around the house, peering at the art, which had sustained her during her mourning, with new eyes. The delicate lines were still pleasing and she found no pain in the method or means of construction. But the deeper joy of them had disappeared. During his dismissive rants about his public, Tine had believed John had a real inability to perceive his own massive talent.

Now she knew he was right. He had produced art to a formula, and the pictures' value lay only in the minds of his buyers. It was not his fault and nor had he hood-winked the purchasers. From obscurity to fame on the back of a hype generated by popular demand, he had grown rich on other people's perceptions. Tine would disclose nothing. It would be unfair to the owners who had paid substantial amounts to buy these works.

She was standing in silent contemplation when the door-chimes roused her, and she walked slowly downstairs. She felt slightly drained, and when she opened the front door the shuffling figure of Demmy did little to cheer her.

Demmy had expanded from a child-like waif into soft, over-generous contours. Her pale eyes were hooded but retained the startling blue, almost turquoise, translu-cency Tine remembered. The girl had coloured her thick, dark hair with wild pink streaks. One side of her head was shaven to bristle, the luscious hang on the other side barely tamed by gel to fall in spikes. A gold stud pierced one nostril and, when Demmy spoke, a gold ring glit-tered and shivered with the movement of her soft lower lip. The effect was compounded with multiple piercings around one ear, each sporting a different metal bauble. Tine wondered how the ear did not detach with the weight.

Demmy was wearing a short black shift dress which hung loosely to mid-thigh and through which Tine could trace no underwear, merely the suggestion that her jewellery was mimicked at the girl's nipple, where an obvious and alarmingly large ring was outlined under the soft fabric. She wore heavy boots with short socks. Heavy leather wristbands and a mass of rings completed the ensemble. An exquisitely executed line-drawing of a fish was tattooed onto her upper right arm. Her face was clear of make-up, her skin pale and beautifully unmarred.

'I came about John's work.' She was unapologetic, the

87

childish soprano of her voice discordant with the picture she presented.

Tine stood aside silently and let her pass. Demmy did not pause, but marched straight through the office door. Not feeling able to confront the girl, Tine continued through into the kitchen. She refilled the coffee machine and sat quietly for half an hour, blankly aware of the intrusion. She presumed that Demmy had logged onto John's machine and was busily trying to find the 'j_piks' directory which Tine had removed. Despite her chagrin, Tine felt sympathetic. Demmy knew John's methods and where he banked the pictures. When she failed to find them, she would be concerned about their whereabouts. It would be easy to suppose the executors of John's estate had discovered them and that they were in strange hands. In the weird world in which Demmy might live, presuming she had some success with her art, those pictures may represent a later threat. Of course, mused Tine, she might simply want to rip off John's successful formula. She would not tolerate that.

When Tine at last entered the office, it was to find Demmy standing by the computer. She was in tears, the back-up tape which Tine had made of the 'j_piks' directory in her hand. Not having cleared the screen, it showed the image of Demmy commencing fellatio. The two women faced each other, Tine calm, bearing mugs of coffee, Demmy trembling with silent crying. Eventually it was she who broke the silence.

'You knew!' Her voice was full of accusation, as if it were Tine who had transgressed.

'Not when I telephoned earlier, but I worked it out.' Tine felt absurd, as if she should apologise. She was uncertain why the girl was crying and her natural instinct was to be kind. Placing the mugs carefully on the table, she removed the tape from Demmy's hand, then gathered the young woman into her arms.

Demmy sobbed against her shoulder for some minutes, pressing hard into Tine as if for comfort. Her nipple-ring pushed into Tine's breast, creating a *frisson* of pleasure. When Demmy buried her face in her neck, the older woman became aware of the lip-ring. She realised the advantage of the jewellery. The nose-stud gently bobbed against her earlobe, the effect gentle and pleasant. Lost in isolating the sensations, it was some time before Tine realised Demmy had stopped crying. The girl had slipped her arms around Tine's waist and was holding her quite firmly. Demmy was slightly taller than her and, when she raised her head, her chin was level with Tine's eye-line. She now stood straight, her length along Tine, her soft curves a warm pressure.

This was the first, close human contact Tine had experienced for months and she was starved. Sharon's friendly hug had been pleasing but this was like sluicing away the thirst of a desert. Tine took from the hug all she could. Now the young woman had stilled, her breathing even, the rise and fall was reassuring. It reminded Tine of the near proximity of another human heartbeat, the hot pulse of life.

Demmy was pleased. She felt little attraction towards Tine, but her visit to the house had upset her. At first shocked by the call, she had then been able to plan an action which she had mulled over for months. She knew how John had generated his art, and she only needed to obtain his program and filters to manufacture a similar product. Oh, she would alter things slightly, leaving her imprint, but as John's acolyte her art would glory in the shadow of his. She was no purist, simply happy to earn generously from the system he had created.

When she found the tape she quickly realised, from the writing on the label, that Tine had learned of her association with John. She also suspected that Tine would have interpreted the picture hanging in the lounge and would have realised the significance of the photographs. That would thwart Demmy's attempt to steal John's formula and cheat his widow out of many thousands of pounds. She had not been concerned that the compromising pictures of her may have fallen into

89

strange hands; she simply did not care. Demmy considered herself a modern woman.

She had been crying simply because she had failed to find the program containing John's formula. Her tears were caused by bitter frustration. She found not comfort but opportunity in Tine's enfolding arms, recognising her sympathy as weakness. She could still work her plan providing she gained the trust of the older woman, and the route became clear as the embrace continued.

As she leaned into Tine, Demmy noticed her ring exercising its charm on the other woman's breast. Through her thin shift she felt Tine's nipples bud against her chest and heard the slightly quickened breathing. She slipped her arms around Tine's waist and waited for a while, holding herself tighter against the small body. There was no rejection, so she carefully began to caress Tine's lower back, working her hands softly to knead gently on her bottom. The denim was a nuisance which she resolved by sliding her hands into the surprisingly loose waistband and resuming her pressure against Tine's bare bum-cheeks.

At last she was beginning to enjoy this. Far from withdrawing, Tine had leaned into Demmy, pressing against the soft woman and trembling under her hands. Unseen by the other woman, Demmy smiled to herself. Tine was reacting well to the slow insistence of Demmy's hands working her bottom. Soon a finger travelled the crevasse, insinuating softly as the other hand cupped her sex, urging Tine to rise to her toes. She did, and gave a soft sob as the explorer touched past her anal pucker and reached under, to seek her more moist divide. The finger was joined by another and they cleverly parted, slid around the outside of her labia, then closed to trap the now swelling lobes.

Demmy was aroused by Tine's small sound. The older woman was hungry for sex and Demmy knew exactly how to please her. She was leaning awkwardly to reach Tine and simply wanted to take her past the point of refusal, then she could entice her to a more easily manipulable position. Demmy was unused to soft sex. She responded to more direct action, and figured she could drop the seduction soon and urge the woman to participate. Afterwards, the replete Tine would be more amiable and willing to share. They could reach an arrangement regarding the program.

Now, however, she felt the wetness increase and was amazed at Tine's responsiveness. Her fingers slid experimentally into the cleft and were immediately drenched. Tine was wriggling to trap Demmy's fingers and uttering little whimpers. Then she suddenly stilled. Her breathing was ragged and she seemed frozen with an effort to bring herself under control.

Demmy immediately recognised that this attempt had failed. Her fingers were redundant, and she slowly eased them from Tine and brought her hands gently from their denim constraint. She was not worried. She recognised that the lust of the older woman was barely held in check below the surface. Within a very short time Demmy could try again but, for now, she simply had to crawl a little. She frantically thought how to turn the situation to her advantage.

Eventually she whispered, 'I am sorry.' She stood with her head hung. Her hands dropped to her sides and she succeeded in forcing a lone tear to trace down her cheek. 'I know how this looks. I was just very close to John, and being with you reminded me.'

Tine had fought hard to bring herself under control. Her body still yearned for the young woman's clever touch, burning for release. There was nothing in this mess which reassured her, and in Demmy she perceived a bad actress. With all the evidence to hand she wondered if the girl's skill had been provoked by John, but decided that the ministrations were too skilled to be merely the practice of one summer's experience; and that was with a man.

Demmy seemed very comfortable seducing a woman.

She had known all the right moves, none of which any man, including John, had practised. Tine was unsure but realised her suspicions had broken through during the sex-play, despite her rampant arousal. Too wise to neglect her inner voice, Tine had broken the embrace and now coped with her physical disappointment. The worst thing was the realisation of her vulnerability. In giving comfort she had also sought warmth. Her betraying libido had overridden her finer feelings.

Nevertheless, Demmy's eager compliance puzzled her. The girl had been terse and unaffected prior to her tears, and now something in the shift of her pale eyes indicated she was lying. To Tine it confirmed the young woman was not in the least interested in John; therefore her concentration centred on his work. Again, she suspected that the girl sought John's formula for filtering the pictures. If that was the case then it was necessary for Tine to thwart her and delete it from the system.

Unused to subterfuge, Tine simply suggested that Demmy leave and, should she wish, return on Tuesday morning.

'Perhaps we simply both need a little time to think about this,' she said, speaking kindly, intending to buy a day to undertake her own search of the files on the computer. She believed she had an advantage over Demmy, who had not administered this machine, merely used its facilities for graphics. She might not understand John's slightly idiosyncratic file structures. Tine made a show of turning off the machine, implying that it would lie idle until Demmy's return. She carefully tucked the tape into the rack and ushered the young woman from the room, ahead of her, to the front door.

Tine watched Demmy leave the yard, her hips swaying sensuously, and felt a pang. She experienced a confusion of feelings in which anger warred with desire. She understood better how she must have appeared to Rupe the previous day, full of need and thoroughly exposed. She felt relieved that he and she had failed to act and,

92

with the memory of Demmy's insistent kneading, of having escaped making a far worse mistake. She did not feel attracted to the young woman but was intrigued by her. Had she succumbed, she felt sure it would have been physically exciting and fulfilling, and perhaps that might have been enough, but she knew what Demmy would have considered fair recompense, and that would have set the cost too high.

Even as she thought this, Tine felt guilty. Demmy was not evil, merely a struggling young woman on the make. Unlike Demmy, she felt it not a matter of sexual morality, more a question of opportunism. Which was worse, she wondered: for Demmy to seduce her while believing her submission would persuade her to part with something as valuable and dangerous as John's formula; or to simply steal it without the deception? She was now sure this was Demmy's ultimate aim; to own the filters. The young woman's change of university course to computing was enough to convince Tine that she had most likely attempted to replicate John's techniques herself.

John, Tine decided, had been a true genius, but it had lain not in his artistic ability but in his computing expertise. Demmy's eager acquiescence to the idea of returning on Tuesday confirmed that she had failed to find the crucial files. Tine was none too sure that she would meet with any more success herself. She realised that she would have to enlist the help of a true UNIX guru, and the one nearest would be Rupe.

She found that she had been thinking while standing at the open front door, and the sounds of pots and pans being sorted now broke through her reverie. She entered the kitchen and found Rupe humming over a mass of ingredients, sharp knives and chopping boards. When she looked at her watch, it showed three o'clock. While Demmy's visit had seemed fleeting, it had lasted over two hours.

'Shall I get out of your kitchen?' she asked Rupe, knowing that if it was her preparing a special meal she would prefer the peace to putter around. It was obvious, given his early application to cooking, that this would be a special meal.

'Yup!'

'Oh, okay.' She grinned at him, happy after her close brush with Demmy, and once more looked forward to her promised treat. She poured herself a glass of fresh orange juice and returned to the office, grimaced at the mugs of cold coffee, and once more fired the computer. She was aware that the minicomputer, unlike a PC, did not respond well to constant rebooting. From now on she would leave it running constantly unless, she resolved, it was going to stay silent for much longer periods.

She settled down to search for the files containing the filters, starting with the system directories and progressing to those containing the graphics packages. Eventually she resorted to running the packages and attempting to trace the sequences which employed the filtering commands, although she realised that the process would not be that obvious.

It was thus Rupe found her. He had knocked on the office door, having seen her disappear through it when she left the kitchen. Failing to get a response, he entered and stood gazing around the room, expertly assessing the computing power on display through narrowed eyes. He watched Tine tussle competently with the graphics package, then exit and run searches on the system files. It was obvious to him that she knew what she was doing but was failing to find what she sought.

Rather than break her concentration, he left. He felt slightly puzzled that, knowing his involvement with UNIX, she had failed to disclose her own expertise. Feeling sneaky, he quietly mounted to her study and peeped in. He noted the equipment included another minicomputer and a PC.

Rupe was aware of John's expertise and success in the computer-generated art world. His name was large in computing legends and his style well known. The computer fraternity had mourned his passing. He knew Tine was John's widow, and had noticed that the house was hung with examples of his work. What puzzled him was Tine's involvement, and what she sought on the computer with such furious concentration.

He presumed she must have a reason for hiding her skill with computers; she had implied a simple understanding during their previous night's conversation. She did not seem the sort of person to be cowed by Rupe's mastery and therefore, he reasoned, something deeper lay beneath the apparent subterfuge. He did not, however, suspect her of anything devious and resolved to uncover her mystery that evening. Get her drunk, he thought mischievously – and get her to reveal all.

Two hours later Tine emerged to delicious aromas invading the hallway. They were stronger in the kitchen and she spied dishes laid out, ready for slipping into the oven. Rupe was setting the table in the dining-room. He had found the fine china and silverware, and was carefully folding serviettes into rosettes. When he noticed her he ushered her out with the admonition that she should not peek, it was all a surprise, and she should be ready to enjoy an aperitif on the patio at seven o'clock. He added that he had met Sharon prior to her departure for work and she had indicated she would be out that evening.

Tine was aware of the effort he was making and decided to reciprocate by dressing for the occasion. It was beginning to take on the aspects of a date, which both of them clearly relished. She primped and pampered herself, critically examining her reflection in the full-length mirror on the wardrobe door. She had chosen a harem suit; black, voile wrap-around trousers with a lacy bodice top. It was casual enough for comfort, yet elegant, and would reassure Rupe that she had made an effort to please him.

She experimented with her hair without success. It

was too thick to tie or tame so she merely brushed it to gleaming perfection and it shimmered with a life of its own, a shining accessory to her outfit. She dabbed *l'Eau d'Issey* on her wrists, and approached the dining room at precisely seven o'clock.

The French windows were both open, the room bathed in sunshine. The dining table was beautifully set, a candle in a silver holder promised intimacy and a champagne flute, white wine and red wine goblets were assigned to each setting. A single red rosebud lay, its juvenile head nestling softly, in the petalling folds of a serviette.

Rupe reclined in a lounger on the patio with his back to her. His hair was wet and he had changed into a soft, black T-shirt and chinos. Like hers, his feet were bare. Another lounger rested beside his. He had found them in the garage. There was a pitcher full of amber liquid, ice-cubes jostling with fruit for a place on the surface, flanked by two tall glasses.

Tine suddenly felt shy. A small breeze played with a leaf on the lawn, lifting and tossing it a couple of feet then sending it scurrying in confusion. When the cat suddenly leapt from behind the rhododendron bush to attack it, she laughed out loud. Rupe turned, smiling.

He saw a beautiful woman, her face full of sweet humour as she turned her attention to him. She stood on the terrace of the patio and the breeze, seeking further mischief, tussled with the voile of her trousers, then lifted it to expose her legs. The soft material billowed slightly and lifted to ride the wind, exposing her slim thighs, before she tamed it with a gentle hand.

Tine saw admiration in Rupe's look and returned it without reserve. It was a serious, open moment and each felt pleased to have the evening ahead. Tine stepped down as Rupe rose to pour her aperitif, ushering her to her lounger, before handing her the glass. It felt cold and the ice chinked a welcome. She sipped experimentally and found it to be a simple fruit punch with refreshing undertones of passion fruit and lemon to combat the sweetness. She sighed her approval.

They sat for some minutes in companionable silence before Rupe broke it.

'I came into your office while you were working today. I didn't want to disturb you, so I left.'

Tine appreciated that Rupe would be curious about the computer and, if the interest of previous visiting nerds was anything to judge by, would be itching to play with it. He would also be aware of her ability, if he had watched her working. For one horrified moment she wondered if he had entered while Demmy was there but she dismissed the suspicion: he would never have mentioned it if that was the case. It was enough that he had witnessed her arousal with the performance in the garden the previous day, without her being caught ravishing a young woman the very next. She chuckled at the thought.

'I wouldn't have minded being disturbed. I was searching for something and couldn't find it.'

It was idle, non-threatening conversation, until he asked, 'Who was the Tank Girl?' He must have seen Demmy leave.

'She was the reason why I was looking. She's also the reason why I need to ask for your help.'

Tine decided to tell Rupe everything about John's involvement with Demmy and the other young women, about his art and the files she sought. It was a long story which lasted through the fruit punch, followed him into the kitchen and accompanied the sweet salad entrée followed by fried camembert with puréed beetroot sauce.

Rupe listened intently and without interruption until she fell silent. He had deliberately delayed opening the champagne, feeling it would be inappropriate, considering the uncelebratory nature of the tale she told.

He felt sad when he thought of her discovery of the secret pictures just as she began a new life, especially when she expressed her doubts regarding Demmy's intentions, but there had been no trace of distress in her voice or expression as she related John's infidelities. He had nodded assent at her entreaty to keep the secret of John's art safe. Her late husband may have been a cavalier artist, but he was a brilliant programmer and Rupe did not presume to judge the man's character. Tine's failure to do so endorsed his attitude and increased his respect for her. Thinking of Demmy, he groaned inside. First Oddball and now Tank Girl – Tine attracted a fair share of weirdos. He took a wry look at himself to see how he fitted in.

He served red mullet with courgettes and fennel sauce, this time pouring Mont Rachet into the glittering, smaller crystal wineglasses. Tine expressed awe at his cooking, and he told her that his father had been a fine chef; running his own restaurant in Sydney. Before gravitating to computing Rupe had trained in catering and was considered almost as good as his father. The two dishes he had served so far were his own recipes. He warred with himself over his love of computers and his love of the kitchen, and attempted to make time for both.

'You know, you are the first woman I have ever cooked for,' he said with surprise, as if this thought had just occurred. 'Thank you for the opportunity.'

Tine stared at him, pleased and stunned. That he had prepared the wonderful meal especially for her was enough; that he had thanked her for being there was astonishing. There is a humility in this art, she thought. To offer thanks for his gift seemed puerile and insufficient so she rose, leaned across the table and planted a small kiss on his lips. She lingered long enough to feel the tremble of his lower lip.

'It is a glorious meal,' she said softly, 'and you are an amazing man.'

'Gift for gift.' He smiled. 'Your truths for my offerings.'

The sharp pain of her deception lanced through Tine

and she was about to blurt her identity as Astyr when Rupe rose.

'Next course!'

It proved to be veal served with a stilton sauce, tiny roast potatoes and a medley of colourful, shaven vegetables. Each course was small enough to delight the palette, yet leave Tine anticipating the next treat. This turned out to be fillet of venison served with black cherries and accompanied by generous glasses of Corbières. While Rupe had tinkered in the kitchen preparing the courses, Tine savoured the wines.

Night had fallen, rich as the venison, and she suspected he had timed the course perfectly to coincide with darkness. Rupe lit the candle and dimmed the dining-room lights. He had switched on the security light attached to the side of the garage and it cast a soft pool over the lawn, highlighting the edges of the flowering shrubs. It created a stage set which waited for the actors to emerge and, perhaps, perform *A Midsummer-Night's Dream*, and yet it did not seem bereft without the players.

The candle flame danced in the breeze, casting tiny rainbow prisms in the cut of the glasses before finding its way to the red, starburst heart of the ruby wine. They drank very little, Rupe swiftly removing the half-full bottles so Tine did not rue the waste. He seemed delighted with Tine's pleasure at the food he served. She said little, but every now and then would close her eyes in soft enjoyment. Her earlier confidences had engaged them both in an intimacy of companionship. Now they sat in silent tribute, sipping the wine and staring into the silent garden.

'Tell me about the computers,' Rupe said softly. 'I mean, your skill with them.'

'I haven't got any significant skill.' This was the truth. 'I simply know my way around them because of John. At times it was up to me to administer them; sometimes fix small problems.'

'And the Internet?'

Again Tine felt a strong urge to confess. She resisted the temptation.

'I used to spend a great deal of time there. Just recently I thought I might start again. Real life intervened and in some ways it's more alluring, and much stranger.'

Rupe told her he understood. Like a great many people, he had been addicted to the Internet for the first two years he had indulged. He spent long nights awake at the screen. Like Tine he had turned from the real world to make the 'virtual' his reality, and had experienced a confusion that took months to resolve. Eventually he established a balance, able to separate the realities. Now he enjoyed both, each in its proper place, and they were of equal value. For him the Internet provided an enrichment. It enhanced his life and provided him with new, technically oriented friends. He talked about Dickens with whom he shared a camaraderie which, he insisted, he had never experienced with 'real' friends. He talked admiringly of Dickens' skill and easy nature.

'You would really like him, Tine.'

She could not think of a response which would be true without giving away her identity as Astyr, so she did not respond, except to smile at Rupe. Her smile was enigmatic, a small lift which slightly creased her eyes. The candleglow urged amber lights to play among the brown of her irises and sent gleaming red-gold shafts along her hair. Unable to help himself, Rupe stroked along the glossy fall then softly traced her chin, along the line of her lower lip, and held his palm to her cheek. His eyes were wide, a dark jade concentration on her face. Tine leaned softly into his large palm, closing her eyes with pleasure.

'You are beautiful,' he whispered. 'When you came onto the patio earlier I thought I had never seen anyone more lovely.' He rose, urging Tine to her feet, his large hands cupping her shoulders, and kissed her. His mouth moved softly, his lips gently trapping hers, upper then lower, then glanced softly from side to side. She could feel the sweep of his thick lashes as he rubbed his cheek against hers. With a huge sigh he wrapped his arms around her and she encircled his waist. They stood silently for some minutes with their bodies pressed softly together.

Tine reached to just under Rupe's chin. Her lips pressed softly against his throat and she could feel him swallow, her mouth sensitive after his kiss. She could sense his heartbeat and, turning her head, she dipped to rest against him so she could hear its steady rhythm. His arms were enfolding, his thighs warm along hers. His groin rested at her stomach. She felt the slight hardness of him, a peaceful half-erection. There seemed no urgency to take the action further, only a feeling of certainty that, at some time, they would. She shivered with delight at the thought.

Rupe slid his hands back to her shoulders and, dropping a lingering kiss on her brow, eased away with a smile.

'Dessert.'

'It would have to be very excellent to follow that.' Tine cocked her head to one side and Rupe shook his ruefully before he let go.

Dessert was a rich chocolate mousse shot through with crushed lemon ice, served with amaretto biscuits and flutes of Piper Heidsieck champagne. Rupe had also slipped Vaughan William's *Serenade to Music* in the CD player, and a sweet choir filled the room. Tine felt replete and, when Rupe pulled his chair nearer and manoeuvred hers to face him, she felt very happy. They sat, legs entwined, sipping the bubbly, dry champagne until the end of the movement.

Rupe had also found the library of video tapes. He led her to the lounge, sat her on the sofa and left, returning shortly with espresso, wafer-thin bitter chocolates and tall glasses of cold spring water. He had already selected *Strictly Ballroom* for viewing and sat on the far side of the sofa to pull her feet to his lap. He commenced a soft massage before he set the tape running.

Tine fell asleep under the gentle ministration of his hands. He stared at her for a long while before lifting and carrying her to her bedroom. She barely woke, muttered softly against his neck as he mounted the stairs, and sighed as he laid her under the duvet. He loosened her clothing but resisted the temptation to remove it. It took all his willpower not to lie next to her and fall asleep with her cradled in his arms.

Chapter Seven

The first thing Tine realised when she woke was that she was alone in the house. There was an uncanny stillness. She had not realised the extent her senses had adjusted to accommodate Rupe and Sharon after less than a week of sharing. Now, strangely, she knew them to be absent. It felt vaguely uncomfortable and yet she liked the idea of having the space to herself. Somehow, after his fine supper and good company, she was reluctant to see Rupe until she had balanced her feelings.

She recalled the beginning of the video and the feel of his hands gently massaging the soles of her feet as she had slipped into a pleasant, wine-induced fugue. Now she felt hot, her lacy top sweat-laden under the duvet, and she noted that her voile trousers were wound tightly around her legs. Her make-up was smeared on the pillowslip. Tine hoped fervently that Rupe had not seen her as a snoring drunk. She vaguely recalled the strength of his arms as he carried her to bed.

His kiss. She pressed her finger to her lips and closed her eyes in remembrance. It had been so sweetly intense that she yearned for more, and the feel of his arms around her. What had been perfect the night before now seemed incomplete. She longed to roll over and feel the naked length of him in her bed, to tuck into his curves and feel him press against her.

At last, with a sigh, she rose to face herself gloomily in the *en suite* bathroom mirror. Pale, mascara-smudged eyes peered back at her in disapproval. Her unbrushed, sleep-mussed hair hung in a messy frizz. She suddenly felt glad Rupe had not stayed to witness her dishevelment.

Showered and toothpaste-fresh, with her hair smelling of apples, she made her way to the kitchen. She found the surfaces gleaming and, on investigation, the dining room cleared and smelling of polish. A package lay on the butcher's block in the kitchen, a note from Rupe taped onto the brown paper:

Had to go to London. Found the files! R x x x
(Your lunch, madam, is in the fridge)

Inside the package she found a back-up tape, unlabelled. She decided not to touch its contents; she would ask Rupe about it later, but she knew it contained the filters. Inside the refrigerator she found a plate of food. A slip of paper, skewered to the plastic film by a wooden toothpick, informed her that the wine was last night's Corbières, and was in the shelf of the door. The plate contained fine strips of mullet, a small pot containing sauce and a generous serving of mixed-leaf salad.

I could grow used to this, Tine thought, with a delighted smile. She was aware that Rupe must have had very little sleep, since her own bedtime must have been well after midnight. He had not only cleared the dinner debris, sorted the kitchen and prepared her lunch, but had still found time to search for the files. She recalled she had left herself logged onto the machine as its superuser, which was bad, but it had given Rupe the freedom to search. She slipped upstairs and placed the package in her bedside drawer.

Over fresh orange juice and toast on the patio Tine decided to rid herself of the picture in the lounge. Her first inclination was to sell all John's art, bar the piece hanging in the bathroom, but it had sustained her during her grieving and she felt attached to it. Apart from her certainty about the work derived from demmy.jpg, she could resist attempting to decipher the others.

Each time John had decided to retain rather than sell a piece, they would hang it and celebrate intimately. Tine had treasured these times even though she now realised that, far from her impression they were alone, they had been a ménage à trois, given the models peering at them during sex-play. Recalling her fantasy after finding the 'j–piks' directory she could not decide whether, had she known of his methods, she would have consented to the celebratory sex. She decided that she felt uncomfortable with the deception, not with the content.

Apart from Demmy. She wished to rid herself of the picture because the young woman was a reality and Tine did not like her. She would always have to be alert around Demmy, or she would be conned. How much of Demmy's attitude could be ascribed to John's treatment of her was important to Tine. It had been her whole reason for contacting the girl in the first place, and she felt partly responsible in John's stead. She realised that this was not logical, but was determined to try to befriend the young woman.

Fresh with resolve, Tine lifted the picture from the lounge, carried it to the hallway and propped it, face hidden, against the wall. She then called John's agent, who was surprised but delighted to learn of the sale of a work from the private collection, and arranged to visit the next day to collect it. He prophesied a quick sale and a generous price. Tine had not really thought of the money and was not much bothered. She simply wanted to be rid of the picture.

To pass time and clear another unlovely task, Tine gathered all the junk mail from the tallboy in the hall and spread it over the breakfast bar. At first she separated it into piles, discards and unknowns, then simply pushed the lot into a black dustbin liner and carried it outside. There was a likelihood she might have tossed something of value but her irritation had overcome her good sense.

Jerry was lurking in the garden and she took the opportunity to invite him to the houseshare-warming dinner she was planning for Friday night. He mumbled and plucked the dead heads from the roses, avoiding her eyes. She walked away shaking her head, wondering how Sharon made sense of him at all. Nonetheless she found herself back at the breakfast bar over coffee, in reverie. The fact was that Sharon did not have to make sense of Jerry, simply enjoy him. The two of them had tacitly agreed their relationship: Sharon would demand and Jerry would supply. There were times in Tine's life when she wished for the same but she knew she lacked the assertiveness, overt sexuality and confidence.

When she thought of Rupe, Tine felt she could have easily overcome her timidity had he not proven to be such a gentleman. Her first impression of him had forced a response in her for which she could not have prepared. She tried to picture them performing in the garden the previous day, in the same way as Sharon and Jerry, and failed. She could, however, easily recall the gentle pressure of his lips, and mentally transfer the sensation lower to touch her stomach, then feel the soft capture of her folds.

Avoiding the onslaught of fantasy, she dashed up to her study to find Dickens, hoping his attachment to IRC would cause him to log on at what would be mid-morning in California. She was in luck and they leapt into #glade simultaneously and happily exchanged an electronic *hug*.

Dickens>   Popped on quickly a couple of nights ago
           and saw you and The Rupe closeted :-)
Astyr>   Oh you should have joined in ... never feel
           you are unwelcome!
Dickens>   Sheesh, tell that to Rupe! I saw him at some
           ungodly hour today. What are you *doing*
           to the lad?

Astyr>   Eating his food, drinking his drink, gawking
            and generally behaving like a kid :-) Besides,
            the way things are going, it is him doing the
            doing.
Dickens>   So I hear. The fellow is much in-lust with
            you, dear.
Astyr>   On a serious note, and you don't have to tell
            me of course, there is no fear of 'love' is
            there?
Dickens>   You worried about that?
Astyr>   Uh huh. Look ... I don't need those sort of
            complications, nor do I reckon does he.
            There is nigh-on twenty years between us,
            and it would just get yukky.
Dickens>   It is up to you, hon. I think he is a sensible
            boy, very affectionate but not nuts. Tell me
            what is he like ... I mean I cannot *see* him,
            can I?

Tine happily described Rupe. She realised, as her
words rolled up the screen, that she was noting finer
details than before, and in a different way. Instead of
merely his physical attractions, she described the touch
of his hands, his generosity and attention to her needs
and the feel of his lower lip, soft under hers. She tried to
portray the feel of his waist under her hands, the way he
moved, the smell of him and the butterfly kiss of his
lashes on her cheek.

Dickens>   Hey, I am almost tempted myself!
Astyr>   Well why not?
Dickens>   No sweetheart, I don't bat that way. Strictly
            girls only, me :-) Now of course there is
            you ...
Astyr>   Yes indeed, and how are your travel plans
            going?
Dickens>   A little this way, a little that way. The gods
            are onto it. I am keeping my fingers crossed.
            Must confess that even if they don't play

nicely I am tempted to simply fly over the
ocean and sweep you off your feet.

Astyr>   I think I would like that, Dickens.

Tine meant it. An image rose in her head. Too good to
waste, she asked Dickens if he wanted to hear it and
received an enthusiastic response.

Her fingers flew across the keyboard, creating a vision
from the moment where Dickens arrives at the front
door, suddenly having decided to drop everything, so
great is his lust, and race across the sea to claim her.
Astyr opens the door:

Astyr>   We simply stare at one another, without
            introduction, each realising immediately
            who the other is. My heart seems stopped;
            you look so wonderful. Tall, your dark hair
            loose, picked up by the wind and billowing.
            You look slightly menacing in the dusk,
            intense dark eyes piercing right through me.
            I cannot help it, I reach to touch you, to
            ensure it is really you, that you are flesh
            under my palm. It is enough, you move
            swiftly at me and pin me against the wall,
            your strong hands grasping my wrists, pull-
            ing my arms straight up.

Astyr felt helpless with Dickens pressing hard against
her. She could hear his breath, ragged and hungry, as his
lips sought hers harshly. He plunged his tongue greedily
into her mouth and she reciprocated, a wave of lust
shuddering through her. They fed on each other like
animals supping at the trough, sweeping deeply for each
other's juices, their mouths wide and wet.

She had showered and wore a short robe, loosely tied
with a looped belt. It rode open and she could feel him,
bulging hard against the buttons of his Levis. He ground
into her, seeking friction, and the buttons bruised her,
the hard metal crushing against her exposed mound.

Dickens trapped her wrists with one hand and plunged the other between their bodies, tearing at his buttons, and then his penis was free.

He smelled of travel, sweat, stale sleeplessness and of sex-need. A rich, slightly malodorous lust rose from him to excite her. When he again reached to grasp her wrists she released her feet from the floor and wrapped her legs tightly around his waist. They met in frenzy and Dickens slid into her with a groan, bowing his head to grip her neck between his teeth, like a dog quelling a bitch.

Pinioned, and in spite of the aid of her legs grasping Dickens' waist, Astyr's arm muscles burned and she felt Dickens tremble with the pressure of holding her.

'Legs tighter!' he whispered hoarsely, and she closed her thighs, her calves pressed around his back. He forced her harder to the wall and, releasing her wrists, he hastily cupped his hands under her bottom.

'Wait!' Dickens' voice was strained, his penis throbbed in her as she sought to ride him. He bit hard to stop her and the pain lanced at her neck, enough to shock her into submission. She froze, feeling the sharp ache recede, then under his warm and sucking lips the wound tingled and became hotly alive. She moaned and forced her head back, drawing it to one side, to expose her neck further to his harsh ministry.

That was when Astyr saw Rupe. He stood in the dim hallway, his eyes fierce and his mouth a harsh gash. Astyr's robe had ridden from her shoulders and, with the release of her arms, had dropped to the floor. She was naked and the pair, framed in the open door, glowed in the evening sunlight. Between her tight thighs Dickens moved once, slowly, testing that he had brought his urge under control and that he would not spout too soon. He drew Astyr's hips towards him, leaving her shoulders for purchase on the wall and leaned back.

Following her stare, he saw Rupe. The men's eyes met, brown on green in a feral clash. Dickens' muscles tensed.

'Hug my neck!' The command was terse and she

109

swiftly encircled his neck, clinging as he lifted her from the wall and turned her back towards Rupe.

Rupe responded swiftly, torn by her need, his own desire an eruption which forced him towards the pair. A male message passed. Dickens retained his firm grasp on Astyr's bum-cheeks but slid from her. Her protest was silenced when Rupe penetrated, oiled himself liberally with her slick juices, then pressed his tip firmly against her starry, rear pucker. He paused and Astyr felt Dickens regain his territory.

Rupe slipped his arms under Astyr's, slid his hands up Dickens' chest and grasped the American's shoulders; thus taking her weight. Then Rupe pressed, his bulb pushed into her, and glided in unerringly to the hilt. Tine burned, then thrilled, moaning with pleasure.

'Release your legs.' Rupe's voice was a soft persuasion, his voice barely in check.

Astyr did. The men were of equal height and she sensed the tacit agreement between them, her weight shared. Her toes could not reach the floor and she hung softly between them, suspended on Rupe's strong arms. The fullness of their shafts inside her was a barrier to her fully closing her thighs. They stilled to allow her to become accustomed to their presence. At first she felt a small quiver of fear, then the amazed awareness that she held them both in her body, her snug heat surrounding their projectile flesh. Through the fleshy wall they shared each other, their shafts lying length on length, their ridges massaging. Both were clothed, but Rupe's firm grasp had slid under the loose neckline of the other man's T-shirt. His palms were naked against the American's flesh, feeling the hot pulse in Dickens' throat.

Dickens' hands still cupped Astyr but the hold was almost redundant.

'Lift her,' he whispered to Rupe. Their gaze held, something new dawning, a complicity, and Rupe straightened his arms. Dickens slid his hands slightly down, cupping and then holding, and Astyr felt her thighs gripped high at her groin and urged slightly

110

apart. He had elected to keep her steady. It would be Rupe who seesawed her small form for their pleasure. The soft movements shifted in her and she felt their hardening. It took no action on her part, just the *frisson* caused by the proximity of their pricks.

As Rupe eased out he felt his shaft slide softly over the backs of Dickens' hands, then he returned to the heat of Astyr's tight channel. His head swam with the sensations, the intensity of being so shared; stroked by his friend and deep in the forbiddenness of the women after whom he lusted. His grip on Dickens' muscular shoulders set the pace. When he squeezed, the Californian withdrew, and when his hands relaxed he thrust.

Dickens felt the tightly packed sack of the Australian press to his hands and he thrilled to the foreign sensation, his penis engorging. He picked up the rhythm at the urging of Rupe's grip. His senses boiled, as much from riding the neighbouring shaft as from delving Astyr.

She was rocked. As Dickens withdrew she felt Rupe horn in. She lost herself in the image of the two cocks riding, their erections huge in her and their bulbs caressing. As her tissue swelled it padded the increasing friction. It was her who yelled 'Harder!' and they who obliged. She was consumed by the disparate sensations, rear and front, the images racing – the two of them fucking her, as well as each other. Not merely a vessel, she was the vital link. Short of the men directly plundering each other, she brought them together, with her, to experience such closeness.

It was Dickens who came first. Unable to control his final thrust he surged, lifting almost her whole weight on his shaft, his cry of release a haunting wail, issuing from the rictus of his corded throat. Its echoes barely died before Rupe's hoarse shout joined and the discordant jolting forced the keen from Astyr, preceding her own ringing climax.

They stood leaning into each other, trembling, their legs giving. Then Astyr could touch the floor, her feet firm on the hall carpet. They slid down her until they knelt, Dickens' face buried in her muff, Rupe's head loose against the soft pads of her bottom.

She could feel the leak of them both easing silkily from her, cooling as it moved along her thighs. The rich, pungent smells of aftersex, the throb of hearts and pulsing organs was a very precious, shared gift.

Tine had forgotten she was writing. She stopped in confusion, blinking at the screen and trying to get her mind back to reality. The scene she had described was very real to her, and she ached as if she had just been, in truth, twice penetrated. Her breathing was jagged and she felt slightly faint, her heart pounding hard.

Astyr>   Uh . . .
Dickens>   Holy cow!

They sat for a long moment in silence.

Dickens>   I am keeping the log of this session. I need to read it tonight, in bed, on my own. I feel shattered.
Astyr>   Yes so do I . . . I don't know where that came from. It was real. I feel all beat up.
Dickens>   I really want to hold you now. Oh lordy, I can *feel* you in my arms.
Astyr>   And I you . . . and Rupe. On my big water bed, between you. We are all tired and almost asleep, all tangled. In fact, sweetperson, that is what I really must do . . . sleep.
Dickens>   My dreams are with you, sleep sweetly, my dear Astyr.

Tine logged off and made her way to her bedroom. It was late and there was no sign of either Rupe or Sharon. She felt as if she was in a dream as she washed and crept beneath the covers. Her last guilty thought, as she fell asleep, was that she had failed to eat Rupe's lunch.

* * *

112

It was morning when she was woken rudely, dragged from deep sleep by a knocking on her bedroom door. She sat up fast, regretted it, groaned and sank woozily back to the pillows as Rupe softly entered, mistaking the noise as permission. With her eyes closed Tine did not see his entry, but heard the door close a moment later. She realised he must have seen her bare breasts, and backed out.

Tine pulled on a T-shirt, went to the door and opened it to reveal a slightly blushing Rupe. She smiled at him which merely seemed to deepen his colour, but he managed a weak grin.

'You have guests. Tank Girl and some bloke.'

Tine heard voices raised in the hallway but could not make out the words. She surprised Rupe by grabbing his hand and dragging him into the bedroom.

'Do me a favour. Keep them apart for a minute,' she said urgently.

Rupe shook his head, stepping back and making a warding-off gesture with his hands.

'No way, she looks fierce! And he doesn't look like the quiet type either.'

They giggled companionably.

'I'll be down in a minute, honestly,' Tine beseeched him. 'Just tell them that, okay?'

He looked down at her, her eyes large and coaxing, and dropped a small kiss on the end of her nose. 'Okay.' He left, leaving Tine feeling slightly startled and rubbing the moist tip of her nose.

She swiftly drew on a pair of jeans, cursing as she peered at her watch and noted the time was ten o'clock. She had slept around the clock and not even heard the front doorbell chime, probably not just once, but twice.

The agent and Demmy were stood sulkily in the hall as she raced, barefoot, down the stairs. Between them rested the picture. Each had a proprietary hand laid on its frame. Demmy was the first to roar:

'He is trying to take my picture!'

'Will you please tell this woman to let go?' the agent pleaded with Tine, pointing at Demmy.

'Over coffee.' Tine marched past them and into the kitchen. 'And leave the damn picture where it is!'

Tine poured four mugs of coffee and then restrained Rupe, who was attempting to edge from the room. They were seated opposite each other at the breakfast bar when the scowling Demmy and the puzzled agent joined them. After a moment Tine turned to face Demmy.

'Demmy, did you see a certificate attached to the painting?'

The young woman nodded reluctantly.

Tine sipped her coffee before continuing: 'It means that the painting belongs to John's estate. Therefore it belongs to me and I am giving it to this man, who is a dealer, to sell.'

'You know it's my picture!' Demmy was barely coherent, her face suffused with anger. Rupe, who was seated next to her, drew slightly away.

'No Demmy, it's a picture of you, for which you modelled. It is not your picture.'

The stool crashed to the floor as the young woman leapt angrily to her feet, causing Rupe to jump and spill coffee over his fingers. He looked scalded and increasingly uncomfortable. Despite the scene which was unfolding, Tine was seriously tempted to giggle, more from tension than at Rupe. The agent had less success in restraining himself and bellowed, his huge belly-laugh shattering the tension.

'I'll fucking get you, Tine!' Demmy roared. She turned to go to the front door, and swung straight into the hard lines of Stevie who had witnessed the exchange.

'Get the fuck out of my way,' Demmy shouted, pushing hard at Stevie who, ladened with two large dufflebags, did not budge. Instead she lifted her eyebrows at Tine, then put down one bag, laying it gently on the parquet floor. Then she gripped Demmy's upper arm in a firm grasp and steered her back to the breakfast bar. Anticipating her direction, Rupe leapt to restore the stool and Demmy was placed firmly back on her seat. Stevie pulled another stool close and, easing the other bag to the floor, sat gratefully. Demmy was trapped, glowering, between Rupe and Stevie. She looked like a small, enraged troll.

'Hi Tine. Door was open.' Stevie smiled and ignored Demmy. 'I've brought my gear round. Is my room ready?'

Demmy stared at Stevie and asked, 'You are moving in here?'

Everyone looked at her. She fell silent, hunching her head between her shoulders.

Stevie peered around, eventually settled on Tine and explained.

'Dembabe and I know each other.' Her voice was soft, slightly scornful. 'She touts at my club.'

'Your health club?' Tine asked, puzzled. Demmy did not look the health club type.

'No, a club called Silky Lizzie's. My gay club.'

'I know it!' the agent butted in happily, then blushed as all eyes turned to him.

'I know you too.' Stevie grinned at him, deepening his colour.

'I am not gay,' Demmy muttered sulkily.

'You are not anything,' Stevie rejoined with a shrug.

'I just don't have preferences. I am bisexual.' Demmy swelled as she said this as if she had just discovered the word and considered it a badge of honour.

'You are not a bisexual,' retorted Stevie. 'You're an opportunist. Were you bisexual I would think well of you. But you're on the make, and you don't give a damn who you rip off.'

The two women glared at each other under Rupe's amazed stare. The agent, sensing his moment, beckoned to Tine and led her to the hallway where he collected the picture and left, with a whispered promise to be in touch. A scrabbling in the kitchen alerted Tine to the probability that Demmy was trying to escape and thwart his progress.

As she re-entered the kitchen, the viciousness of Demmy's glare caused a chill to run through her. It did not escape Stevie's notice. She drew the straining young woman to her feet, again sending the stool crashing, and dragged her from the room. Tine watched them enter the lounge. The door slammed and loud voices immediately began.

Rupe and Tine studied their coffee thoughtfully.

'Tank Girl is going to be a problem.' Rupe's voice was sympathetic.

'You should have seen your face!' Tine exclaimed, shouting at last with laughter, bubbling to a stop then gurgling with renewed vigour at Rupe's expression.

'I'll have you know that coffee was hot.' He was indignant but his mouth twitched in betrayal. 'She's a lot of girl, the Tank.' He gave up and chuckled, 'That agent could have been more diplomatic!'

The pair collapsed, arms akimbo on the breakfast bar, and howled with laughter. The situation was not as funny as all that but it served to defuse recent tension. Tine also realised it was inappropriate, especially as her new housesharer was battling angrily with Demmy in a nearby room. Eventually she hiccuped to silence.

'And you did not eat my lunch.'

It set Tine off again, under Rupe's grinning gaze.

'I'll eat it now,' she apologised.

'The cat had it for breakfast.'

'You gave the cat my lunch?'

'Yup, so dinner is on you. I reckon you have a few hours to sort it.' Rupe rose, smiled sweetly and blew a kiss at Tine. 'I've got to sleep. No need to prepare anything special for me, but I do like chicken.'

There was silence from the lounge and Tine hesitated by the door, wondering if something dreadful had happened. It opened and Stevie ushered Demmy out. The young woman paused before Tine, her eyes red-rimmed and downcast.

'I am sorry,' she whispered, her voice tearful.

116

Stevie was leaning on the doorframe.

'I think she means it, Tine.' She beckoned to Demmy, who padded softly outside with her to a hired van and started to lift bags.

Tine watched for a moment. She was not as certain as Stevie of Demmy's contrition. It is going to be another of those days, she sighed to herself; then went upstairs to shower.

Chapter Eight

*I*t was three o'clock before Tine re-entered the kitchen, wondering what to prepare for dinner. As she had crossed the landing from her room she could see through the open doorway, to where Stevie and Demmy were sitting on Stevie's bed. They seemed in earnest conversation but broke off to peer absently at Tine. Without thinking she invited them to dinner, then cursed herself all the way down the stairs for a fool.

Giving in to the inevitable, she wandered into the garden where Jerry was mumbling obscenities at the weeds. The barbecue was his idea.

It was incredibly hot. The temperature had soared to 34° Celsius at midday and seemed little better as late afternoon approached. Given shade, the idea of a salad-laden meal was tempting and Jerry's enthusiasm persuaded her. He had found the barbecue grill in the garage. John had used it once and it was designed for a party of ten. Providing the complicated assembly instructions were decipherable, it was impressive and ideal. Jerry tapped Tine for twenty pounds to get charcoal, oak chips and whatever else was necessary to adhere to his promise that he was an expert with 'this sort of thing'. She gave him a further twenty, admonishing him that, if he did not return in the next half-hour

118

with at least that many boned chicken breasts, she would set Sharon on him. He paused long enough to let Tine know that the realisation of her threat would be welcome, then raced away with a grin.

Tine worked fast, enjoying the idea of an impromptu party. She mixed a marinade for the chicken with fresh tarragon, honey, red wine and soy sauce, warming it in the microwave oven. Jerry returned triumphantly as she sorted her ingredients, brandishing the poultry as if he had personally brought it to maturity, plucked it and prepared the pale breasts. He watched Tine slip two portions in the marinade then took over and completed the task for her.

Tine found it difficult to reconcile the gardener's boyish prancing with the image of Sharon's lover. He seemed endearing, like a boy scout suddenly given the opportunity for a new badge. Alive with energy, his sun-streaked curls flew as he dashed to assemble the grill, his hands feverish with activity as he accurately slotted the parts together without the aid of the manual. She felt as if she should take him milk and cookies.

Tine had forgotten how much she enjoyed cooking as she prepared avocado in spinach jelly with chilli, new potatoes with anchovies and chives, tomatoes in basil and a large mixed, green-leaf salad. She decided that dessert would be an exotic fruit salad with ice-cream or cream, but popped banana bread into the oven in case stodge was preferred. As she was mixing crushed, fresh garlic into butter, in preparation for garlic bread, Rupe walked into the kitchen. He was wearing little, merely loose, thin cotton shorts. His hair was wet from a shower and the dark curls on his chest stood out; softly enticing. There was enquiry in his eyes as he gazed at the full bowls which Tine was lifting into the refrigerator.

'I know I'm a big boy, but this could feed an army!'

'Let's just say it's a premature Friday houseshare-welcoming party.'

'Uh oh.' Rupe noticed Jerry messing with the barbecue and smiled.

'Tank Girl too.'

'Sounds good.' Rupe was cautious and Tine chuckled. She drew two bottles of Piper Heidsieck from the refrigerator, waved to indicate the remaining bottles, and pushed them at Rupe.

'Shall we start now?'

The dinner was under control and Tine finished preparing the garlic bread, while Rupe expertly popped the corks. She grabbed one bottle and two flutes from the cupboard.

'Back in five.' She raced up the stairs and through Stevie's still-open door, surprising the pair by thrusting the champagne at them, telling them to be downstairs in an hour.

Tine was hot from the kitchen. She had a cool shower and slipped on a strappy black summer shift, then raced back to the kitchen. She drew the banana bread from the oven and left it to cool on a wire rack. Rupe had already stacked china, serviettes and silverware on the table in the dining-room, and was on the patio playing with the cat. Sharon had returned home and was poised in the wide doorway with her back towards Tine. She was wearing, as far as Tine could make out, absolutely nothing but a string around her waist. The men had not yet noticed Sharon and Tine paused, her breath held, waiting for their reaction when they did.

It was Rupe who looked up first. His eyes widened and then moved firmly back to the cat as he muttered a greeting. Jerry was transfixed when he saw her. He stared in open admiration, his eyes sweeping Sharon with naked lust. It was sufficient for her to sway down to the patio to his side and pat him lightly on the bum.

Tine collected a flute of champagne and wandered over to the pair, anxious to prevent their degeneration into open sex-play. She was relieved to note that the 'string' Sharon wore was a sun-suit of sorts: a white fabric all-in-one with a halter top and thong bottom. From the front it was daring enough, barely covering her

120

breasts which threatened to bounce out of the sides, the legs cut high to the waist. All that held it in place were strings around the neck and waist, and the thong string rising between her bum-cheeks to tie with the waistband.

It seemed that her close proximity merely served to provoke the pair, rather than dissuade them from action. Jerry took the gleaming tongs from the barbecue tools and traced them up Sharon's stomach, then under her breast, to catch her nipple in the pincers. The long handle allowed him to angle the tool downwards so his hand brushed Sharon's vee. He tucked his little finger under the material covering her mound.

Tine could see his movements worming under the fabric and the slight tilt of Sharon's hips as she urged them forward to enjoy the tickling. She was aware that her complicity was a repeat of the previous encounter, and that Rupe was again present. Despite her misgivings she was held to the spot, her excitement already mounting. She was so close to Sharon she could hear the blonde woman's quickened breathing and smell her perfume.

Tine tore her eyes from Sharon long enough to cast a glance at Rupe. He smiled enigmatically and fluttered his fingers around the glass. She realised that he was going to stay and watch. Effectively, he was telling her to get on with it. It added to her excitement and she swayed slightly, touching Sharon's shoulder briefly. The violet eyes sought hers and held them in a bright gaze. Then the woman leaned towards Tine and softly kissed her, her lips opening slightly and her tongue flicking.

Tine had never kissed a woman before and, despite the permissions implicit in Rupe's behaviour, felt a moment's doubt before she was lost in the sensation. Sharon's mouth was gentle and wide, her tongue softly insistent. Tine let the mouth move over hers, savouring the moment, then parted her lips. Sharon's tongue-tip slipped along Tine's soft inner lips, tracing along her teeth. Sharon cocked her head slightly and positioned her open mouth firmly on Tine's, slowly pushing with her tongue.

121

When Tine reciprocated it was with the same, slow motion. The women edged to face each other, leaning but not touching, to prolong the kiss. When they drew apart they stood gazing at each other, Sharon licking her lips, Tine catching her lower between her teeth to enjoy the sensation of the sharp bite on the swollen flesh.

Jerry had moved behind Sharon, his eyes wide, and peered over her shoulder at Tine. He was barely in control, excited by the women's contact. His hands crept around the blonde woman's hips and tucked under the thong, pulling her back towards him so he could rest the length of his erection between her bum-cheeks. He rode, sliding along the crevasse, in tiny lifting movements. His hardness was still trapped beneath his shiny running shorts but the silky fabric served to increase the friction, and his pleasure.

Abandoned by the tongs, Sharon's nipples were sharp exclamations under the white fabric. Tine, barely able to control her movements, brought her hands to the blonde's waist and slid them softly upwards until her thumbs crept beneath the fabric and tucked under Sharon's breasts. She urged the slightly elastic material inwards until the pale orbs were exposed, the stuff of the garment trapped between. Releasing her hold, she picked up her discarded, half-full flute and poured the pale champagne on the naked mounds. Sharon gasped as the liquid trickled over her, then trembled when Tine drew her fingertips softly up from under her breasts to circle her nipples.

Fascinated by the smooth, soft texture, Tine felt a moment's retrospective jealousy. This is what men felt when they touched a woman, the velvet give of flesh, the rounded lend to the palm and the hard, excited tips. She felt powerful and overcome with a sensual curiosity. Her lips sunk to trace Sharon's teat, feeling the little ridges, tasting the sheen of champagne and the woman's own perspiration. She hefted the globes in her palms, enjoying the weight and give of them, then buried her face in the valley between, pressing the mounds into her cheeks and inhaling deeply.

Tine felt she could meld with the soft, fragrant flesh for a long time. A part of her noted Sharon's increasing arousal, and that of Jerry who was leaning hard into Sharon so he could peer over her shoulder to watch Tine. His hands still worked softly on her mound, and the blonde had her head tilted back onto his shoulder, her long neck exposed, eyes closed. Sharon's length was open and available.

Tine pulled reluctantly from Sharon's breasts and, placing her hands softly on the swanlike neck, eased them slowly downwards. She floated over the swollen nipples and brushed along Sharon's fluttering stomach. Jerry stilled, his hands easing slightly to allow Tine access when her fingers met his over the fabric. Through the material Tine traced Sharon's mound, its gentle hummock, then the vee beneath. She pushed so the fabric caught and grew swiftly damp in the cleft, outlining the vulva.

Then Tine knelt on the hard flagstone and forced her tongue into the crease of the damp cloth. She tasted Sharon, her sweetish musk, through the barrier and felt heady. A strange, wondering hunger rose through her, followed by impatience. She placed her hands between Sharon's thighs and they parted. Tine plucked the material aside to reveal the blonde's wispy mons, swollen pudenda and clitoral nub.

Jerry, not able to see her from his angle, had all but withdrawn his hands, surrendering space, but Tine trapped his fingers. She urged his fingertips into position so they held Sharon's folds apart for Tine's view. She stared for a long moment then leaned forward, her tongue extended, and swept the length of Sharon's crease with long, slow laps, like a child with an ice-cream. Soon her laps became more demanding and her tongue pushed deeper, riding hard amongst the damp folds and pressing against the nub to force back Sharon's clitoral hood.

Sharon groaned. Her hands sought and locked Tine's

123

head, forcing it hard against her as she ground wetly into Tine's face. The older woman obliged by crouching further underneath, feeling the urgency of Sharon's excited pressure.

Jerry, no longer able to control himself, caught Sharon on a backsweep and, holding her firmly, freed his prick from the loose running shorts, and urged it into her corridor. Tine watched for a moment, then reached to cup his balls and massaged them softly, fascinated with the explicit view she received of his slippery penetration and the pull and release of Sharon's flesh around Jerry's shaft.

Tine tilted her head, laying the bridge of her nose firmly against Sharon's clitoris. Needing a hand to balance her awkward angle, she relied on Jerry to control the choreography. He responded to the different feeling tracing along the out-slide of his cock and slowed. Tine eased back, caught Sharon's clitoris gently between her teeth, and sucked softly. Her hand urged Jerry forward, squeezing to set the tempo, then releasing him as his own driving need took hold.

She refused to release her teeth, and Sharon's hands forced Tine's head hard against her. As Sharon came she felt Tine bite hard and the painful, dull flow joined with and heightened her throbbing. Sharon barely noticed Jerry's climax until she felt his wet withdrawal and, freed, she joined him, slumping to sit on the hard flagstone. The three gazed at each other.

Tine felt at a great distance, confused by her recent intimacy with Sharon. It seemed inconceivable that it had actually happened, and she witnessed the same bewilderment in Sharon's eyes. Both expected that there would be no repeat. It seemed a singular libidinous act. Jerry appeared an even more remote part of the triad, and in Tine's eyes was now back to being the gardener. She resolved to try to keep her distance in the future, erecting a barrier to prevent further such interplay. While she did not regret the experience, it seemed alien, thrilling only for its rarity.

Sharon reached out a hand which Tine grasped. It was a friendly act, one of consent, endorsing the recent experience and taming the boundaries.

It was Rupe who surprised Tine most. He lifted her to her feet with exquisite gentleness, enfolded her in his arms and held her tightly for a moment. She leaned into him gratefully, aware that his act was one of support. His lips brushed her forehead and he slipped away. There was no hint of an erection but she noted a damp sheen on his cotton shorts.

It seems, she thought wryly, that I am the only one who did not come.

Rupe needed time alone. He had watched the scene, at first alarmed then roused to fever-pitch when Tine's tongue sought and caressed Sharon's muff. He had been so entranced that he did not take account of his own hardening, except to absently slip a soothing palm to his shaft. He was amazed at his empathy. Jerry had seemed merely a passer-by to the action, which had all centred on Sharon. Tine was the protagonist. He had urged Tine on in his mind, almost proud when Sharon shuddered to climax. He felt generous, and when Tine sat on the hard flagstone he all but applauded, except his hand was busy easing him to stillness.

Tine had looked so pale and confused, somehow lonely and very small, that he had been driven to hold her. She had seemed grateful for his reassurance and he knew, even whilst slightly bewildered by what had happened and why, that the attraction between them had heightened. A bond was forged, a trusting closeness. He left to shower and change, walking silently with Sharon into the house and up the stairs. They did not say anything, merely exchanging puzzled looks, then he continued to the attic while she entered her room.

Jerry settled back to normality with disconcerting swiftness. He was soon shoving at the coals with a steel prod, and demanding the meat for cooking. Tine sluiced her

125

face at the kitchen sink to wash away the evidence of her recent involvement, smiling at the taste still in her mouth, then carried the chicken to the patio.

She poured more champagne for herself and Jerry, and settled on a lounger to watch him jiggle the chicken breasts expertly on the grill, occasionally spooning marinade onto the cooking flesh. It was still very hot, although the long shadows had started to cloak the lawn with cool evening promise. A part of Tine's mind still reviewed the earlier sex-play, but it was a distant picture. Given the excitement of the houseshare so far, it merely seemed a prelude to something more profound.

Tine recognised that through her recent fantasies, her voyeurism and her manipulation she had rediscovered her libido, but had thus far failed to experience her own fulfilment. She felt frustrated and uncertain, displaced and a little afraid that she had erected a barrier to prevent her own, real involvement. Perhaps she was absorbed in some mind-world, a fantasy without responsibility. She felt concerned that, were she to actually surrender her control in sex-play, it would fail when compared with her fantasies. While she could clearly recall the soft feel and taste of Sharon she knew that some part of her had kept aloof. Waiting for what, she wondered, waiting for Rupe?

When Stevie and Demmy appeared, Tine was startled. She had forgotten they were there, but was sure they had not witnessed the patio scene. She swiftly placed the salad bowls on the dining-room table, put the garlic bread in the oven to heat for ten minutes and laid the fruit salad and banana bread on the sideboard.

The air was full of aromas; the smoke from the barbecue overlaid with oak, the charcoal, hot honey scents of the cooking chicken and the warm scent of the banana bread seeping through the house. Tine made her way to the lounge and placed Beethoven's *Piano Concerto No. 5 'Emperor'* in the CD deck. Returning, it was easy to judge from Demmy's expression that the music was not to her taste, nor that of Stevie. However, it lifted Tine's

126

heart when Rupe reappeared, his expression rapt and approving.

He had changed into his 'Programmers' vest and cut-off jeans. Anticipating the demand, he also flourished two more bottles of Piper Heidsieck. The party began well, with Tine retrieving the garlic bread to add its own pungency to the dining-room, and Jerry's insistence that people collect meat from the barbecue.

Sharon entered amidst a flurry of hungry diners and was quick to join in, seemingly uncertain whether to flourish the glass or a plate. She wore another sun-suit, a black halter-neck, with skorts; soft swirling shorts. As she twirled, the material floated up to leave no one in doubt of the absence of underwear.

Demmy had not encountered Sharon before and was spellbound, the turquoise of her eyes deepening in admiration. Stevie seemed more Rupe-like and aloof but was still unable to resist staring. They all settled companionably on the patio, each finding a perch on the terraced edge or at the table, and silence fell while the meal was consumed. They worked their way through the barbecued food and dessert, finishing the champagne and two bottles of Chablis, before Jerry announced he was tired of the 'witches' piss' and was going to drink beer.

He had stocked up when he fetched the coals and, retrieving a six-pack from the kitchen, tossed cans to anyone who wanted one. Tine and Sharon declined; the former because she felt she had drunk more than enough alcohol, the latter preferring wine. The strands of conversation wound around Tine as she settled comfortably into a lounger.

Sharon was quizzing Demmy and Stevie on Silky Lizzie's, eventually soliciting an invitation from Stevie and a sulk from the younger woman, who seemed to feel left out. Demmy had found a seat at Sharon's feet and stared up adoringly, like a small, love-struck spaniel. Rupe chatted about motorbikes with Stevie when he learned she owned a Kawasaki. Jerry kept his peace, his bright eyes roving the company, settling butterfly glances here and there.

Long after the meal was finished and they had soaked up the excess alcohol in their systems with banana bread, Tine rose to collect the debris and take it into the kitchen. She got as far as the dining-room door before she was blocked by Stevie, who marshalled Demmy, Jerry and Sharon and marched them, laden with dishes, into the kitchen to wash up.

Re-emerging, Tine found Rupe slumped in her lounger and so she settled into its neighbour. Despite the long day and the stress she felt alert. The meal had helped and the champagne had added its own zest. Tine was slightly drunk, and Rupe seemed not far behind her. He entertained Tine with stories of his life in Australia, hamming up the 'cobbers and sheilas' angle to amuse her. When the rest of the party emerged they all sung 'Waltzing Matilda' very badly. It emerged that Stevie played guitar and produced one, amid good-natured catcalls and derision. She soothed the group with a medley of African lullabies. Demmy was the surprise. She had a fine, deep voice and a range to rival any country singer. She competently dealt with a selection from k d lang and got the party to sing along with a medley of Irish songs.

Tine fell silent amidst the voices, her contentment sweet. Her angst and lusts had faded and her conviction had returned that opening up the house to tenants had been a perfect idea. The good-natured joshing, warm companionableness and ease which seemed to flow through the small gathering seemed very sincere.

It was hot, in spite of the cool shield of black night. Dazed by champagne and lulled by the murmuring conversation around her, Tine felt an urge to seek the cooler environment of her study, with its high ceiling and open windows promising a less oppressive temperature.

As if some invisible hand had gestured, the group started to disband. Stevie gathered Tine in a firm hug, thanked her for the party and dropped a small kiss on her lips.

Demmy muttered, 'Oh yeah, thanks,' and trailed after Stevie, demanding a space on her bedroom floor for the night.

Sharon and Jerry moved across the patio and rounded the corner of the house with small, farewell waves. Tine wondered where they would go in the dead of night, and shuddered to guess. As if in echo, Rupe voiced her thoughts aloud as he followed her to the base of the stairwell.

'Probably the graveyard,' Tine laughed. 'After all she is the Oddball.' She continued up the stairs, leaving Rupe to stand for a moment with a small, disturbed frown on his face. He shrugged, reaching the landing as Tine disappeared into her study and the door swung shut. He stood, his hand poised to knock, still thinking deeply. Then he shook his head and continued to the attic.

Tine logged onto IRC. She kept pushing at the heavy fall of her hair, to ease it from her sweating nape. Eventually she rose in irritation and sought a hair-clasp in her bedroom, winding the chestnut fall into a loose topknot. She felt agitated. A thought nagged at her but slid away every time she seemed to grasp it.

Returning her attention to the screen, she found it blank. She felt disappointed because she had thought that Rupe would log on, as had happened on previous evenings. After a few minutes she joined her old channel #midlife but, disinclined to talk, she simply watched the screen scroll with the conversation of the chatting group. She checked to see if Rupe was around.

Rupe, she thought, who would tell Astyr all about the party and the revellers. Suddenly Tine shot to attention in her chair, her mind whirling. He had never called Sharon 'Oddball' outside of IRC. She felt aghast at her blunder.

It was some time before she realised that she had

curled up, her feet on the chair, hugging her knees hard. 'Damn, damn, damn!' her mind repeated. A paranoia cloaked her. Of course he had not logged on. Right this minute he would be angrily stuffing clothes into a bag to leave, calling her a scheming bitch. He would be wondering at her shallow amusement as he had laid himself bare, his generous self-exposure in response to her cock-teasing, pathetic seduction.

A voice reasoned that perhaps her comment had passed over him, or that he would convince himself that he had, in fact, used the term 'oddball' with Tine. They had talked a lot outside of IRC. Even if he was puzzled he would, perhaps, give her the benefit of the doubt. If not then she would face his contemptuous rejection and the icy coldness of his glare as he left the house to find a more trustworthy place to live.

Tine chastised herself. She barely restrained her urge to race to him and face him with the truth; risking his censure in the chance that she could convince him of her own dismay at the situation. No, he would see it as an attempt to crawl out from under her gaffe and would be even more hostile.

Perhaps she could disappear. Feeling guilty and self-serving, she swiftly examined this option. She had told him the previous night that she was thinking of rejoining IRC. Why not, but as the tamer persona 'Leeter', her previous character? She could simply kill Astyr, log off now and never appear as her again. If she actually sought Rupe, calling herself Leeter, it would be honest. She would let him know she was actively looking for him, having returned at last to the chat arena. The question of Astyr would simply be open-ended, but she would have to beg Dickens to support her betrayal. Guilt upon guilt.

As the options jumbled in her head her screen flickered and then it was too late:

Rupe>   Busy? I see you are on #midlife.

Tine could not kill Astyr now. If he had realised her mistake, and she tried to disappear, it would compound the deception. He had approached her and she would have to face it out. His words were not threatening and she could not guess whether he had noticed her slip, or not.

Astyr>   No, I am actually just lurking ... not joining in.
Rupe>   #glade?

Tine mistyped her exit from #midlife three times, her fingers trembling on the keys. Eventually she managed to join #glade.

Rupe>   Hi. I am glad I found you here. Mind you, I sort of expected it.
Astyr>   Tell me.

It seemed to Tine that he was suspicious and uncertain, hinting that he was aware of something amiss but not wishing to confront her. Her heart lifted a little at his next words.

Rupe>   Nothing really. We had a party, it was great. I guess it just seems an anticlimax to be here. I don't mean that you're an anticlimax! I simply anticipated something different. I feel disturbed. Something is bothering me but I just can't place it.
Astyr>   Want to talk it out?
Rupe>   No not really, but I do think it's about time we talked about you. You are a little mysterious, you know?

Tine's heart sunk. He was suspicious. If she could show herself to be someone other than Tine, he might be satisfied. Perhaps then she could abandon the Astyr persona. It would involve her in a much more elaborate lie, forcing her to create another Astyr in some other city, with another life, just to placate Rupe. Suddenly sick of all the lies, drained in the heat and nauseous in the aftermath of her panic, she went blank. The idea of seeking somewhere cool seemed overpoweringly important. At that moment, more so than Rupe.

Astyr>   Fine, but right now I am sick with the heat.
           I absolutely have to find a cold place to be. I
           shall return in half an hour. Then we can
           talk.

Tine logged off. Feeling slightly faint, she staggered down the stairs and through the dark kitchen, where she yanked open the refrigerator door. She grasped the top shelf, arms straight, her body a taut line as she leaned into the cold air. Breathing deeply through her mouth, she quelled her nausea and felt her heartbeat slow to an easier pace. The soft material of her shift clung to her, glued by perspiration, and the cool, refrigerated air soaked through her hot dampness.

With her eyes closed she did not notice that she was no longer alone until she sensed, rather than felt, a presence close behind her. Rupe's voice was low, traced with pain, and held a much deeper, stranger element. His breath brushed her ear.

'Astyr ... you crossed over. Now who are you going to be?'

Chapter Nine

*T*ine grappled feebly with his question, before deciding it was irrelevant. What was important was the
nearness of the man behind her, the reality of his breath;
soft coffee-fragrant clouds, wisping and misting in the
refrigerated air.

She played his voice in her mind, seeking the strange,
tight undertone. Reproach? Yes, but the tone was deeper.
Beneath his words she could sense his desire. He still
wanted her and was available to her. He was guileless
and uncertain but still generous enough to withhold
judgement. She was swept with a humility, knowing
that if she pursued him now it would be on his terms –
without barriers. Lowering her guard and giving her
trust was a risk but, in all honour, she could do no less.
Even this rationalisation was irrelevant. Rupe was mere
inches from her and she had no intention of walking
away. It would be impossible to drift from the golden
cage they had been building over the past days. The
time was right.

Tine released her hold on the shelf and stood up. She
turned towards Rupe, searching his face. In the calm,
pale light his eyes were translucent, a watchful green;
still uncertain. Hers were dark, wide and vulnerable.

'What's in a name?' she whispered.

They stood, stripped of pretence, facing each other at last on an equal base. She felt him a stranger, but somehow familiar, and knew the inevitability of their pairing. He seemed vulnerable, his arms loose at his sides and his chest bared.

Tine felt empowered. It felt so natural to raise her hand to touch Rupe's face, trace her fingers over his temple and along his cheek. She felt the slight, rough stubble of his evening beard contrast with his silken, soft lips. His mouth twitched in an involuntary hiss, as he suddenly breathed again.

When Tine caressed his chin, Rupe tilted his head back, exposing the pulse in his neck. She pressed her fingers softly into his throbbing vein, delighting in his blood-rhythm. Her eyes swept over his chest, anticipating so much to explore. She felt an impatience at war with the languor which flooded her. Her hand dropped and her palm came to rest over Rupe's heart.

His chest was lightly cloaked in sweat, the effect of the heat of the evening. Tine leaned forward and dipped her tongue in the cup of his collar-bone. He tasted of salty ferns and smelled gently musky. She swept her tongue upwards until she pushed at his pulse, her tip probing his vein, her mouth seeking the hot throb of his blood. His groan vibrated through her swollen lips and he eased his head to hers. Tine swiftly caught his lower lip between hers, holding his flesh as if to savour his desire.

She swayed to him, at last meeting his firm flesh as his hands spanned her waist. His hold was too tight, betraying his barely contained lust, and his heart pounded beneath her palm. His mouth was a harsh demand on hers. They fed. Their hunger and thirst seemed unquenchable as each plundered the other's mouth. They paused only when Rupe crushed her to him with arms of iron, jamming her face into his neck as he, likewise, buried in hers.

She leaned into him, glorying in his strength and the depth of his passion. She flowed perfectly along his hard contours, rubbing against the thick, silky pelt of his chest through the thin fabric of her shift. His neck was hot and yielding against her mouth and his shaft was a hard rod trapped against her mound through his tracksuit pants. Tine's dress rode up in the rough embrace and her naked thighs pressed against him.

Rupe drew away and held her firmly from him, his thumbs twisting beneath the thin straps of her dress. He drew his palms over her shoulders, pulling the straps with him until the neckline fell away. The material slid moistly over the slope of Tine's breasts, meeting some resistance at her nipples, then settled at her waist.

Rupe stared, his eyes roaming over Tine's breasts, then settled at the thrusting tips. He eased her back against the refrigerator. A shelf cut below her shoulder-blades, the cold metal harsh but not painful. His hands cupped her small bosoms, weighing them softly before he brought his mouth to cover her perking nubs. Rupe suckled at Tine, his lips pursing and working each nipple in turn. He supped liked a starving child, with strong, wet and noisy demand until her areolae puckered and hurt. Tine crushed his head to her, thrilling to the ache as she encouraged his hunger.

Lust tendrilled in her, forking like small lightning shafts, and she moaned and shifted trying to force his head down. He seemed immovable, then stared full into her face, grasped the fabric of her shift and tugged. The material swathed over Tine's hips and thighs before settling in a soft, dark puddle around her feet. Apart from a lacy scrap of panties, Tine now stood naked before Rupe in the silvering, refrigerated glow. Her face was shadowed, framed by a cascade of auburn hair, plucked through with coppered threads. Tine appeared carved, a marble statue, her hips thrust slightly forward for balance.

Rupe caught the light, his face strong-lit planes and his lips swollen and red. He had moved slightly back from Tine to release her clothes, but his hands remained at her waist. His eyes were intent on the tiny lace barrier embracing her hips. He sunk to his knees before her and encircled her thighs, his face pressed to her stomach. Then he rubbed, like a cat against her soft flesh, inhaling deeply. He felt her tremble, shift her hands to frame his head and twine her fingers in his hair.

Rupe recognised Tine's need. An explicit memory rose of her bending at the front door, her blushing pudenda open to his view. He linked the image to the taste and texture of rose-flavoured Turkish delight. Then he recalled Tine worshipping at the Sharon's blonde altar.

He rose swiftly and, clasping Tine's waist, swung her to sit on the edge of the butcher's block with her legs splayed. She lay back and pillowed her head on crossed arms. She could now see down her length, viewing the uplifted mounds of her breasts, the taut curve of her belly and the dark presence of Rupe urging the lace panties from her. He tussled with them, then groaned, and tore them from her. He held the flimsy fabric to his face and inhaled deeply as he stared between her thighs. At last he bent and sucked her swollen lobes.

The strain on Tine's back was excruciating and she felt she could not hold the position long without support for her legs, so she brought her heels to rest on the edge of the block. She was then spread more widely for Rupe's noisy feasting. When at last he drew back, he stared for what seemed a long time, his eyes shifting in minute exploration of her wet and shining lower lips.

Rupe felt vulnerable. The ache in his groin was a strident demand, urging for release. Almost absently, he loosed the string of his tracksuit bottom, slipped the fabric over the tip of his bulging, upright penis and kicked the fallen garment from his feet. His slick, purpling bulb waved proudly atop his quivering shaft, in Tine's full view as it lined up with the sloping landscape of her furred mound.

Despite his own need, Rupe was not yet visually sated. He gently pressured Tine's thighs further apart until her delicate, damp vulva parted before his gaze.

136

With one finger he traced over her clitoris, its hood pulling back to reveal the tiny, rubbery focus within. He dipped among her warm folds and continued his exploration until he found deeper access. He slowly slid his finger in and twisted it as if to examine the length and width of her, then added another finger, then another, until she was full and stretched.

Almost as a backdrop he became aware of Tine's whimper and her urgent push on his hand. She was drenched and swollen, wide open under his ministration and now vocal in her demand. It seemed that, although he penetrated her with three fingers, she was still hungry and writhing with an urgent need.

Rupe turned and reached into the refrigerator, seeking a surrogate. He worked himself close between Tine's thighs to hold her wide to his view, allowing the refrigerator light to fall boldly over her. His one hand gently nursed inside her, his other drew a courgette along the soft flesh at the top of her inner thigh.

As he eased the cold, green-veined substitute inside her, Tine's muscles clenched hungrily, surrounding the icy cold intrusion to welcome its invasion. She gasped, puzzled, and rose to her elbows to stare in fascination as Rupe directed the chilled rod into her. After the cold came a numb delight and, peering at the hilt of the manipulated green object, Tine felt a relaxing of barriers and an intimate bonding with the man who stood between her knees.

Rupe watched Tine's vaginal ring tug softly at the courgette as he withdrew it, her elastic flesh stretched and pursing around the mottled girth. He felt as if he was watching Tine's intimacy with another man, a usurper, and the mental image of another penis caused his grip to falter on the now warming vegetable. His wrist brushed his own erection with an electric thrill. His own need was becoming more urgent. He glanced at Tine's face, her eyes staring down, viewing his manipulation. There was a fascination in her expression, not repugnance but excitement at the intruder.

When she raised her eyes to meet Rupe's, her gaze was wide and lucid, her lips almost impossibly swollen and her excitement blazing across her face. He urged the courgette from her and drew it, glistening with her juices, under his nose like an exquisite Havana cigar. He slid his tongue along its length, then leaned over and eased it across her lips, leaving a viscous trail of her own pomegranate sap for her to lick and savour.

At last Rupe gave in to his need. His heavy erection curved out from him, stretching towards the soft cushion of Tine's mound. He edged closer, stilling her hips with firm hands. His eyes never left her face as his rod pressed at her entrance, its tip seeking permission to enter.

Tine widened herself as much as she could to assist his penetration. He paused a moment, then slid slowly into her velvet embrace, hearing his own groan of pent-up pleasure echoed in hers. Buried to his hilt, he stopped and stared at Tine, his expressions changing between triumph and humility. When Rupe started to thrust, Tine shed her remaining reserves and her cry was one of freedom and surrender.

Deep inside her, merging with the rampant physical tide, was a welling of exhilaration. She felt her naked lust and boiling needs explode in her conjunction with Rupe. She made animal cries and her throat, unaccustomed to the strange language, growled around them. She mewled and whimpered as she found her release. Her senses pulsed, absorbing Rupe and spreading the delight of his pitching member to her limbs; her muscles burned with effort as she ground her hips and bucked against him.

At last she reached the vortex of sensation, the deep pleasure whirling and throbbing through her. Rupe rode the final distance as Tine's clenching intensified. Her muscles sucked him to release, drinking from his flesh in thirsty demand, creating a vacuum that was almost painful. He felt as if his root was being torn and he ebbed in her strong grip as their fluids mingled inside her.

As their harsh breathing abated, Tine reached out to Rupe. She craved closeness in the aftermath of pleasure, the mingling of scents and the press of warm, intimate flesh. He eased himself limply from her and she shifted lengthways along the butcher's block so he could join her there. He slid one arm under her neck, resting his head close to her cheek.

Tine lay quietly beside him, her eyes soft, her face and neck rosily flushed. In surrender she was peaceful, her fears flown. She had been able to relinquish control, not merely submitting to Rupe but joining him with abandon. She felt very close to him and, as he eased himself up to rest on one elbow at her side, she recognised the perfect torpor of afterglow, the intimacy following untrammelled lust. Her hand traced softly along his chest and waist as she felt a great languor overcoming her.

As she drifted into sleep she could sense him trying to shut the refrigerator door with his foot. She felt a mild alarm when he failed the first time and a series of cracks and thuds alerted her to the avalanche of contents to the floor, then the silver light blinked out and the kitchen dropped into the soft grey of early dawn. Tine's last sense was of smell, the sweetish odour of spilled milk almost overlaying the heady musk of sex.

She was disoriented when she woke, her head aching and her neck and shoulders stiff. It took a while before she adjusted, shivering, despite the harsh morning light which promised another blistering day. Beside her, Rupe lay asleep on his side, one leg thrown over her thighs. The butcher's block seemed too small to accommodate the two of them and Tine wondered how they had not rolled off.

She edged to a sitting position, trying to slide from under the weight of Rupe's leg without disturbing him. She was unsuccessful, and his eyes sprung open to stare at her, reflecting her own waking confusion. After a moment his expression softened with awareness and he drew her over him. Tine straddled him, bent over and relaxed, her breasts cushioned against the carpet of his chest. Between her legs, he stirred and settled half-erect along her cleft. It was a peaceful, silent moment broken only by pleasurable awareness and thoughts of the night's coupling.

The air was full of smells; milk souring in the heat, stale sweat and the slightly cloying musk-sweetness of sex-spills. Their morning breaths mingled. Tine felt sticky and chafed, yearning for a shower, yet roused and unable to resist sliding herself along Rupe's hardening shaft. She curved her hips gracefully, aligned, and edged down as Rupe's tip pushed at her. She was not yet lubricated and his penetration caught and burned against her, a sensation which delighted her and made her force herself harder on him.

Rupe groaned, but he raised his hips to assist her movement until he was fully inside Tine. They stilled and she concentrated on clasping the muscles of her vagina, encircling his girth until her juices started to flow and soothe the tight corridor. Then she forced one knee between his, parting his thighs until her right leg lay between them. She eased downwards until his penis was bent slightly back in a position that must be uncomfortable for him. He lay very still, trustingly, as she began to move her hips, her waist moving gracefully. With an effort she straightened her arms to take her weight, and Rupe instinctively grasped her elbows to assist.

As she rode Rupe's stiff shaft it became hard to distinguish who was penetrating whom. To Tine it felt that she had acquired an extension, which she now buried in Rupe. He felt pushed inwards at the root, passive under her control, and aware of how vulnerable he felt both physically and emotionally.

It was a difficult and exhausting movement for Tine to sustain, and she soon rose to straddle Rupe. She sat hard on his hips and rode him, her thighs straining to maintain a steady, tight rhythm. When she faltered slightly it was because she felt the call of a different beat, the demand of her clitoris for pressure. She cupped her mound, and slid two fingers around Rupe's root, then rose until the heel of her hand pressed against her clitoris and she could ride her wrist. The pressure on Rupe's penis was intense, almost painful, as she moved to gratify herself. He was torn for a moment between withdrawing to ease his torment, or remaining to witness Tine taking her pleasure.

Her eyes were dark, wide and glistening, slightly unfocused as she watched him watch her. He had frozen in submission, his expression careful and fascinated as her orgasm flashed through her. A bloom spread along her cheeks, washing down her neck and staining her breasts as her mouth opened in a harsh, primeval cry. She bucked once more against her wrist and Rupe felt her clench him inside her.

He felt a mounting, animal excitement as Tine lost control. He had been used and was thrilled to be a mere cock, an instrument for her pleasure. The sensation made him feel free to take the same liberty with her. As Tine still throbbed against him, Rupe shifted, pulling her under him, and mounted her.

Tine's head and shoulders lolled over the edge of the block, her neck exposed. Her hair fell in a rich chestnut swathe, one lock caught across her throat like a dark gash in the pale flesh. Her breasts were pulled almost flat as her back was curved, her arms spread, falling loosely. Her thighs were widely and submissively parted as Rupe thrust in her.

Rupe felt powerful. Rearing above Tine's limpness, he experienced the savage joy of an animal strength; a mindless, predatory victory. Echoing her selfish use of his body, he thrust for his own pleasure, weaving from side to side to gain the best traction, pulling back until his tip almost slipped from her, then plunging to ever-greater depths. With each thrust, Tine jarred backwards. Rupe's demand was furious and he grabbed hard at Tine to pull her up the slope of his slightly parted thighs until

141

he held her close, pinioned on his rod. He hardly felt the pain of his penis's acute angle. A red mist seemed to glaze his sight as he glanced down along the impossible incline of Tine's body.

Rupe groaned in frustration. His climax seemed as frozen as the muscles which strained, sharply corded, with the effort of restraining his prey. His arms burned with Tine's limp weight and his penis seemed to be merely hot, throbbing and unsatisfied. In response to his moan, Tine stretched herself up to him, her arms around his shoulders. Her legs circled his waist and she sat astride his thighs. She began to rock slowly, her thigh muscles straining. It was clearly an effort as she moved against him, whimpering slightly.

Rupe did not release the harsh hold on her hips. His penis ground hard in her, twisting with her rolling. He was desperately uncomfortable, with his weight on his ankles, pressed hard on the block. His organ felt raw and torn, but stayed hard. Then heat spread through him, crept across his scrotum and rose through his shaft as he erupted, releasing his white lava. As he gouted, he forced Tine away from him as if he might burn inside her if he remained in the volcano of her quim. His member flailed in release, ribbons of come spurting over her until Tine captured his bulb in her cool mouth. His last tired thrusts were between her soft lips and then he relaxed under her nursing, gentle tongue.

Rupe felt drained and confused. He was shocked by his brutal use of Tine and felt emotionally raw. His cheeks were wet and he realised, wearily, that he was crying. Beyond this, he perceived Tine still alive with need. He urged her, with comforting murmurs, onto his aching thigh and tucked his fingers into her, his palm cupped so she could ride the ball of his hand to completion. Tine cooed and murmured as she moved against it, then stayed on his hand to share the small tugs of her spending.

* * *

It was only when Tine felt the soft cloth being placed over her shoulders that she became aware they were not alone. Almost absently she pulled the edges around her and peered at the debris from the refrigerator which scattered the floor. She eased from Rupe to sit tiredly on the block and he groaned loudly as he straightened his legs, rubbing them to restore circulation.

Both were now cloaked in pale blue sheets, and soon mugs of coffee were pushed into their hands. At last Tine sought their benefactor and looked up to see Sharon, clad in an austere business suit, exiting the kitchen. She paused at the door, turning, a small smile playing across her mouth.

'Like I said, a wham-dinger.'

There was no way of knowing how much she had witnessed.

Tine studied Rupe as he bent his head to sip his coffee. His hair hung in dark, untidy tendrils, wisps snagging on the rough bristle that shadowed his jaw. He looked tired yet peaceful, his eyes downcast, his heavy lashes stark against his pale cheeks. The sheet shrouded his hips as his hands, strong and gentle, clasped the mug. The muscles of his arms were soft slopes in contrast to the straining, exerted sculptures she had seen during their lovemaking.

He seemed less of a stranger now. Her body still felt the heat of his invasion, and his scents lingered. They sat cross-legged, knees touching, in silent companionship. It seemed to Tine that the most natural next move would be to sleep, and a part of her wished to snuggle into his curves between crisp, cotton sheets. However, in spite of their torrid union she still feared the real intimacy of waking with him.

Her back and neck were stiff from sleeping on the hard, wooden block and she yearned for the relaxing sluice of her shower, the clean perfume of soap and the freedom to stretch, unrestricted, and be lulled to sleep in the gentle wash of her waterbed. Mostly she needed privacy, to be able to wake alone and review the events

143

of the early morning. Rupe, who she had known for less than a week, was now her lover, confidant and conspirator. The tape on which he had hidden John's precious filters was as significant as the lovemaking they had shared. It seemed, as his jade eyes now met her brown gaze, that Rupe had invaded every part of her, and Tine felt she had to establish a separate control. She needed to define her parameters or she could easily lose sight of the life she wanted to live from this point on.

Rupe gazed at Tine. Her eyes were steady and he could see her thoughts were busy. She looked as she did when she had first opened the door to him; mussed, sleepy and endearing. He was thankful for the gentle pressure of her knee against his, without which the previous hours would have seemed unreal. He felt that this was not about sex; that mystery had been laid to rest. Now everything was way more personal. He had never felt so close to a woman before. As he replayed them in his mind, he felt how the expressions and demands of the woman who now lay quiescent before him had altered his perceptions. A part of him yearned to follow through with his emotions, to commit to her in every way. He knew, however, that Tine would not allow herself to commit the same way. She had shown him enough to make sure that he realised that their time together was temporary.

Another part of him relished the freedom this gave him. Their relationship was based on affection, lust and a trusting, deep friendship which he would not compromise. Her example had encouraged him to begin a new stage of life, and from here on he too would emerge into fresh adventure and risk-taking. They shared a bond which would hold, no matter whether they were together or continents apart.

In the meantime, he looked forward to re-establishing that bond regularly over the next months. The thought brought a smile to his lips, which caused Tine to arch her eyebrows.

'Sleep?'

Her query caused Rupe to realise how tired he felt. He nodded.

'Walk you home?'

Rupe eased stiffly from the block. With Tine at his side, hand in hand, they mounted the stairs. At Tine's bedroom door Rupe drew her to him in a tight embrace, his mouth grazing her forehead. She snuggled into his chest, the tight curls tickling her lips. They stood, enjoying each other's breathing for a moment, and then he held her from him, smiling softly at her.

'Sleep.' His voice trailed off and he kissed the corner of her mouth lightly, then pushed her gently through the door.

Tine smiled and made her way to the shower. She was pleased to be alone and yet disappointed that he had left, in spite of her earlier conviction that she needed this time to herself. As the spray engulfed her she had a vivid picture of Rupe, standing in the other shower, with the water washing away their night's exertions.

She dried her hair and then crept into bed, amazed by how easy it seemed to build someone into her life. She sighed. Feast or famine; she hoped that eventually the choices would not seem quite so absolute.

Chapter Ten

*T*ine woke, still stiff but charged from deep, dreamless sleep. She felt very alive and energised, an eager restlessness demanding that she get on with the day. Forsaking underwear and pulling on a loose sun-suit, she dashed barefoot to the kitchen. She felt acutely hungry.

Stevie was busily clearing the last of the debris from the kitchen floor. She had stacked the vegetables carefully on the freshly scrubbed surface of the butcher's block and her broad grin left Tine in no doubt that the night's shenanigan's remained no mystery to her. The kitchen smelled of pine cleanser, almost blotting out the faint, remaining tang of soured milk.

'Um . . . sorry.' Tine felt contrite. While there was no possible way she could have found the energy to restore the kitchen earlier, the last thing she wanted was for someone else to be faced with the mess.

'I like to clean.' Stevie hugged Tine gently and urged her to the breakfast bar where she would be out of the way. Demmy sat there, nursing a cup of coffee. The girl wore a knowing, leering expression and Tine avoided catching her eye, feeling a now familiar guilt that she did not like Demmy.

'I thought I might get some work done on the computer,' the girl stated.

'What work?' Tine was genuinely curious. There seemed no reason for Demmy to go near the system.

'Well, there might still be unfinished art to uncover.'

Tine stared at Demmy. For one bizarre moment she found herself almost convinced the girl was right, then recognised the manipulation behind the words. Of course Demmy would not know Rupe had removed the filters from the machine, so she would assume there was still a chance she could steal them. Suddenly tired of the game, Tine gave into her dislike.

'Look Demmy,' she sighed. 'The filters are no longer on the computer, okay? There's no point in looking for them. From here on you are barred from using any machine in this house.'

Demmy glared as she absorbed Tine's words and her expression grew more hostile until she leapt to her feet, shouting:

'You bitch, Tine! You stole my picture and now you're stealing my future!'

It was apparent to Tine that Demmy was convinced that she was the victim here and nothing she could say would instil reason, so she simply said nothing. As Demmy stormed from the room, Tine stared after her in puzzlement. She heard the girl rush to Stevie's room and slam the door.

'I'll sort her out later and make sure she no longer hangs around here, okay?' Stevie sounded sympathetic. 'I'd do it now, but I have to go to work in a moment.'

In a few hurried words, Stevie told Tine she was concerned and uncertain about Demmy. The girl had slept next to her in the night like a child, whimpering with bad dreams, and determined in her propinquity. The dark woman had instinctively kept Demmy in line over the last two days, using mainly threats, and her presence seemed to stop the younger girl from hassling Tine. There was something injured about Demmy which made her hostile towards Tine. Stevie was worried about leaving her alone in the house, yet she was hesitant to cast her out. She was also reluctant to continue shoulder-ing any responsibility for the girl.

Tine nodded, assuring Stevie that she was not concerned.

'If I see her, I will try and talk to her.'

'No, just avoid her for now ... trust me, she is not right at the moment.'

Something in Stevie's tone communicated her unease. Tine suddenly felt nervous and agreed. She resolved to question Stevie later but wished that Demmy was not in her home. It felt as if the happy, purple room was harbouring a dark, malicious shadow.

Stevie hugged Tine to reassure her, but found herself burying her nose in the fresh-scented chestnut fall, her good intent thwarted by a resurgence of desire. Tine stiffened for a moment and then relaxed. Seated on the stool, her head was level with the dark woman's breasts and she allowed her cheek to rest softly against the swell.

Stevie wore a white T-shirt, emblazoned with the health club's logo, and dark blue shorts. It seemed that, however she moved, her strength shone through; not merely in the careful honing of her muscles, there was something inside her which radiated a calm power.

As Tine rested, enjoying the measured rise and fall of Stevie's breathing, she longed to be absorbed, to take cover and seek sanctuary. She thought it fanciful but felt as vulnerable as a child. She was also aware of the easy, calming stroke of Stevie's hands on her back and shoulders. It was no wonder, she thought, that this woman controlled Demmy; she had the sort of presence which diffused anger. Tine was also slightly uncomfort-able with the awareness that Stevie attracted her. She was tempted to put her arm around her waist but, luckily, Stevie pulled away before she could do so.

'You are a good person, Stevie.'

'Perhaps not so good.' Stevie carefully planted a soft kiss on Tine's lips. 'But good enough to know your muscles are stiff as hell. I'll give you a massage to loosen out those kinks in the next couple of days.'

Tine felt confused. Fresh from her intimacy with Rupe, she now found herself drawn to Stevie. Had she stopped to observe her stance, as did the other woman, she would have noticed she was leaning towards her, her nipples eager and her lips swollen with invitation. Her imagination had conjured pictures of Stevie, hands oiled, kneading her naked back. More than she wanted Stevie, Tine instinctively recognised that Stevie wanted her. Her mind's eye pictured the dark girl leaning over her, stroking firmly along her spine, kneading her buttocks and pouring scented, warm oils between her thighs. She could almost feel the spill being captured by clever, circling fingers and worked into her skin.

Tine pulled away, blushing as she recognised her fantasies taking hold again. Stevie was unabashed, gazing at Tine with interest and noting the slightly unfocused arousal in the older woman's eyes. She brushed her hand softly over Tine's nipple, then cocked her head to one side, watching arousal war with embarrassment in Tine's expression as she trailed her fingers along the underside of the now forward-thrust breast.

Tine's breath had quickened and her lips had parted. Stevie groaned in frustration, stepped back and shook her head to clear her mind, casting an almost despairing look at the ceiling. When she looked down again, Tine had closed her eyes and pressed her hands to her midriff as if to contain herself.

'I don't understand this at all,' Tine muttered miserably and Stevie could not avoid chuckling.

She placed her lips forcefully on Tine's mouth, thrilling to the hungry give and warm moistness. Then she edged her hand behind Tine's head and under the thick fall of hair, which draped in a heavy, pleasing sweep. Her fingers instinctively probed the skin there, and eventually her professionalism won through. She pulled away and exclaimed:

'Your neck muscles are as stiff as fence-posts!'

Tine looked bewildered, then refocused, staring in almost comical puzzlement at Stevie, while trying to reconcile the change of events. Her expression altered from sheer, unabated lust to dawning comprehension, but before she could say anything Stevie placed a finger firmly over Tine's lips.

'Later, okay? Work now – talk later!'

Before she could object, Stevie sped from the room. Tine sat for a while, attempting to analyse her wanton, irresponsible behaviour, then shook her head dismissively. There seemed to be too many things going on in her life all of a sudden; denial seemed best.

In cleaning up Rupe and Tine's mess, Stevie had carefully stacked the salvageable items in bundles on the butcher's block. After getting herself a cup of coffee, Tine studied the ingredients before her. Racked together were courgettes, tomatoes and an onion. Unable to resist, Tine sniffed each of the courgettes, trying to work out on which one her scent still lingered. She set about preparing a light supper. Later she would reheat the dish and serve it to her young lover, in memory of their first sexual encounter. She chopped the ingredients, added garlic and fennel, white wine and seasoning, and created a sautéed courgette dish to be served with dark, German rye bread and cheese.

As she worked she noticed Jerry trundling around the garden with buckets of water. He made several trips between the tap and the flower-beds, carefully feeding the thirsty plants. At last he upended a bucket over his head, the deluge flattening his hair and chasing over his naked chest to soak through his shorts.

He made a great fuss of kicking off his wet tennis shoes and rubbing his feet dry on his calves, before he entered the kitchen to sniff appreciatively at the cooking smells.

'Hosepipe ban,' he observed without further comment.

He downed a bottle of water from the refrigerator, his throat working hungrily. Dribbles escaped from the sides of his mouth and trickled down his neck. Tine had to smile at his profound sigh of pleasure when he finished drinking. He beamed and indicated he would return later, then ogled Tine appreciatively, gathered up his shoes and left.

The house was quiet. Tine sensed the sleeping presence of Rupe, the sulking of Demmy in Stevie's room and the departure of Jerry. A calm settled and she made her way to the patio where she sat cross-legged on the hot flagstones, munching an apple. She felt that there was something bizarre in her acceptance of the chaos that had erupted since the first of her tenants had arrived, but realised that if order did need to be restored, its time had not yet arrived. The wages for her awakening were in taking risks, and she was prepared to pay the price.

For the first time in days she yearned for rain. The plants looked long-suffering and impatient with their meagre quota of water. The earth was starchy and brittle. With the announcement of the hosepipe ban came a feeling of disappointment. Her garden was struggling and she felt an empathy with it. Some of the plants seemed to have thrived and bore gaily coloured heads, others were wilted but refused to surrender. Several were blackened, dried and dead. Jerry had done wonders, and Tine was surprised he had not removed the skeletons and instead watered around them. She thought he was merely being hopeful but considered that he might know something she did not. In either case she was willing to accept his faith.

Her mind turned to Demmy. Clearly the girl was starved of something that she needed to thrive, just like the wilting plants. In her case, the deprivation had induced a mean hunger. Tine intended to honour Stevie's request and keep away from the young woman, but she hoped that she could, in time, redress any wrong John may have committed. Even though she was sensible enough to realise that her late husband might not have been the cause of any harm, she felt that he could have augmented the damage. The girl seemed unlovable, and that challenged Tine; she resolved at least to be tolerant. She wished that making Demmy blossom into a beautiful person was as simple as throwing a bucket of water over her.

These thoughts revived Tine. She re-entered the cool of the house and made her way up the stairs, intending to change her clothes and then seek the company of Rupe. She was surprised that her mind was not filled with him but she was pleased to think of spending the evening ahead in his company and aware that an anticipatory tingle accompanied her expectations.

As she entered her bedroom she stopped, puzzled, and stared. Her cupboard doors were open, clothes pulled from the hangers and lying heaped on the floor. Drawers were yanked open, their contents strewn. Her first coherent thought was of burglary, and it was only when she heard the slam of the front door that she was startled into racing to the window to peer into the front drive.

She was rewarded with a view of Demmy moving swiftly over the gravel and through the gate. The girl cast a swift glance over her shoulder, raising her eyes to rake the windows and, seeing Tine, she stopped and turned. Her expression was twisted with victory, vindictive, and she deliberately opened her hand to ensure Tine would see her booty, then pivoted on her heel and raced off. In her hand she held the unmistakable rectangular, opaque plastic box of a computer back-up tape.

Tine was furious. Her private room had been invaded and her hospitality abused. All her resolutions to be tolerant had been shattered by Demmy's messy theft. Feeling a little dizzy, she rested her forehead against the glass pane and took several deep breaths.

That was how Rupe found her as he descended the attic stairwell moments later. He could see her through the open doorway, a small, despondent figure slumped against the window. His first inclination was to race to embrace her; then paused with the thought that perhaps

152

Tine regretted their coupling. As he hovered, uncertain, on the landing, he noticed the mess of strewn clothes across her floor and he acted instinctively, moving swiftly behind Tine and encircling her. She twitched in surprise then leaned into him, her head falling back against his chest.

Her body felt pliant and warm against him, like a child, and he felt protective and concerned, although he had no idea what the problem was. He felt a moment of relief when Tine said:

'Demmy has stolen the tape.'

Rupe paused. He felt angry, but chuckled. 'It won't be any good to her. The files are encrypted.'

'She's bound to know the encryption codes. She worked with John for long enough.'

'Perhaps, but she won't know mine.'

'Oh lord. She'll be back when she works that one out.'

'Then,' Rupe muttered, 'I shall talk with her.'

His tone made Tine hope that Demmy was smart enough to keep well away. There was something terribly soothing in the rich basso of Rupe's lazy vowels, despite the threat implicit in his words, and Tine turned to rub her cheek against the fabric of his T-shirt; an acknowledgement of his concern and thanks for his protection.

'She made rather a mess of the room searching for the tape,' she said.

Rupe slid his hand over Tine's breast, cupping and squeezing sympathetically. They stood quietly for a moment, both peering at the street outside the window, while his fingers sought and trapped an emerging nipple, to roll it softly through the fabric of her sun-suit.

'I suppose I should tidy up.' Tine's voice betrayed a sensual languor which indicated she had no intention of moving.

Rupe rubbed his chin on the top of her head. She followed his gaze as it concentrated on a trio of chattering students as they made their way past the house, their voices muted by the double glazing. With normal curiosity one of them peered at the house, her gaze glancing over the windows, then her eyes widened slightly as she caught sight of Tine and Rupe. She turned to clutch the shoulder of a male companion, whispering urgently, and he peered up and smiled broadly. They disappeared from view.

Tine shifted slightly in embarrassment, but Rupe stopped her from hiding from the passers-by. He dropped his head and whispered, his breath tickling her ear:

'I am going to take your clothes off.'

He squeezed her breast, as if to warn her to remain still, and then released her.

Tine stood in a torment of indecision as she felt the straps of the sun-suit being slipped from her shoulders. The trio of students had gone, but were followed by a deluge of teenagers making their way homewards in the late afternoon. The pavements were alive with raised and laughing voices. Tine hoped that these pedestrians were so caught up with their companions that no one else would look up. A part of her, however, was excited by the thought that someone would witness the illicit display which Rupe had initiated.

'I want them to admire you too,' Rupe murmured and tugged the cloth free from her hips. His sigh revealed his delight at the absence of underwear, his hands sliding and circling over her bottom, and trailing his fingers over the tight cleft between her bum-cheeks. Already familiar with the speed with which Tine became aroused, he was anticipating the moment when she would lose sight of her surroundings.

He drew away and Tine heard the rustle of fabric, then felt him press behind her, now as naked as her. His arms once more embraced her and his penis, half erect, pressed against her. She wriggled to urge it to harden.

'Oh no, not yet,' Rupe muttered, his hand sinking over her mound. His fingers buried in the dark curls and sought her clitoris. 'Part for me.'

His voice was a mere whisper, his excitement clearly mounting as more students approached. Despite his intention, he hardened against her, and Tine thrust her bottom back at him instinctively. In spite of her misgivings, she recognised she would soon become blind to the passers-by on the pavement so she closed her eyes, blocking the view of the street and surrendering to Rupe's fingers. She parted her feet so he could reach further into her.

'You get so wet. I wish they could feel how wet you get.' His voice deepened, his breath quickening as he probed, spreading her juices so his fingertips would slip more easily among her folds.

Tine felt him tremble. She knew he was trying to keep his hips still, as if any movement which caressed his stiff penis might break his restraint. His excitement was so palpable that Tine felt herself losing her last inhibitions. She rose to her toes, circled her hips so that his rod lay against her entrance and then captured it, so it lay between her thighs.

Rupe froze, fought to retain control, then surrendered with a helpless groan. He grasped Tine's hips with both hands and urged her to bend forward. She placed both hands on the window-sill and prepared for his mounting with a feeling of triumph. Now she opened her eyes and willed someone to look up at them. Her wish was met when a lone male student seemed to respond to her mental command. He lifted his eyes from the pavement, to stare directly at the window.

At that moment Rupe slipped inside her and Tine moaned with pleasure, her eyes hard on those of the watcher, who had stopped in his tracks. He moved just inside the gate, exercising the presence of mind to pretend he was merely waiting. He dropped a rucksack to the ground and quickly slipped his hand inside the pocket of his loose chinos. Even from the distance of the first-floor window Tine could make out the urgent stroke of his fingers along his hidden length. She wondered if he had been fantasising as he walked down the street; whether he was hard before he noticed the movement at the window, and his prayers had been answered.

Rupe was moving softly inside her, his own gaze shifting between the view of his prick pumping and the young man leaning against the gate pillar, enjoying the show.

'He wants to be me. He wants to be fucking you now.' Rupe's voice was deep with insinuation. 'Would you like that, huh?' As if to punctuate his words, he thrust hard, stilled a moment, then re-commenced his movement.

The young man, frustrated by the restrictions of his pocket, had now undone his flies, and dipped his hand through the gap. He was only partially shielded by shrubbery and seemed aware of the possibility of being seen from the street, so he slipped further into the garden. Once safe, he eased his penis through the opening in his trousers. His long blonde hair flopped untidily as he peered down to ensure he was free and accessible. Then he looked up, his blue eyes fixed and slightly challenging as Tine licked her lips. She felt her saliva flow, knowing that, were he in front of her, she would not hesitate to take his smooth, hard length in her mouth.

As if he had read her mind, Rupe suddenly slipped from her and spun her around, so now her bottom faced the window, her quim on display. The young man flinched and faltered in his self-administration, and Rupe wondered briefly if this was his first clear view of a woman's secret places. At the same time he slipped his bulb between Tine's lips. While he knew the student could not see her circling tongue and working lips, there was no mistaking that he was aware of what she was doing. Rupe leaned forward, grasped and parted Tine's cheeks, then slipped his fingers along the rift. Once his fingers were soaked with her juices, he brought them to his mouth and sucked.

The young man began to stroke faster and Rupe, wanting Tine to witness the voiding, spun her around in time to see the white ejaculate trace through the air and the slump of release in the student's stance. Seconds later the young man tucked himself away and looked about wildly as if to re-establish his surroundings. He stared in amazement at the window then moved off in a hurry, gathering his rucksack and speeding down the pavement without a backward glance.

Tine turned to face Rupe and stared into his eyes in an attempt to decipher his actions. He had surprised her by revealing a side she had not suspected. His pupils were dilated, betraying extreme excitement, and his erection quivered. He had been unyielding in the acting-out of his exhibitionist fantasy and she found the hard, unapologetic jade of his returning stare painfully stimulating.

'If he had been closer,' she whispered, licking her lips, 'I would have fucked him and made you watch.'

Anger flickered across Rupe's face. He carefully grasped Tine's chin, forcing her head to tilt back, his fingers digging painfully into her cheek.

'You love it, don't you?' His accusatory tone was attempting to mock her, but failed as he merely betrayed his wonder.

'Oh yes.' Tine smiled softly. 'I love it.' Her eyes narrowed and she promised, 'Any way you like. I love it.'

She pushed Rupe backwards and onto the bed, straddling him just as the telephone rang. For a moment they stared at each other, then glanced at the offending instrument jangling on the bedside cabinet. Tine lifted the receiver, listened a moment, and offered it to Rupe.

'It's for you,' she said, and pushed him flat when he tried to rise. Rupe cleared his throat and closed his eyes in despair as Tine slipped his penis into her. He covered the mouthpiece and hissed at her:

'It's work!'

Tine nodded sympathetically and rode softly, tightening around his base then rocking her body gently. Lost in her own pleasure, she barely registered Rupe's attempt to ward off the caller. When he started to look desperate and had softened in her, she slid from him, ignoring his look of disappointment. Frustrated, Rupe settled back against the headboard and Tine rested her head in his lap.

Rupe gazed at her while he spoke, stroking her hair and easing a lock behind her ear, which he then circled gently. Tine felt him relax and smiled. When he replaced the receiver with a disappointed sigh, she quietened him.

'The night is young. Stay there and I shall bring you supper.' She slipped from the bed and tugged on the discarded sun-suit, exiting the room with a crumpled grace.

Tine entered the kitchen to find Sharon and Jerry seated at the breakfast bar drinking bottles of Trappist Ale. Between them lay bowls containing taramasalata, tsatsiki and humus, and a large supply of red-hot tortilla crisps. Both were naked, and there seemed to be a competition as to who could spread the greater amount of the dips on the other's body. Sharon's hair was scooped into an untidy knot, held in place with wooden kebab skewers. A few escaping gold locks were spattered with food and a smear of pink paste covered one downy cheek. She grinned at Tine, waved an invitation to take a beer, and took advantage of Jerry's distracted greeting to plop a humus-smeared tortilla chip on his nose. It stuck and he squinted at it before curling his tongue to dislodge it, and then trapped the sliding crisp between his lips. He absently dipped his fingers into the tsatsiki and painted stripes over Sharon's breast, then leaned forward to sweep his tongue over his artwork.

Tine smiled and shook her head. It seemed a sign of the times that their naked fun did no more than arouse a mild curiosity. She set about warming the courgettes and slicing the dark rye bread as the games continued.

'I notice Demmy's gone,' Sharon observed after a moment.

Tine nodded, explaining the theft briefly.

'We're going to Silky Lizzie's tomorrow night. Want to join us? Perhaps she'll be there.' Sharon's voice showed she relished the prospect of cornering the wayward girl.

By this time Jerry had captured and was exploring one pink nipple with his circling tongue and Sharon seemed to be growing distracted. Tine grinned as she collected bowls and spoons on a tray, added the crock of courgettes and a bottle of Yarra Yering, an Australian Shiraz she had been saving for a special occasion. She tipped the bread into a basket and, balancing goblets carefully, lifted the tray. As she slowly mounted the stairwell she considered Sharon's invitation.

Stevie had described Silky Lizzie's to her at the barbecue but Tine, lost in her own thoughts, had missed most of her words. The thought of going out with Sharon and Stevie was intriguing, but she decided not to. There would be future outings.

She did not regret her decision when she entered her bedroom. Rupe sat naked and cross-legged on her bed. Tine recognised that, for many nights to come, she simply wanted to explore this lovely young man. She set the tray carefully on the sheet and Rupe smiled as he lifted the lid of the pot containing the courgettes.

'I'm very hungry,' he stated, staring at Tine and leaving her in no doubt that the food would sate only part of his appetite, and that the balance lay with her.

Despite Rupe's innuendo, his appetite for food overrode his lust for Tine. Together they wolfed the meal, scattering crumbs. After the tray had been safely moved away they sat enjoying the wine and talking companionably. Tine was disappointed to learn that Rupe's telephone call meant his departure for London for a couple of days. While this left her free to reconsider the trip to Silky Lizzie's, Tine still resolved to stay at home. It would be strange to have the house to herself, but she felt compelled to take time out.

'You could come with me.' Rupe looked at Tine hopefully.

She thought with delight of a trip to Harrods while he

was working and the offering of Chinatown restaurants; perhaps Soho at night. But:

'Next time.' Tine was set on having the house to herself and enjoying mundane domestic chores, feeling it would somehow anchor her once more. It crossed her mind that her reluctance to emerge into the world outside her sanctuary was cowardly but she felt no need for haste. She felt happy to proceed at her own pace for at least one night. She felt warm and peaceful, unable to avoid blurting:

'Hey, I'm glad you moved in!'

Rupe lifted Tine's glass carefully from her hand. He set the crystal bulbs carefully on the bedside table and pulled her across the bed, then carefully eased over her. Kissing her softly, his lips sliding moistly along hers, he said:

'I didn't stay put when you went downstairs, you know.' His eyes twinkled. 'I logged on quickly. Dickens wants to speak to us.'

Chapter Eleven

*T*ine stared at Rupe. She had anticipated an evening snuggling and lovemaking. Rupe's wish to chat with Dickens on IRC was unexpected and disappointing, especially as he was disappearing to London the next day. Still, she reasoned, it served her right for having expectations of someone who might have his own agenda. She set aside her misgivings and decided it would be nice to catch up with Dickens; who no doubt would be feeling rather left out.

There seemed to be something rather odd about Rupe's behaviour. He was excited and restless, obviously eager to get to the computer. Tine had never seen Rupe prior to logging onto IRC and perhaps this was his normal behaviour, but it seemed rather juvenile, and she was reminded again of their age difference. She felt slightly remote as she agreed to join Rupe in the attic where, he promised, they could use IRC side by side. He bounded away with enthusiasm, blowing a kiss from the doorway as she settled back thoughtfully to finish her wine.

Tine took her time. She tidied the mess Demmy had made, then showered and washed her hair. It was late evening when she tugged a T-shirt over her wet hair, drew on some panties and descended to the kitchen to tidy away the supper tray. No evidence remained of Sharon and Jerry, and the house seemed strangely quiet. Despite the hour it was still light, the garden visible, though the sharp edges had softened in the dusk. There was a sultry, electric promise in the air. A bank of swiftly moving clouds built in the west.

The cat was stretched sleepily under a shrub, eyeing a bird with lazy interest, and Tine was tempted to forsake Dickens and lounge on the lawn to share the tranquillity. She was surprised at her fickleness as she succumbed to the whim, promising herself no more than half an hour, and made her way outside and onto the lawn. Underfoot the grass was dry and brittle, alive with insects. A bumble-bee steered a drunken course towards her, veering off clumsily to avoid collision, and the cat rose, stretched and sauntered towards the promise of company and a tummy-rub. Tine sat cross-legged on the grass and obliged, soothed by the purring vibrations under her fingertips.

The sun was low and weak when the sky greyed, and it was almost abed when the rain began. It was a soft, unsatisfactory outpouring which threatened no climax, although the air seemed dense with the promise of a storm. At the first drops the cat raced away and disappeared over the fence. Tine shrugged, hugged her knees and felt the wet seep over her until she was drenched and shivering. A wonderful smell of damp, hot earth rose around her and she could feel the garden unfurl from its sleep to drink.

The rain enlivened Tine. She felt that she was awake and alive, with the thirsty, whispering leaves and the promise of a sated night ahead. It was dark. The only window alight in the house was the attic; pale behind drawn curtains. Behind them she imagined Rupe, lounging in the leather swivel chair, his terminal screen alight and the words pouring as his eyes raced over them, his fingers poised over the keyboard to respond. She wished she could fly, rise to peek through the curtains and observe him at play, unaware of a watcher. How differently, she wondered, would he behave?

At last, with her hair glistening and her T-shirt cold and clinging, she made her way silently to the attic. The busy clicking of a keyboard reached her as she approached the doorway.

The attic lounge was transformed. The existing furniture had been pushed back against the walls and cables snaked like wayward ivy across the carpet to mate with three terminals. One, resting atop its computer base, glowed green with importance, betraying its administrative status. Tiny pinpricks of red light on the base flickered urgently as words scrolled on the screen. Tine guessed that Rupe had been working and the machine was compiling a program, running without human intervention. As she watched, it uttered a plaintive bleep and froze, the green glow settling in accusation at Rupe, the red lights tapping their digital fingers softly.

Rupe's hands stilled and he swivelled his chair to face the terminal. Too far away to reach it by stretching, he had to rise and cross the room to attend to the machine, allowing Tine a view of a further two terminals resting on the desk. One was logged onto IRC, displaying a screenful of chatter, and the other rested quietly, presumably awaiting her attendance. With the main lights dimmed, the room was bathed by the glow from the terminals, an outpouring of mute whiteness which spread the virtual environment into their world.

Rupe tapped out a command on the keyboard and the screen smugly resumed activity. He watched for a minute and then straightened, turning to face Tine. Pleasure warred with concern in his expression.

'You're drenched!' He crossed to her and drew his hand over her hair, across her shoulder and over the damp cloth clinging to her breasts.

Tine hugged him, deliberately rubbing against his naked chest, then stood back, satisfied, to note his thick mat was dewed. She gave him a cheeky look.

'I've been playing in the rain,' she stated.

'It's raining?' Rupe concentrated. Over the hum of the computers he could make out the patter of drops at the window. 'Nice.'

He drew Tine to the desk and, once reseated, pulled her onto his lap. The old chair creaked a small protest at their combined weight. Tine sat sideways, stretched her legs over one arm and nestled her head on Rupe's shoulder, so she could read the screen. Rupe stretched his arms around her to reach the keyboard, typing accurately but slowly:

Rupe>   Found her! Astyr is now curled up all damp on my lap.

Dickens>   Damp? The mind boggles. Hi Astyr :-)

Rupe>   She says 'Hi'. Yup, she played in the rain. Drenched through she is, dripping all over me.

Dickens>   To be fair, from what you have told me, you have done your fair share of dripping over her these past couple of days!

'Oho,' muttered Tine, 'and what have you told him?'

'Everything. In great and gory detail.' Rupe was unapologetic.

Dickens>   Well, you have this gorgeous woman on your lap, so what are you going to do with her?

Rupe>   Kick her off?

Dickens>   Nerd!

Rupe>   You tell me then :-)

Dickens>   Ask Astyr. As I recall, she has a rampant imagination.

Tine imagined Dickens, sat at his computer thousands of miles away, the Californian sun pouring through his windows. The contrast: Dickens alone in the sunshine, she and Rupe together and intimate, with the rain thrumming a duet with the computers. It was still a moment the three could share. She had so often felt the realness of her electronic liaisons, the words projecting images which seemed to reach from the machine and finger her softly. Rupe was articulate and therefore she knew he could shed 'fingering' images into Dickens' space.

'Tell him what I am doing.' She slipped from Rupe's lap and stepped to the side of the chair, quickly stripped off her T-shirt and dropped it carefully outside of the range of cables and computers.

Her sheer panties, wet through, were translucent and outlined her pubis with its wispy hair. As she drew them from her, they felt clinging and reluctant. Tine urged them over her legs, bending to slip them from each foot in turn. Still leaning over, she turned from Rupe and parted her feet to allow him a full view of her pudenda.

Rupe>   Astyr has stripped her clothes. She is now
            bent over and I can see her quim.
Dickens>   Tell me how it looks.
Rupe>   Pale and delicate, pink lobes descending into
            mauve. She is at rest.
Dickens>   How does she taste?

Rupe swivelled the chair to face Tine. Her soft spread was almost level with his eyes and he studied her for a moment, then leaned forward and delicately buried his tongue in her folds. She trembled a little but stood firm. She had heard Rupe stop typing and the creak of the chair as he turned, so his attention was not entirely unexpected. She conjured the image in her mind's eye; Rupe, dark hair swirling around his naked shoulders, his face buried and his tongue massaging her to urge forth her juices. She imagined Dickens watching.

Tine wondered what Rupe had written. Unashamedly she thrust backwards and met the resistance of his mouth, feeling herself open and swell as his tongue-tip found and circled her clitoris. To her intense disappointment he withdrew and, moments later, she heard his fingers moving over the keyboard. She remained in place, anticipating more attention.

Rupe>   She tastes like oyster sauce, smooth and slightly salty, with the same slickness. There is also something sweet. Perhaps like rose-flavoured Turkish Delight.

Dickens> You tasted her. Just then?

Rupe>   Yes. She is leaned over beside the chair. I licked and sucked her and pushed my tongue into her. Her nether lips are starting to blush and become very wet.

Dickens> How does she feel?

Rupe returned to Tine and stroked his fingers along her rift. He closed his eyes and concentrated. There was a gentle spring of sparse curls as his fingers crept over her mound, then the soft texture of her labia. He urged his index finger between her folds and her moisture enveloped it as her tissues parted under his probing. His finger sunk into Tine. Still tight, though wet, he felt the ribbing of her inner walls, the elastic muscle at her entryway and the curve of her passage. Unable to resist, he twisted his hand so his thumb rubbed her starry anal entrance. He pressed harder and the firm muscle clutched around his thumb-tip.

Rupe opened his eyes, surveying the scene with an almost clinical detachment; his hand captured finger and thumb in Tine. He noted that her thigh muscles were clenched and her hands, surrounding her ankles for support, had tightened, her knuckles white. He pushed into her and was rewarded with a sharp, delighted moan as his thumb penetrated. There, she seemed more firm and smooth, slick but not wet; satin as opposed to silk. He withdrew and noticed her legs bend slightly to release tension.

'You can stand up now.' His words came out as a whisper, and he cleared his throat. Then he returned to the keyboard, taking pleasure in the fact his wet fingers left traces on the keys.

Rupe>   She feels like satin and silk. Silk soft and giving, shifting easily – that is her cleft and cave. Her little, tight arse is like satin; firm and smooth.

Tine had risen, stretching to ease her muscles. As Rupe typed, she read the screen. She felt strangely peaceful, slightly remote from the scene, as if she were observing rather than participating. She recognised the detachment as the same feeling she had experienced with John when they made love in front of a naughty video. It seemed an impersonal but arousing event, the provocation outside of the rutting reality. This was for Dickens, he was the instigator and they were merely the tools.

'My turn,' she said. 'Take off your pants and kneel beside the chair, facing it.'

Rupe obeyed.

Tine grimaced at the stickiness of the keys as her fingers travelled over them. She changed the nickname to Astyr, so Dickens would know it was now her who typed.

Astyr>   Hello. Rupe is now kneeling beside me. He is naked and very beautiful, his hair wild and loose ... his body soft in the light from the screen. He can read as we type.

Dickens>   How do you feel, Astyr?

Astyr>   Strange, as if you should be here and aren't. I am aroused and wet. I feel swollen and squashed against the leather of this chair.

Dickens>   Oh God, I wish I was there! I want you to tell me how Rupe tastes and feels. Touch him and take him in your mouth.

Tine turned to Rupe. She smiled and tapped her fingers along his already excited cock while she looked into his eyes. His foreskin offered spongy resistance over the harder, veined tube which quivered beneath. He seemed so large as her fingers circled his girth, pumped gently to test the elastic stretch and give, then eased back his foreskin to expose his bulb. At last she leaned to lap at the pearl of pre-cum, then licked along her lips to coat them.

She slid her tongue around his satiny, rounded head, tucking under to press against the lip of skin there, then tightly surrounded Rupe's shaft with her pursing lips. As Tine took him in she tried to memorise how he felt under the slide of her lips, how she felt his occupation of her mouth. She sucked in her cheeks to encourage more fluid from him, succeeding when it leaked thickly into her throat.

Rupe laid his hands on Tine's head, stroking her hair as he looked down. He was experiencing the same dislocation as she, almost amazed, despite the reality of his aching erection, to find her head bowed to him. A part of him wanted to force into her and take possession of her throat, working hard in her until he released. He wanted to use her but was made vulnerable by her helplessness. She seemed fragile and unaware of his more massive strength, and yet she seemed in control. She tamed his beast and he felt weak, supplicatory and overwhelmingly thankful for the pleasure which was expanding from his groin as her mouth and tongue trapped and manipulated him.

When Tine suddenly ducked her head, with her throat wide open, he slid hard into her throat. He whimpered at the unexpected, hard clench then moaned, with anguished disappointment, as she swiftly withdrew.

Tine sat up. Rupe's penis bulged furiously, the head engorged and purple. It weaved, as if seeking a nest, then settled in a sullen, rising arch. Tine leaned to cup beneath him, her palm hefting the weight of his testicles in their loose pouch. She rolled her fingers, thoughtfully feeling the soft balls, then let go and returned to the keyboard.

Astyr>   Rupe is large. He has a thick, loose foreskin
          and I look forward to slipping my tongue
          beneath it as I suck his tip one day. He
          arches upwards and his bulb is shaped like
          a Shitake mushroom, sharp-domed then
          widening to a brim. He tastes bitter at first,
          sharp and thin ... then thick and salty-
          sweet, like yellow bean sauce.
Dickens> Is he still kneeling?
Astyr>   Yes
Dickens> I want you to fuck. But I want to hear about
          it.

Tine glanced at Rupe, who was reading the screen. She
rose, pushed the chair out of the way and knelt on her
hands and knees, edging under the desk. Despite her
earlier exposure to Rupe she now felt more vulnerable.
She was roused and willing, but was also feeling depersonalised. She imagined, with her accommodating,
doggy stance, her bottom exposed and her cave open for
penetration, that she was merely a convenient hole for
Rupe's tool. Fancifully, she imagined a line of men
queuing, each taking their turn at her. It sent a perverse
thrill of excitement and shame through her and she
suddenly became eager for the first customer, pretending
it was not Rupe, but a stranger whose hands would part
her bum-cheeks to gain easier access.

Rupe lined up behind Tine, still on his knees. His
penis lay slightly higher than her flushed quim so he
grabbed their strewn clothes and created a bolster which
he pushed beneath her knees. The effect was to raise her
and trap her against the underside of the wooden desk.
Viewing her like that was strange. He could see nothing
but her spreading need, the soft line of her parted thighs
and smooth curve of her calf down to dainty, bared feet.
He was alive to the fact she could be a stranger and it
seemed warped and perverse, as if he should throw
money to her before rooting for his own pleasure. He
found himself thinking with slight repulsion of Demmy,

whose sturdy rear and short skirt had caught his eye the first time he had seen her.

Slightly ashamed he transposed Demmy onto Tine. The position seemed more suited to the dark girl. More honestly, he recognised his desire to pump heedless and spew his seed without the obligation of closeness that he enjoyed with Tine. Before him he saw only disassociated sex, wet and ready for his entry.

He turned his attention to the waiting screen, changing back to his name.

Rupe>   She is crouched under the desk. I can only see her bum. She could be anybody.

Dickens>   To her, you could be anybody too – perhaps even me. I would take her slowly. Make her wet and push your tip into her, then stop.

As Dickens' words appeared, Rupe rubbed his fingers along Tine. It was a clinical effort to slicken her for his entry; a fact of which she had to be aware. He bent his member to her opening and thrust forward, feeling his tip slide in. Then he stopped, as instructed.

Rupe>   My cock-head is in her. When I look down I can see my shaft. It seems a long way away, as if it has nothing to do with me. She is very still.

Dickens>   Not your shaft buddy – mine, okay? Now I am going to fuck her slowly.

Rupe felt displaced. He projected, divorced himself from his body and imagined Dickens knelt there in his stead. Thrusting slowly, he watched the wet juices coating his penis, which seemed like something alien, not a part of him. He felt the soft friction of Tine's core tease along his length and almost wished that he were watching Dickens softly plough into her, rather than experiencing this strange detachment. With an effort he brought to mind the image of Demmy, his Tank Girl, with her ready rear and stocky thighs. It felt somehow easier, and he could not resist an exploratory, harsh plunge, which caused Tine to clench her buttocks.

Under the desk, Tine crossed her arms, grasped her elbows and rested her chin on the bridge created by her forearms. In the dim light she could make out a tangle of cables and the hard edges of a power source. A computer just above her generated a loud hum which blocked the noise of the keyboard. She felt Rupe sliding in and out of her, and wondered how her body stayed so willing while her mind was elsewhere and cool. Closing her eyes, she resurrected one of her fantasies.

She imagined the stranger . . .

He was the first of two, stocky, his broad chest straining at the cotton of a half-undone and sweaty shirt. A mass of curling, blond hair escaped at the open neckline. A labourer, with hard features and callused fingers, which were rough as he groped between her thighs to test her readiness. As he probed rudely he muttered words at her, as if calming her in case she chose, skittishly, to prevent his access. From his voice she could tell he was mature, possibly middle-aged. He warned her to be good, that he was just trying her out for his son, who was next in line and a virgin. He wanted quality, a good sturdy rear and a wet, wanting hole. While he spoke he fingered, obviously enjoying his own foray, then he sunk his prick into her.

He was big, and consumed the space within her with little regard for her own comfort. She could feel the length of him deep inside her, and it hurt her slightly. He had imprisoned her hips with his large, strong hands. As he thudded, he breathlessly uttered obscenities interspersed with encouragement.

'You love it,' he grunted, burying hard in her. 'Wet and willing. My son is gonna shaft you good.' He described in graphic detail the joy he would have watching the teenager enjoy his slippery 'seconds'. He would tell him how to do it, he promised, how to stick his prick in her and pump. He reminded her that soon he would reward her for being a good girl by dumping his load of 'precious' in her lovely hole. Despite the crude shafting, Tine found herself frantically aroused. Trapped as she was, she could not return the pressure against the sweep of the hard length plunging at her. She anticipated the invasion of the young man, imagining him slipping along her entryway, aided by the thick ejaculate left by his father. Persuaded that the relentless pounding was the gift to his son, Tine hoped the offering would be treasured and felt herself blend into the game, willing a strong and rich pour. She feared the young man would be repulsed and timid.

With a harsh grunt the man completed and, as promised, his coming was full and rich, leaking along her thighs as he slid unceremoniously from her. He slapped her sharply with an open palm and tendered a final, crude compliment as he beckoned to his boy.

The young man was ready and willing. He slipped, unable to enter easily due to the mingled wet of Tine's juices and the overflowing ejaculate. Trembling with eagerness, he fumbled at her entry and Tine, frustrated at his lame attempts, eventually stretched her arm back through her legs, grasped his penis and tugged, to provoke him to jab. He slid along her cleft and with the momentum caused by a mighty thrust, slid off-course and swiftly past the hard, muscular boundary of Tine's lower star, heaving to a stop when deeply buried in her anal passage.

Rupe>   She is telling me she wants me to fuck her
           rear.
Dickens> Do you want to?
Rupe>   Yes.
Dickens> Then do it.

Tine felt Rupe's withdrawal and then the hard press of his tip against her rear pucker. He pressed hard until he slid past the tight band and then stilled, feeling her tightness clench, then ease, around his penetration. Rupe

172

had begun his thrust to climax prior to his change of passageway, and seemed unable to prevent his hard drive.

Crazed from her fantasy, Tine yelled encouragement, thrilling to the different possession, the lawless joy and shame of being taken in her most shy of places. Deep within her she felt wrenched, a riding dullness seeped around the hard probe burying in her. It felt as if her whole inside shivered with the thrill of her impalement. She cried out moments before the harsh, bass shout that preceded Rupe's expulsion. He gouted, driving hard until he was drained and then he stilled, panting, crouched between the tremble of Tine's buttocks. Shifting slightly, he slipped his fingers beneath his shuddering penis and probed Tine's vaginal passage. He felt shamefully curious but was reassured by the residual, circling tug on his fingers.

As he had come, Rupe had slumped, his forehead hitting the keyboard with some force. There was a massed jumble of letters and numbers creating nonsense on the screen.

Rupe>   We are done.
Dickens> And I too, but that is another story :-) I think,
          now, that you two need to be alone.

Not bothering to log off, Rupe slipped from Tine and helped her out from beneath the desk. As she emerged he gathered her to him, his arms gentle and enfolding. They slid the small distance to the carpet. Rupe curled and Tine backed, trembling, into his safe contours. For a long time neither spoke.

It was thirst which finally caused Rupe to release Tine, with the promise that he would return with drinks. He pulled on a pair of denim jeans and made his way to the kitchen. He realised that he needed sugar, and was sure that Tine would share his craving. They had used a great deal of energy, and she was as tired as him.

Rupe collected two bottles of mineral water and quartered oranges, which he had chilled in the refrigerator. On his way back to the attic he paused at the bathroom, unloaded his cargo and set the bath taps to run. He found some bath crystals in a glass jar and poured a generous amount into the flowing water. The room soon filled with pungent vapours, which followed him out to the landing and up the attic stairs.

Tine had not moved. She lay curled and sleepy, and did not protest as Rupe lifted and carried her to the bathroom. He slipped her into the warm water before shedding his jeans and easing into the bath to face her, then stretched his legs around hers. She smiled and tucked her toes into his scrotum, chuckling as his limp penis bounced, buoyant in the water.

They sucked the orange quarters noisily, the sweet juices escaping down their chins, and greedily gulped the water direct from the bottles.

'Can we talk about it?' Rupe felt unsure. He felt confused and slightly guilty, as if he had committed Tine an injustice.

As Tine rose, the water slopped untidily and threatened to spill over the edge of the tub. She pushed Rupe down so he relaxed against the end of the bath, then slipped between his thighs and leaned back to rest her head on his chest. Her hair trailed in the water, spreading in chestnut whorls over his hips. He had not thought they could be so comfortable. He rested his head on the cool, mirrored wall and stroked Tine's hair.

She told him about her fantasy, sharing the explicit details and embellishing with details of the smells and noises. Her voice was soft and intimate and her confession provoked his.

'Tank Girl.' Tine sounded intrigued. 'Would you like to fuck her?'

'No. It just seemed more the sort of thing she would do.'

'Ah, but she didn't do it, I did. You find that surprising?'

'Yes. As I find myself surprising.'

Tine lifted Rupe's hand from the water and kissed it.

'You see, you can't predict me. You can't create images instead of seeing people. I'm older than you, and you thought I seemed like a nice woman, but just now I acted like a whore – and I felt like a whore. And I loved it.'

Rupe did not miss Tine's criticism. He had created an image of her which pre-judged her. He thought what they had done was dirty. Because he could not reconcile his mental image of Tine with the act, he had substituted an image of Demmy.

'You are a dirty lady,' he mused.

'And you're a dirty boy!'

Rupe heaved himself from the bath, this time drenching the floor. Grabbing towels, he threw them over the puddles, then knelt on them beside the bath.

'I think I should give you a good wash – get rid of some of that dirt?'

Rupe was gentle, treating Tine like a fragile child, soaping the parts he could reach thoroughly then rubbing her down with a damp flannel. He urged her to her knees and stroked soapily between her thighs, noticing her wince as his fingers rode between her bum-cheeks and over her anal star. He rose and pulled her to her feet, lifted the hand-shower from its cradle by the taps and turned it on, directing the warm needles to rinse her. He turned her around then, parting her bum-cheeks, ran the water over her tender pucker. It stung at first and Tine flinched, then it eased and Rupe could stroke his finger over her without it hurting.

'How did you know about that?' Tine asked, referring to the healing of the sitz-bath.

'I read a lot.'

'Oh? I can't wait to know more.'

'I am sore, you'll have to!' Rupe's protest made her chuckle.

Tine stepped from the bath and pulled fresh towels from the airing cupboard. As she patted herself dry, Rupe bathed himself, splashing happily. He sat on the edge of the bath as Tine towelled him roughly, ignoring his remonstrations. Eventually pink and clean he pulled her to him, looking up at her with bright green eyes as she stood between his thighs.

'Tonight,' Rupe planted a kiss on her tummy before peering up again, 'we sleep together.'

The house was asleep when they exited the bathroom and climbed, naked, to the attic. Tine longed for a hot drink despite the late hour and Rupe, seemingly clairvoyant, pointed her to the bedroom and disappeared.

The bed was crumpled, the duvet skewed and thrown back. The rain still pattered, more noticeable now she was away from the computers, rivulets chasing down the pane of the skylight. Risking the entry of water, Tine urged the sloping window open a couple of inches. The air rushed in, cool and fresh. Moving into the shower room, Tine found a toothbrush still in its plastic tube, unwrapped it and brushed her teeth. She used Rupe's hairbrush, leaving her chestnut strands wound around the bristles with his thicker, black hair.

Tine pulled the bed straight and snuggled in, breathing Rupe's scents on the pillowcases and sheets. She plumped up the pillows and leaned back against the headboard as Rupe entered, bearing two mugs of fragrant tea.

'No milk, no sugar.' He placed a cup in her hands, set his on the bedside table and brushed his teeth with her toothbrush, then unthreaded a copper strand from the hairbrush with a smile. She watched him through the open doorway, admiring his body as he unselfconsciously completed his ablutions.

He leaned against the doorpost and stared at her, arms crossed, his expression serious.

'This gives a whole new meaning to coming to bed.' His eyes were admiring and warm.

He snuggled in beside her, sipped his tea and enjoyed the feel of her warm thigh against his. Eventually Tine drew the pillows from behind her and turned to lie on her stomach, her face towards Rupe. He drew himself down beside her, his hand resting on her bottom.

'I have to leave really early tomorrow.' He sounded mournful, which made her smile. 'I won't wake you.' He dropped a kiss on her lips as Tine's eyes closed and she drifted into contented sleep.

Chapter Twelve

*T*ine woke, confused. Accustomed to the steady give of her waterbed, the sprung mattress seemed unyielding under her. It took a few seconds before she recalled where she was, then she curled on her side, buried her face in Rupe's pillows and inhaled deeply. His side of the bed was cool, which indicated that, as promised, he had risen and left without disturbing her. What had woken her was the steady hum of the vacuum cleaner on the landing below. As she listened the tone changed, unmistakably mounting an attack on the lower stairwell. The clock on Rupe's bedside cabinet beeped the hour, eight o'clock.

Further sleep was thwarted by the domestic activity below and Tine, resigned, slipped from the bed. She spied a T-shirt on the floor, and pulled it over her head. It turned out to be Rupe's worn, programmer's top, which hung loosely on her. It was creased, smelled musky and felt reassuring.

Tine descended to find Sharon energetically plunging the vacuum cleaner half-way down the stairwell. The blonde woman looked radiant. She had tied a scarf around her hair and donned a halter-necked top and denim shorts in an attempt, Tine guessed, to look like a domestic char. She had merely succeeded in looking as charming as ever. The effect was heightened by the pink flush of exercise blooming across her cheeks, which enhanced their contrast with her violet eyes.

Tine stood grey and crumpled, her arms crossed, and tapped her foot until Sharon noticed her. An expression of dismay crossed the younger woman's face.

'Oops! I saw the ravishing Rupe exiting with rucksack in hand, and I knocked on your door but there was no answer, so I decided you had both gone out. Sorry.' She grimaced, gesturing at the machine. Unable to maintain an apology for long, she glanced up and down Tine, eyes narrowed. 'So you've taken up Rupe's couture as well as his hormonal imbalances then?'

Tine laughed and edged past as Sharon switched off the vacuum cleaner. They both entered the kitchen to find Stevie munching a bowl of muesli. The dark girl wore a blue track suit and was still damp from a shower.

'Does everyone get up early in this place?' Tine demanded.

'Apart from you, yes.' Sharon raised her eyebrows. 'Anyway, I have a day off work and was bored before I'd got up, so I decided to clean. And now I am going to cook you a high-calorie fried breakfast, Madame.'

'Sounds good to me.' Tine settled at the breakfast bar opposite Stevie who looked disapproving but did not start a lecture on healthy diets.

As Sharon cooked, Tine told the two women about Demmy's behaviour the day before. Stevie looked furious and Sharon unsurprised as she explained the nature of the theft and the significance of the stolen tape.

'I suspect she's not going to leave it at that, especially when she finds out she cannot access the filters,' Tine finished just as Sharon slid a plateful of fried foods in front of her. She felt ravenous and tucked into bacon, egg, sausage and tomatoes while Stevie raged about Demmy. It was obvious that she was sorely disappointed and very angry with Demmy, and Tine hoped that the girl would stay away. It was frightening to witness

179

Stevie's anger, though not frightening enough to upset her appetite.

'Change the locks,' were Stevie's final words before falling silent.

Tine stared at her in surprise. 'You think that's necessary?'

'Look,' Sharon interrupted, 'we have no idea what that girl is going to do, so why don't we all just go shopping in London today?'

'Not with these locks.' Stevie seemed to think the proposed trip not as astonishing as the idea of leaving the house unattended.

'The locks aren't really a problem. You've all got Yale keys for the upper lock on the front door, but I'm the only one with the mortise key, and a key to the back door,' Tine said. 'So if Demmy has stolen or copied a key, it'll be useless if the mortise locks are locked.

'So then, let's go. We'll use the Porsche. It needs a run anyway,' Sharon persisted.

'Aren't you two going out tonight?' Tine peered at them.

'We'll be back in time. We weren't going to go out until almost midnight. It isn't nine now. A couple of hours' drive either way gives us a few hours in the city.' Sharon paused. 'And of course I need something to wear tonight.'

Tine laughed at her lie, not believing that Sharon's extensive wardrobe ever lacked appropriate clothing. She liked the idea of an impromptu shopping trip and driving to London added zest to it. She had not wanted to go to Silky Lizzie's but the idea of a shared day with Sharon and Stevie promised to be fun. Realising she was winning, Sharon quickly cleared away the breakfast clutter.

'I know this great shop in Soho for all sorts of gear!'

Stevie's interest was sparked. 'Oh yes? What sort?'

'Leather, silk and gadgets. Plus I get a discount.' That seemed to close the deal, having persuaded Stevie and piqued Tine's curiosity. They looked silently at each other for a moment, then nodded and laughed in unison.

'Okay, coffee! Then we change and go?' Sharon was victorious. 'Over coffee we can also discuss Rupe's prowess in bed. You two make enough noise anyway.' She glanced cheekily at Tine.

'I thought you were asleep!'

'Oh that's an excuse is it, mummy, the kids are asleep?'

Tine shook her head in mock despair. Sharon's irrepressibility was the very reason the woman was so likeable. She sipped her coffee thoughtfully.

'Actually he is rather saucy,' she admitted.

'Tell.' Sharon shuffled onto a stool beside Tine and elbowed her conspiratorially.

Stevie groaned. 'If these poor blokes could only hear how you women discuss them, it would fry their brains! Ah well, tell anyway.' She grinned at Tine.

'Well,' Tine warmed to the task, 'he has a great body.'

'Cute buns.' Sharon nodded.

'He is uninhibited, you know, with that genuine enthusiasm blokes have before they get too experienced? They do it naturally and then get all sophisticated and start being selfish.'

'You know the wrong chaps, honey!' Sharon retorted.

'You,' Tine protested calmly, 'would get the ones who would worship you anyway. Us less gorgeous individuals have to make do and grovel a little.'

Sharon looked puzzled. She was aware she was attractive because she had been told it often enough, but she had never actually felt that she was beautiful. In spite of her obvious success with men she always felt slightly surprised when they fell for her. Men responded to Sharon, she felt, because they thought her a vamp; a situation she thoroughly enjoyed, along with the game-playing involved. However, there were times when she just wanted to put on her flannel pyjamas and snuggle up, with a mug of warm cocoa, to chat with a partner. She envied Tine's easy, caring association with Rupe because it was the kind of relationship she had never shared with a man.

To her surprise she found herself telling this to her listeners, now quiet and serious. As she spoke her eyes widened, casting about as if seeking escape from her mouth, from which the words poured, seemingly unstoppable. Eventually she subsided, staring at Tine and Stevie with wide-eyed, violet incomprehension.

Tine blinked, then threw her arms around Sharon.

'Welcome to the world,' she chuckled. 'We're going to have to work on your self-image, though.'

'I have no idea where that came from!' Sharon recovered her composure swiftly, astonished at how vulnerable she felt after her outburst. She realised with amazement that, for the first time she could recall, she actually trusted the people she was with. Not that she ought to be surprised, she thought; she had felt at home ever since she moved into this house. Tine's warmth and Stevie's solidarity embraced her.

'I have women friends!' she exclaimed at last.

'Now don't get carried away,' Stevie teased. 'I, for one, am not genderist.' She sniggered. 'Or perhaps that's something we should also work on.'

'I've got a better idea. Let's go tidy up and get on the road.' Sharon regained control and slipped from her stool. She wagged a finger at Tine and added, 'Maybe we can continue our conversation about Rupe in the car.'

Tine found her bedroom strange. The bed seemed aloof after her night's absence, and lonely. She realised that apart from holidays with John, she had not slept outside the room in years and had not realised how familiar surroundings could so easily become alien. Her memories of John were still very real and she could, even now, picture him curled and gently snoring in that bed. But now these images were more vividly overlaid with the image of Rupe, sat cross-legged, eating sautéed courgettes.

Conscious of her recent loss of weight, she slid open

the cupboard doors and was immediately disappointed. Her clothes were tailored and would hang miserably on her now; not the image for sophisticated London. Eventually she stopped worrying, shrugged, and found blue jeans and a denim blouse; she would wear a bright silk camisole and leave the shirt loose and open. They were shopping, she reminded herself, not appearing on a catwalk.

After showering, dressing and applying a minimum of make-up, she tied her hair back with a silk scarf and returned to the kitchen, where she was forced to reconsider. Sharon and Stevie were waiting, both clad in style. Sharon wore a red, halter-necked catsuit, seventies fashion, with large, white polka dots. Her hair was wound into a French pleat. White stack sandals, a huge white bag and daisy ear-rings completed the ensemble. Stevie was splendid in black; wearing a tight, sleeveless top and leather waistcoat, skin-tight lycra leggings and bomber boots. A wide belt, studded with a huge, dull silver buckle, spanned her waist.

Tine felt slightly lost. She recognised that if the others projected an image then so did she, and the nearest she could identify was 'housewife'. No bad thing in itself, but she yearned to reflect an identity which brought her out of the shadows. She had been locked away for too long. Without a word she turned and stomped from the kitchen, raced back to her room, and threw open her cupboard.

Sharon glanced at Stevie with her eyebrows raised and prepared more coffee. She admired the dark woman, not so much for her perfect muscle-tone and gleaming good health, as for the still certainty which settled like deep calm wherever Stevie happened to be. There was an aura of safety in Stevie's company, and of tolerance. Sharon realised that this was probably the outcome of painful experiences and an acceptance of self; a process she knew she would have to undergo herself, if she was ever to reach the same calm.

'You think too much,' Stevie guessed.

'It's the only way to keep one step ahead.' Even as she spoke Sharon knew it was untrue, and she was prevaricating. Like Tine, she had to shed the past and re-emerge. When she moved into the house she had been aware of John's death; the newspapers had been full of it the previous year. What she saw in Tine was her own coming-out, but Sharon had simply buried herself in false images rather than confronting herself in solitude. What had worked for Tine could work for her.

She attempted honesty.

'No. I don't think things through, and usually too late.'

'It's never too late.' Stevie's voice was understanding. 'It is about deciding what you want. That can change at any time.'

'You want Tine.' Sharon was direct.

Stevie nodded. 'Sure, but that doesn't mean I can get her, and that's okay too. Mind you, it doesn't mean that I won't keep trying.'

Tine reappeared at that moment, looking slightly defiant. She had changed into a sheer black bodystocking, with a minute green and black tartan mini-kilt, and she had braided her hair. She wore laced ankle-boots of fine leather, with wineglass heels. She looked waif-like; delicate enough for a gust of wind to sweep her away. The material clinging to her betrayed each curve, the slight etch of her ribs and her rounded breasts and areolae; it could have been painted on. It was an unusual outfit, made more eccentric when she hefted a huge, black leather bag to her shoulder. It made her look more frail.

Stevie whistled her appreciation, and Sharon clapped her hands gleefully. 'It works!'

Tine blushed. She felt pleased. Unlike before, she had simply selected colours and textures she felt to be right. The sensual hug of the body-stocking appealed to her, and under it she was naked. The skirt, absurdly short, was her only concession to decency. She felt thin and sexy, hoping, in her walk through the London streets

184

that a gust of wind would lift the tartan pleats to reveal the outline of her pubis to passers-by. Just to sit in a restaurant or bend over a counter, knowing her own nakedness, would be pleasing. An illicit glimpse that might be granted to a stranger was exciting.

'And,' she said, as if continuing a conversation, 'I shall buy a leather waistcoat like yours, Stevie, in case it gets cold.'

'No better shop for it than where we're headed!' Sharon jingled the car-keys.

The trip down the M1 was uneventful. Tine, because she was petite, was bundled in the rear of the Porsche and was surprised, given the apparent lack of room, at its comfort. Before long she had curled up, her head resting on the cool, soft suede, and dozed. As she drifted in and out of sleep she was amazed at the conversation she overheard. Stevie had commented on the car and, as they entered the outskirts of London, Tine heard the tail-end of a highly technical discussion about the engine performance and gear ratios of various top-range cars.

Sharon was a dextrous and confident driver, weaving in and out of the traffic with casual sureness without breaking her conversation with Stevie. When Tine sat up to peer with interest at her surroundings, she caught Sharon's glance at her in the rear-view mirror.

'Hello sleepy, good timing!'

They parked in a multi-storey car-park. Sharon eased the Porsche into a reserved parking bay, much to Stevie's apparent alarm. Before her passengers could comment, the blonde woman ushered them from the vehicle and shepherded them towards a security cubicle. A young man watched their approach with obvious relish, grinning broadly when Sharon suddenly executed a pirouette before him, her arms outstretched.

'Hello miss,' he said. 'Your dad was here earlier asking if I'd seen you recently.'

'Well, now you can say you have. He's not at the shop, is he?'

'No, he was leaving in the tank,' the man muttered cryptically.

'Perhaps I'll catch up with him.' Sharon waved and led Tine and Stevie on, now mystified but obedient followers.

There was something in Sharon's attitude which forbade inquiry, a defiant set to her shoulders. When neither of her followers sought information her tension seemed to ease and she returned to good humour, pointing out small landmarks as they made their way along Brewer Street into the heart of Soho.

Tine was busily peering into the window of a small bookshop when her companions suddenly disappeared. Sharon returned a moment later to grasp her arm and tug her through a doorway. She got an impression of black lacquer and gold door fittings before she was plunged into the cool, dim interior of a hallway which led through to an up-market boutique. She caught a glimpse of Stevie turning a corner ahead and, following her, stopped and stared as an assistant approached to fling her arms around Sharon.

The woman was incredibly tall; over six foot in height, Tine guessed. She wore an elegant and tailored grey suit. Her red hair was carefully coiffured to hang in a luscious fall over one shoulder and her generous mouth was painted a bright, provocative red.

'Shar! It's been far too long, darling. Your father was here a mere half-hour ago.' Her voice was rich and deep, 'plummy' as Tine's mother would have described it. The woman hurried on: 'We've got in a whole new range since you last dropped by. Would you like a preview? I've got two girls who were here for Richard.' Tine noticed she was smiling at Stevie while addressing Sharon.

Sharon introduced the woman, Magda, as a silent exchange passed between her and Stevie. Tine understood it signified mutual recognition, but of something she could not discern. She dismissed it, and sent a quizzical look at Sharon, who pursed her lips and encouraged Magda to display the new range. The tall woman rung a bell and, at the appearance of a young girl, rattled off instructions which sent her scurrying from the room. Magda followed, disappearing through a solid mahogany door, after urging the trio to make themselves comfortable on the sofas.

The room was elegant. Large, with lofted ceilings, the walls clad in white and gold Imperial wallpaper. The carpet was springy; a massed, soft gold fibre. They settled on tapestry loungers while Sharon explained that her father, Richard, owned the boutique, amongst other things, and that Magda managed the chain and bought the stock.

'Chain?' Tine was determined to suffer Sharon's mysteriousness no longer, reasoning that since she had brought them here, she owed them an explanation.

It emerged that this boutique was one of six. The sister shops were scattered, two on the continent, two in America, and another in Scotland. They were known only by their street numbers, and their clientele was very select. As Sharon spoke the young woman returned, bearing a silver tea service and bone china cups. They had a choice of freshly milled coffee, the rich vapour making Tine salivate, or tea, its perfume vying with the earthier grounds. The tray also bore a gold-edged menu. It invited the guests to snack, offering an entrée of *paté de fois gras*, Beluga caviar with pumpernickel bread, and *crudités*. The smaller girl was stood patiently nearby and, at Sharon's nod, moved off soundlessly, leaving them to pour their own drinks. She returned minutes later with salvers laden with the delicacies promised by the menu.

Tine was charmed. She helped herself to small triangles of the rich, black bread and heaped on the cool grey eggs. She closed her eyes softly in appreciation as she popped the morsel into her mouth, savouring the flavour as she chewed with pleasure. Tine wondered if the trays were always kept ready for guests. Perhaps, she thought, the mysterious Richard's visit had something to do with it; the staff would be sure to maintain their professionalism if the boss had a habit of appearing unannounced. But she was sure, however, that this was the sort of establishment one would expect to visit only by appointment.

'You made an appointment!' Tine stared at Sharon. 'That was why your father was here. And we were late because I went to change.' Everything seemed to slot into place: the reserved car parking, their reception at the boutique and Magda's readiness, with models to hand. Tine was hugely impressed and hugged Sharon impulsively.

'How wonderful!' She settled back to enjoy the unexpected and extravagant treat, resolving to simply go along with whatever happened.

Sharon smiled her relief, and draped herself over a *chaise longue*.

'Hang on to your hats, dears!' she warned, as soft music started and the mahogany door swung open to admit two young women. Magda's rich tones introduced the models over hidden speakers:

'Sandy and Cheryl – for your pleasure.'

Tine assumed it was Sandy who led the way over the lush carpet. Tall, dark and very beautiful, her ample breasts were uplifted by a scarlet, cupless basque. Her long, rounded legs were clad in sheer red-tinted stockings, which clung to her thighs with the aid of elasticised, lacy tops. She wore a delicate scarlet thong to match the basque and, when she turned, her generous bum-cheeks trembled saucily. The thread disappeared, with implied promise, between the shivering globes. She moved with languid grace, her eyes warm and half-closed, seeking smoky contact with the prospective customers.

Tine watched in fascination. She had never witnessed such a fashion show, and was equally impressed with the model's professionalism and the blatant sexuality of the outfit. Recognising that her own petite build would not sustain such a creation, she tore her eyes from Sandy to concentrate on Cheryl, a delicate, ash-blonde young woman who appeared to be wearing royal-blue baby rompers. As Tine leaned forward Cheryl noticed her interest, eased towards her and drew to a silent halt. She slowly turned on her toes allowing Tine a full view and revealing that the outfit was, indeed, rompers. Created in fine, soft leather, they moulded over Cheryl's small breasts then flared into bloomers from the waist. They were gathered high in the thigh with lacy elastic and carefully pleated to fit the crotch. With a naughty smile Cheryl slowly parted her feet. The folds parted to reveal her shaven pubis, pale and softly inviting between the open pleats of the crotchless bloomers. She seemed gratified by Tine's sudden giggle and swift blush, and smiled warmly as she quickly turned and followed her companion out through the door.

In the moment before Magda appeared, Sharon glanced at Tine. The older woman was captivated by the outfit, no doubt imagining where she would wear such an item. She had a faraway expression that Sharon had grown to recognise under her father's tutelage. Sharon made a mental note that, before Tine enquired, Magda would be told to quote only trade prices.

Magda was stunning in black leather. She wore a dominatrix outfit which clove to her like a second skin. Laced at the front, it plunged at the rear to cup under her bare bum-cheeks. Laces spanned her naked back. The muscles of her legs bunched and eased beneath the fine-quality leather and her mons was clearly outlined. She wore thigh-length boots with stark and heavy silver zips. To Tine it seemed an unnecessarily complicated outfit but, as she was working out the practicality of dressing in such a fashion, she noticed Sharon's eyes shining, riveted on Magda as the tall woman sauntered before her.

It seemed that the models were inexhaustible, parading a myriad of complex creations, mainly leather, before the trio. Magda appeared frequently, clad in elaborate, dominatrix styles and looking as if she was thoroughly enjoying her participation. Eventually she emerged in her familiar grey suit and eased onto the *chaise longue* beside Sharon.

'We have introduced something new,' she murmured, 'for interactive viewing.'

Cheryl came through the door, carrying a small leather suitcase. She was followed closely by two young men, wearing only leather posing pouches, and each toting rather larger cases. They assembled before the sofas, busily unpacking and arranging the wares across the carpet. There was a carefully practised order in their movements, the articles revealed and placed in such a way to make them accessible and attractive. On one side Tine viewed a starburst of dildos and vibrators, ranging in hue from soft oyster to blushing purple. On the other side they scattered a glistening pile of sheer underwear in leather and silk, scraps of pulsing colours which invited investigation and promised pleasure to any seeker who should dig her fingers amongst the delicate fabrics. Fanned before them were catalogues with rich, embossed gold covers depicting elegant models, a single name embossed on the lower right corner: *Richard*.

Once the wares were arranged the models retreated, to pose comfortably on the carpet. They murmured amongst themselves, seemingly oblivious of the company. No doubt, thought Tine as she surveyed them, to enable unembarrassed scrutiny.

The men were certainly as gorgeous as the women. One, olive-skinned, with long, tousled black hair and a suggestion of generous proportions under his pouch, was introduced as 'Tyson'. The other man was slim, lean and pale with a shock of red hair; unsurprisingly named 'Red'. He seemed slightly remote, smiling softly as if enjoying an inner joke, his grey eyes friendly and aware. Tine felt drawn to him, appreciating his mystery and surprising herself with the idea that, were he at her disposal, she would simply like to be pleasured by him. She feared that this was an attitude which would draw criticism, were the genders reversed and, feeling slightly ashamed of herself, she consigned the image to fantasy

190

and concentrated on the sex-toys. Magda was inviting them to take a closer look and Sharon was already fingering each in turn with an experienced air. Far from titillated by the thrumming vibrator now alive in her hand, she seemed to be studying it with the narrowed, calculating eye of the entrepreneur.

Tine watched her, with the dawning appreciation that Sharon, most likely the inheritor of her father's empire, had a keen sense of business. The mystery of her rift with her father would remain her secret unless she chose to reveal it. While the blonde continued a muted conversation with Magda, who seemed delighted and even deferential, Tine fingered the pile of underwear. Stevie was leafing through a catalogue and seemed engrossed, her finger marking a place as she slowly turned the pages.

The tiny garments sliding through Tine's fingers seemed ludicrously insufficient to her. In some cases they were mere strings which she turned this way and that to work out how they should be worn. The fabrics were delightful, the fine leathers as soft and crumpling as the satins and silks. She brushed one tiny scrap across her cheek, eyes closed in appreciation of its warm, sheer caress, and imagined the garment nestling against her rift, softly soaking up her juices. Her imaginings stopped abruptly with the realisation that she had overlooked her own lack of underwear, and was presenting the view between her parted thighs to Red. When she opened her eyes to look, he was not there. She felt a warm presence behind her moments before his words brushed softly past her ear.

'This is only a very small selection.' His voice was gentle, deep and discreet. 'Would you like to enjoy more choices?'

Tine turned to face him and, searching for any sign other than friendly enquiry in his expression, felt relieved when she could trace no innuendo. She glanced at the strewn ribbons of underwear. Delightful as they were, she was neither accustomed to nor particularly attracted by such garments. However, she was entranced by the fabrics and, if more traditional designs were offered in the same materials, she would be tempted. She smiled and nodded, allowing Red to help her to rise to her feet.

It seemed that no one paid any attention as Red ushered her through the mahogany door. Stevie remained engrossed in her pages, Sharon in low conversation with Magda. Cheryl and Tyson relaxed, waiting to be summoned if they were required.

A corridor stretched beyond the door. Red led Tine to the second door on the right, inviting her through with a gallant sweep of his hand and a charming smile. She faced a large room, empty bar the presence of a maroon velvet love-seat which sat solidly on the white pile of a thick carpet. Three white walls gave way to maroon drapes covering the fourth. While stark, the white was not glaring, it was softened by dimmed light which spilled from a crystal chandelier, hung high from the vaulted, ornate ceiling.

Tine perched on the love-seat as Red crossed the room. He moved with grace, his lean, long thighs flexing softly, his shoulders square and relaxed. She could imagine him in a tuxedo, elegant and assured, yet he was not made ridiculous by the posing pouch. She wondered, if he was actually wearing a tuxedo, would she have been as quick to mentally undress him as she was to clothe him in his present, nearly naked state. The thought made her smile, and he saw her expression and returned it as he grasped the cords of the drapes and pulled. They opened to reveal an Aladdin's cave of tastefully displayed underwear and sex-toys. Having revealed the treasures, Red returned to her side, silently examining the panorama with her.

Tine spied a collection of creamy rich satin and lace teddies. Her eyes travelled over black silk lingerie crumpling soft leather sets in vibrant colours and an artful arrangement of pastel separates. Displayed at the far end was a selection of men's underwear; posing pouches, thongs, penis sheaths and some whimsical silk boxers in primary colours, scattered with heart patterns. She tried to imagine Rupe wearing such items and failed, aware that the lean smoothness of the man at her side was the sort of model the designers had in mind when they produced their sketches.

'It is all image,' she muttered, hardly realising she spoke aloud.

'Any image you fancy?' Red smiled.

Tine nodded. 'The cream teddies.'

Red swiftly removed items from the display, his long, tapering fingers caressing the fabric. As he draped the garments over his arm he turned slightly to her. 'Would you mind a recommendation?'

Tine agreed, intrigued to see what he would produce. It would give her an insight as to how someone else saw her, and perhaps provide a hint on how she should regard herself. Red grasped a handle beside the cabinets which held the colourful leather goods, and the shelves pivoted to reveal hanging rails at the rear. These carried more leather, but all black. Not meant for display, the clothing was not easily viewable and Red selected a couple of garments which he added to those already draped over his arm.

Red swung open two more sets of shelves. One held a selection of sex-toys, and although many were a mystery, Tine's imagination supplied adequate interpretation. She drew nearer and was fascinated at the variety of designs produced for human titillation. Videos were stacked on one shelf. As she scanned them her eye caught the likeness of Red on one spine, entitled *Water Baby*. She reached for the case and turned it over to view the cover. It was Red, or at least a naked, rear view of him, standing in the unmistakable pose of a man relieving himself. He seemed all elegant long lines, tight buttocks and graceful casualness. Unable to avoid it, Tine murmured, 'You are very beautiful.'

She had not thought she would ever hear herself say

193

such a thing to a man. She could not help compare Red with her image of Rupe, his dark largeness and animal grace. She was drawn to conjoin with Rupe, but Red seemed more aesthetic and her appreciation of him was quite unlike the way she felt about her Australian lover. She longed to touch the redhead, to draw her hands over his almost translucent skin and test his lean tightness under her fingers. He reminded her of a Pre-Raphaelite portrait; heavy, smooth-lidded eyes and a rosebud mouth. She gazed at him with the admiration she would accord a painting by an old master.

Red remained silent, and seemed slightly taken aback by the sincerely given compliment. Then, after a moment, he asked, 'Would you like to see the tape?'

She paused, feeling slightly disorientated. She took in the surroundings, thought of her friends in the other room and grappled with the proposed intimacy of watching Red on video, with him present. There seemed to be no challenge in his tone, more a return of her compliment, a proffering of thanks. It seemed complicit, as if they shared an adventure. She dismissed the notion that he might have shared this experience before.

'Yes,' she answered simply, watching his face. 'I would like that.'

Red beamed, and to Tine it suddenly seemed that he was terribly young, much younger than she had at first supposed.

'There is a viewing room next door. It's only a short movie.' Red looked expectant.

'Okay. The film first, then the clothes?'

'I am at a disadvantage here.' Red gestured at Tine's clothes, then his own near-nakedness. 'Perhaps ... ' His voice trailed off, eyes seeking her permission even as he undid the large, silver safety pin holding the flaps of Tine's kilt.

She stood silently as he eased his hand beneath the open edges, drawing his palm softly upwards along the curve of her hip until he reached the waistband, then flicked open the clasp with his thumb. The skirt fell away while his hand remained at her waist, his thumb now circling softly.

He sighed loudly, spanning her small waist with gentle hands and squeezing softly before reaching for the tape. Then he drew her from the room with him.

He chose the door opposite, ushering her in with the instruction to make herself comfortable and pulled the door closed, leaving her alone in the room. As he turned, Magda entered the corridor, her expression questioning. Her eyes dropped to the video case and held it up.

'She wants to see it.'

Magda kissed him quickly on the cheek, whispering, 'Are you okay with this?' Red knew she had a fondness for him. He rarely interacted with customers in the way in which Tyson was predisposed, and perhaps she was concerned about him. He knew she was aware of his particular interest but in the past she had been inclined to trust his young judgement.

He thought a moment. 'Yes. She's different. There is something special about her.'

'Well, be careful, okay?' Magda told him she had called Richard to alert him that Sharon had arrived. On his instructions she had cancelled two appointments to keep the salon clear of other custom. His clear message was that the staff should endeavour, in every way, to ensure that these visitors left happy.

'Oh,' she said, 'and don't talk prices, okay?' She smiled into Red's eyes. 'This is not business. Think of it as a family matter.'

Red softened, his shoulders eased and a warm light entered his eyes. He hugged her impulsively and dashed into the clothes room, crossing swiftly over to the cabinets and, having chosen an item thoughtfully, he exited the room with pleasurable anticipation.

As he re-entered the viewing room he could see Tine's head above the back of a large, black sofa. He dimmed the lights then slipped beside her after carefully dropping the item out of sight.

Tine sat cross-legged on the sofa and seemed comfortable. This was a much smaller and more intimate room than before. Spotlights in the lowered ceiling cast soft pools of light over the sofa, and a television set and small bar were recessed into one wall. The walls were covered in dark maroon silk and oriental rugs were strewn over a dark wood floor. The sofa was the only place to sit, or lie. Its deep, puffing leather was scattered with bright silk cushions.

Red placed one hand on Tine's shoulder and pressed gently, turning her face away from him. He unbraided her hair then fluffed his fingers though the rich tumble appreciatively, smiling softly as he teased the rippling locks over her shoulders. She looked tiny, her slimness emphasised by the snug black body-stocking. The rich chestnut fall of her hair was shot through with gold beneath the spotlights.

Tine felt totally at ease. She had surrendered herself willingly to this new experience and was avid to see the video, even as she relished Red's careful, planned ministration. It was clear that he was creating an ambience, structuring the hour with forethought. She was not aroused but pleased, the touch of Red's hands gently thrilling but mute.

Red brought her a drink from the bar. It tasted like perfumed water, slightly fizzy and, she suspected mildly alcoholic. She felt her palate refresh as she sipped watching him slide the tape into the video slot. He was soon nestling beside her, his eyes fixed on the screen as it came alive, then, satisfied all was in order, he slid to the edge of the sofa, swung his legs up and pulled her to him. She lay with her head resting against his smooth chest and her hips couched between his thighs.

Chapter Thirteen

*T*he screen filled with a close-up of Red's face. He looked relaxed as the camera panned away to reveal him seated in a comfortable armchair, wearing a loose, dark sweater and jeans.

'Hi,' said the image. 'I am Red, I am eighteen years old and I am a water baby.' He smiled without apology. 'People often ask about watersports. I show them.' He unwound from the chair and the camera followed him across the room. He stripped, turned and exited through a door. The camera followed, concentrating on his tight bottom.

The view widened to reveal a tasteful bathroom; a champagne-coloured corner bath with gold fittings and a matching lavatory, bidet and basin. Large, fluffy dark towels were piled on the edge of the bath and Rupe wrapped one around his waist, sarong-style, and perched on the edge of the tub. He gestured, waving his hand to encompass the room.

'This is a good place for watersports, the great outdoors even better – as you will see later.' He seemed to be waiting, and before long a woman entered. She peered around in bewilderment at the camera, then at Red.

'I want to use the toilet!' She looked uneasy.

'Hi Andrea.' Red smiled at the woman. He cocked his

197

head to one side. 'Remember our conversation last night?'

He informed the camera that Andrea had asked him about his interest. Their long discussion had persuaded him that she would enjoy helping him to make this movie. He confessed that he had arranged an appointment, then kept her plied with liquids during her half-hour wait. She had been directed to the bathroom when she eventually felt the need to relieve herself.

During this explanation Andrea stood staring at Red but, as he concluded his introduction, her expression showed that she seemed to be enjoying the idea. There was no doubt Red had researched his subject well, and her surprise was more than compensated by her growing enthusiasm.

'So.' She smiled at Red then grinned broadly at the camera. 'What do we do?'

'You wanted to go to the toilet, didn't you?'

She nodded.

'Then do so.'

Despite his seemingly peremptory attitude, Red radiated warmth. He rose and placed his hands on Andrea's shoulders, before lifting them to cup her face. His eyes assured her he thought her wonderful and, as his towel dislodged and fell away, his erection provided a more clear endorsement. As pale, long and elegant as his body, it quivered in sympathy with her growing need.

'Here, I can help you.' His voice grew deeper, his fingers already undoing her clothing, efficiently stripping away her blouse, skirt and underwear. All the time he spoke softly and persuasively. Her eyes were large and she was passive as she was undressed. Once naked, Andrea displayed a slight, slim build, her sparsely clad pubis bearing out the authenticity of the short, blonde curls tumbling around her forehead.

Red eased behind her and drew her backwards. The camera now held a full view of Andrea, clearly excited, her waist spanned by Red's hands as he guided her. He sat down on the toilet seat, his legs apart, and pulled her back to sit on his thighs. His hands slid forward to part her legs until they rested either side of his. Her quim was now widely exposed to the lens and almost at once her need for relief overcame any reservation about public exposure, and the golden pour began. As his fingers felt the wetness Red cupped her bottom, urging her to rise slightly and bend forward a little. Now the flow was redirected. It ran hotly over Red's erection, coursed down his shaft and tickled over his scrotum before easing into the bowl. He slipped his fingers into the pale cascade and, once Andrea stopped, he urged her from him and rose to face her, tracing his fingertips over her lips. She licked them dry as she watched him suck his fingers with evident pleasure.

Tine moved restlessly against Red. She could feel his excitement as she leaned against him, his rod hard at the base of her spine. His video had produced a surprising response in her and she had become involved and interested, before her own excitement manifested itself. As Tine unconsciously pressed towards him, Red slipped his hand around her, his fingers circling patiently over her mound.

When she squirmed and attempted to edge from him he quickly switched off the tape and allowed her to sit up and face him, calmly awaiting rejection.

'No, it's not that,' she said breathlessly, betraying her arousal but aware of his concern. She recognised the wary look in his eyes. 'It's just that . . . ' She paused as if embarrassed, and then almost wailed, 'I really do need to go to the loo!'

'Can I come?' Red held his breath.

'Yes, but get me out of this thing!' Tine pulled desperately at the body-stocking, now clenching her thighs. The garment was one piece and she would have to remove it altogether to obtain release.

'Oh no, no.' Red propelled her to the door, swiftly bending to retrieve the item she had noticed him plant earlier beside the sofa, before hurrying her down the corridor. It was the same room depicted in the movie, but Tine had little time for appreciation. Realising she would not make it in time if she stopped to unclothe, she plumped firmly onto the seat as the wetness started to seep from her.

For an extraordinary moment Tine felt unable to continue, despite the pressure of her bladder. The leak started then froze; and Red took this as a signal to produce a buzzing vibrator which he pressed firmly into Tine's cleft through the crotch of the body-stocking. He nuzzled the head against her clitoris. The sensation was a painful, sharp intrusion against her sensitive button and she tried to move away.

'Stay with me!' Red demanded, his eyes shining as he expertly wielded the vibrator. He lifted his head and firmly planted his mouth over hers, his tongue rudely filling her mouth. His forceful intrusion surprised Tine and she became torn by sensations. She forced herself to relax into the thrum of the vibrator head and immediately felt the burning pleasure become a hot-centred demand. Her need to urinate became a dull, bloating wash and her lust rose, concentrating on the penetration of his sopping tongue.

She returned Red's kiss with force as she felt herself gush uncontrollably over the buzzing device. Red swiftly withdrew the vibrator and slid his palm to catch her pouring. A surge shot through her and she lifted her hips of her own volition. She felt she was still watching the video but directing her own involvement, as if from a distance. Red's sheer delight in the drench of her hot waters provoked in her a dark desire to soak him and she shot forward.

Surprised, Red tumbled back and Tine crouched over him. She circled her hips so her gush splashed his face and chin and seeped over his neck. The trickles stained his copper curls. Tine peered between her thighs to watch her elixir pool and glisten. The intensity of the image drew her to ringing climax. At last, relieved in all senses, apart from a strange wonder, she tumbled from him and slumped by his side.

Red looked radiant as he turned to face her, studying her with an expression akin to worship. Despite the bizarre circumstances Tine felt moved, a protective feeling creeping over her. At her age she regarded him as a mere man-child, barely mature and yet his behaviour was so experienced; it produced a conflict in her. She noted that his erection had not subsided. Following the direction of her gaze, Red shook his head, smiling.

'Don't mind that,' he said happily. 'It does not matter.'

Tine felt puzzled, realising that there was much more at play than she could imagine from her previous experience. She had questions but surrendered to Red's evident pleasure following her 'accident'. He peeled the body stocking from her and, while she sat damp and naked on the toilet seat, ran the bath full with water. He lifted her in, laughing at her protests and watched her sink back with a pleased sigh, before he carefully rinsed her garment in the hand-basin. His concentration on the task was absolute. It seemed to Tine that he became involved in a tiny world, concentrating on the sheer fabric which glistened as it slid soapily through his fingers.

His erection had not died. It remained proud and angry until he rinsed and wrapped the silky fabric in a warm towel, pressing to extract the water. His penis then hung, soft and vulnerable, between his pale thighs.

Tine experienced a moment's regret, wishing she could arouse him again. It seemed that she had not pleasured him, at least not in the manner which she was used to; yet he seemed sated. She realised she would have to revise her perceptions. Not entirely ignorant about 'golden showers', it was not something she could ever have envisaged enjoying. She felt bewildered in the aftermath.

Red was aware of her confusion. He leaned over the bath, soaping her small form with now friendly hands. His face seemed alight, as if sunshine now filtered through to his world. His touch on her was intimate, complicit and familiar and he soaped between her legs with the same intensity as he had shown while rinsing her sodden garment. His fingers slicked among her folds in the same way as they had slid along the glistening, black fabric.

'It would take too long to explain now,' he whispered, his attention distracted by his task. 'A lot is in the video, and there is a book I would like to give you.' He paused, looking deeply into her eyes with something akin to love, and whispered, 'You were wonderful. All the more because you do not even realise why.'

He explained that, to him, it was like a fabulously beautiful woman not realising she was ravishing, her actions pure and innocent, without vanity or manipulation. It made her painfully desirable. This, he said, was Tine's present to him: in her innocence she had given him the greatest gift. He towelled her dry, helped her into the slightly damp body-stocking and vigorously rubbed her down. The garment dried under his ministration and, as they left the bathroom, it was as if the scene had never occurred; except that Red was gentle, almost worshipping, as he led her back to the showroom. He wound her tiny kilt around her waist and secured the pin.

The teddy she had chosen and Red's recommendations seemed forgotten but she experienced no regret. She no longer felt like shopping. Her head was filled with her recent experience, a pleasant memory still shrouded in questions. Overlaying her curiosity was a strong sense of self-interrogation and a secret wish to experiment more. She returned to the main salon alone.

When Tine re-entered, she knew that the others would be able to tell that something had happened. She was clearly sated, with an embarrassed pinkness to her cheeks, and her smile was tentative while she reassured Stevie that she was okay. She had sat down close beside the dark woman before she noticed the remnants of an obviously explicit interplay.

Tyson and Cheryl were naked, both wearing the pleased smugness of afterglow. Around them were littered the tools which had apparently led to their satisfaction: dildos; handcuffs; creams and limp garments. Tine raised her eyebrows at Stevie, who merely shrugged and smiled. In the far corner of the room, Sharon was engaged in a low conversation with a man. She noticed Tine's return and broke off in mid-sentence to approach, followed by the man.

This, unmistakably, was Richard. Their relationship was betrayed by his eyes, the same startling, violet slants inherited by his daughter. Tine noted they did not seem at all effeminate but she was startled by their keen interrogation.

Sharon hugged Tine.

'Are you okay?' She peered at the older woman's face with a smile.

Tine nodded, suddenly shy. She exchanged a glance with Richard. In his expression lay a wealth of understanding and, for a moment, Tine felt herself laid bare. It was as if she had suddenly grown, moved from ignorance into a state of knowledge. Richard would know Red's proclivities and Tine's uncertainties. His expression assured her that all was well.

He was an elegant man, resting lightly on sprung heels in Gucci shoes. Silk shirt; classic and expensive, grey suit. His tanned face was relaxed though watchful. His hair silvered at his temples. Tine believed him to be the most handsome man she had ever seen. It was no wonder, she thought, that he owned this chain of salons, his empathy with them was perfect. Despite his allure she was guarded after her initial, open response. He seemed to sense her reserve and was courteous and seemingly amused, which hid his intrigue.

As he had followed Sharon to meet Tine, he waved surreptitiously and the models had quickly gathered everything and disappeared. Apart from some mild ruffling of the pile of the gold carpet, the salon was restored. Magda returned to drop a quick kiss on

Richard's cheek and proffer him carrier-bags, with a whisper. The bags were gold with woven handles, his name embossed in the bottom right-hand corner.

It seemed the shopping trip was at an end. Tine felt slightly disappointed that Red had not re-emerged to say farewell but she followed the group into the street without comment. A metallic-grey Silver Cloud Rolls Royce sat arrogantly on the yellow no-parking lines.

'This must be "the tank",' Stevie whispered to Tine, unable to keep the admiration from her voice.

Richard must have overheard her, and opened the front passenger door, then beckoned to Stevie who leapt into the vehicle without a backward glance at her friends to see if they approved. Sharon smiled in defeat as she ushered Tine into the spacious rear and followed her as Richard took the wheel.

They did not travel far, but Richard took a circuitous route to allow Stevie maximum enjoyment, talking enthusiastically about the vehicle in response to her questions. He ended up offering her the steering wheel on the drive back to the car-park after coffee, which caused Stevie to fall quiet at last, stunned and delighted.

The cafe chosen by Richard for high tea surprised Tine. It was unassuming and not as glamorous as she had anticipated. The staff obviously knew father and daughter, and bustled around until the table was laden with tiny sandwiches, scones, steaming pots of coffee and good feeling. Tine could detect no undercurrent of tension between Sharon and Richard, which left her feeling more confused, having imagined a bitter family parting. In fact the episode was interspersed with friendly banter, fond looks and cheerful charm.

Tine found herself enjoying Richard's company. He seemed to blend into the group and was self-deprecating and witty, causing laughter and goodwill. He did manage to elicit an invitation to the shared house, including a meal, and Tine grinned at him, recognising the clever manipulation he had used to obtain the offer.

He was complicit, smiling back ruefully as Sharon punched him on the arm in jokey frustration.

Stevie stayed mostly silent through the meal, caught up with her proposed treat. She watched Tine, wondering what had transpired at the salon and admiring her appearance. Tine had not re-braided her hair and it swung in heavy chestnut waves around her shoulders. Her dark eyes were alight with mischief and humour as she chatted with Richard. It struck Stevie that Tine was thoroughly enjoying herself. She compared Richard with the raw, dark charm of Rupe and could not avoid thinking that Tine was better suited to the older man. He would provide her with more intellectual stimulation and possessed a depth of understanding not yet available to the inexperienced Australian.

Red, Stevie surmised, was something else. She had observed the young man closely before he had left the room with Tine. He was a specialist, involved in a world beyond the one Tine inhabited; a nice place to visit but she would not want to live there. She figured that, whatever had happened between the two of them had not damaged Tine; the woman was alive with laughter. Stevie suspected Tine was on a voyage of discovery and the richness of her current experiences would lay the foundations for her new life. Much as Stevie wanted Tine, she willed her forward, even if her freedom carried her away. With surprise, she realised she could almost be falling in love with Tine, if the definition could mean that she cared more for another than for herself. She took pride in the generosity of her feeling, promising herself that she would do anything to ensure Tine made the most of her own enjoyment, and, if it was necessary, provide a shoulder for any bad moments.

When they rose to leave, Stevie leapt to her feet, eager to get behind the wheel of the Rolls Royce. With proper ceremony Richard surrendered the keys and offered a minimum of instruction as Stevie slid onto the luxurious leather of the driver's seat. The vehicle surpassed her expectations. She automatically allowed for its size and power and sought, despite protests from Richard, the safest and fastest route back to the Porsche. As she slid into the neighbouring parking bay she sighed with approval and was awarded a round of applause from the others. Richard promised her full use of the Rolls when he came to visit the house, eliciting in return an invitation to Silky Lizzie's. Mention of the club piqued his professional interest and it seemed a new conversation would ensue, but it was cut short by Sharon tapping her watch.

Tine and Stevie politely left Richard and Sharon to make their farewells in private. They leaned against the Porsche, each lost in thought. Stevie, fresh from her delight with the drive, was thrilled by the small form nestling beside her. It felt that the most natural act would be to embrace her but she cautioned herself to remain calm.

Tine was absorbed in contemplation of the afternoon with Red. She was still trying to make sense of the experience. Now she was on her way home, and to Rupe, she wondered how he would react to the suggestion of such interplay. She felt he would be willing but recognised that Red was truly dedicated. For him it was an act in itself; to Rupe and Tine it would be foreplay. For a moment she rued the fact that she would return to an empty house; one in which she had an evening planned, alone.

She shook her head. Richard was standing before her, seemingly reluctant to break her reverie. He allowed Tine to refocus slowly, then offered her the two carrier-bags he held.

'The small one is from Red, and is a present,' he said. 'The larger is from me, to try and buy.'

Tine studied him gravely. Without thinking too much she leaned forward and placed a small kiss on his lips. As he had spoken he had shed his sophistication. She noted that expression in his eyes was one of gratitude, and somehow realised she had been an unwitting catalyst in his reunion with Sharon. The invitation to visit her home had promised him that, whatever had created the rift between father and daughter, the relationship could be mended. With her kiss she accepted the bags. Surprisingly, his lips moved beneath hers. It was the merest flutter but, as they pulled apart, they both knew that in time they would share more. Then they were all in the car, Sharon waving a farewell to her father who stood beside the Silver Cloud, his eyes seeking and finding those of Tine.

Tine repeated her doze up the M1. She had intended not, but drowsiness overcame her just as the A41 gave way to the northbound slip, the steady purr of the Porsche lulling and secure. She did not wake when Sharon stopped at a motorway service station to fill the car with petrol, nor when her companions disappeared to have coffee. When they pulled into the drive of their home she sat up, noting that Stevie was now at the wheel, her eyes gleaming in the rear-view mirror with the pleasure of having driven two top-quality vehicles in one day.

While Tine enjoyed coffee at the breakfast bar, Stevie and Tine dashed off to change. Both were clearly looking forward to the night out at Silky Lizzie's. Tine had no doubt that much of Stevie's delight arose from the anticipation of entering the club with a beautiful woman on her arm.

Tine refused to open the bags until she was alone. Something in her wished to savour her gifts without company. The trip had been a brief, glittering side-track in her life and seemed remote now that she was seated in familiar and quiet surroundings. She wondered at the energy of her companions. Despite her recent nap, she was tired, or perhaps because of it. Her desire was to delve into the carriers then spend some time on IRC, perhaps soak in a bubble bath and contemplate her strange, new experience with Red.

As she daydreamed, the last of the day disappeared.

Darkness revealed her reflection on the pane of the kitchen window, the light from the hallway throwing a halo of gold around her head. She chuckled softly to herself, feeling that one crown she had not earned was a halo. Red seemed as distant as Dickens, and her adventure felt as unreal as the ones she enjoyed via the computer screen rather than in real life. Tine wondered at the reality of IRC, and its profound and very important place in her life. She had not met Dickens in the flesh but his impact on her was as intimate and real as that of Red. More so, because Dickens was still in her life, but she knew that she would never re-encounter Red.

Stevie entered the kitchen softly while Tine was pondering. She turned on the light and stood quietly, waiting for Tine to examine her. For the first time the dark girl was aware of 'coming out' to the older woman. Her image on the trip to London had been slightly camp, and her dress around the house had otherwise been the utilitarian garb she wore to work. Silky Lizzie's was where Stevie felt she most belonged, and to go there she wore comfortable clothes which denoted her preference: plaid shirts; black trousers; and wide leather belts. The clothes were all male, bought in men's shops, even her shoes. She moved differently, not as though she were acting, but with the easy stride and swing most natural to her. At Lizzie's they called her 'Steve'.

The transition was not difficult for Tine. Before her she saw a man, handsome, well built and tall. It was her response which caused conflict. Rationally she knew Stevie was female but her eyes perceived the maleness of the figure before her and found it pleasing. She realised that her posture had subtly altered and she had shifted in her seat to take a different, more feminine stance. Before, Tine had merely accepted Stevie as a woman who preferred love with her own gender, now she was a man; and attractive to her.

When Sharon entered, Stevie's masculinity was heightened by contrast. The blonde woman wore a simple white, sleeveless shift, the hem falling just above her knees, with simple white sandals and no make-up. Her blonde hair fell around her shoulders in glossy waves. She looked virginal, young and exceedingly beautiful.

Tine had expected Sharon to wear leather, something radical, but she realised she had underestimated her friend. Dressed as she was, she would create far more impact in the club, especially when she entered with Stevie. From the look of pleasure on the dark woman's face, Tine did not doubt she relished the entrance. Sharon would be a jewel on her arm.

She felt sad when they left. The house hugged silently around her and she hurried to the study to find Dickens on IRC. There was much she wanted to discuss with him, but he was not to be found. She was startled when a message flashed on her screen:

Rupe>   Hey! I tried to ring several times today. Your phone is always busy!

Astyr>   It is? I wonder who could be trying to reach me. I have been away all day. I went to London with Sharon and Stevie.

Tine cursed herself for not remembering to turn on the answering machine. She had been away from the house so little that it had not occurred to her to do it. Her telephone rang so seldom that a sudden deluge of calls was definitely unusual. She shrugged, curious but confident. If the callers were that anxious, they would try again the next day.

Rupe>   I miss you. I want you to sleep in my bed tonight, to know that where we lay is still warm with your presence. I cannot stop thinking about holding you, hot and wet beneath my hands.

Tine stared at the screen, imagining Rupe at work in London, the night dark around him. She conjured a picture of his office, the neighbouring computer terminals unmanned, the only light shed by his screen, painting him palely as his fingers communicated his need via the keyboard.

She glanced around her study and strained to catch any noises in the house beyond. It seemed strange that Rupe was not upstairs; in the last few days she had grown used to his presence and accessibility, and he now seemed very far away. She wondered how she could tell him this without sounding romantic. She would not sleep in his bed; that implied a commitment which she was anxious to avoid. Close as she felt to Rupe, with her senses alive to their mutual needs, she shied away from any attachment other than close friendship. She did not tell him this but, wary of his response, kept her thoughts to herself.

They talked for an hour, sharing the delight of their last encounter and the anticipation of his return home at the weekend. The closeness returned, her anxieties fled and they brought each other to orgasm with a shared virtual fantasy. Tine revealed her experience in London with some trepidation but Rupe's response was enthusiastic.

Rupe>   Go now! Put your hand in the flow and tell me how it tastes. I want to imagine and then, when I return, I want to share this with you.

Trembling, Tine rose and entered the bathroom. She slipped her fingers between her thighs and felt her wet pour over them. She tasted, concentrating hard, then returned to the quiet screen.

Astyr>   It tastes clean, subtle. A little like one of those flavoured, still waters with herbs and ginseng.
Rupe>   I long for you. I am sitting here alone in a huge office and I am throbbing, hard with need.

Tine described a scene in which she and Rupe shared the shower. They clung to each other, the water cascading to slick their hair, channel over their naked bodies and mingle with their hot pourings. She extended the fantasy to complete their conjunction in a way she had missed with Red, her legs surrounding Rupe's waist as he plunged into her until they both came.

Her monologue on the screen carried Rupe to satisfaction. At the other end of the connection, free from the demands of the keyboard, he stroked himself, his head alive with images, until he felt the warm seep of semen over his fingers. He stared at his shining fingers then licked them clean, imagining them slipping in Tine's mouth, her eager tongue lapping at his precious spill.

He felt very tired, but released. He would work through the night, the demands of the project falling heavily on his young shoulders. The next day he had to present a progress report in a meeting, and he had to attend interviews. The work demanded two new programmers. He was unsure what this would mean to his involvement but felt nervous about the responsibility. While the job was important to him, he was afraid that a restructuring of work would endanger his relationship with Tine. She had shared a sexual passion he suspected he would seldom encounter, a physical adventure he cherished and a friendship he thought he would never experience with a woman.

Vulnerable, Rupe shared his fears and thoughts with Tine. She nurtured him, encouraging him to see that future fears had no place in their friendship. What was happening between them was precious and present, and should be enjoyed to the full.

Astyr> Nothing lasts for ever. Let's just cherish what we share now. It is wonderful for me and you are special. If we question too much we shall lose what we have and that would be a tragedy!

211

Rupe smiled at his screen, cast aside his fears and looked forward to Saturday and his home-coming.

Tine broke the connection with fond farewells and made her way to her bedroom. The carrier-bags rested invitingly on the bed and she forced herself to brush her teeth and slip into a T-shirt before snuggling under the duvet and drawing the packages to her.

The larger bag, the one that Richard had offered as a gift, contained the soft, blue, leather bloomers Tine had so admired on Cheryl. The rich hide was warm and soft as she passed it through her fingers. It was unmistakably expensive, and she was wary of accepting the present. Then she remembered his reconciliation with Sharon, and realised that to him, the garment was a morsel which had been offered with thanks. She determined to accept it in the same spirit, even though she had no doubt that its retail value was far beyond what she would have ever spent on a piece of clothing. She knew he would appreciate a written acknowledgement; so much had seemed to pass between them without words.

The carrier-bag offered for her to try and buy contained the cream teddy and a black leather miniskirt and waistcoat. The latter items were the ones that Red had picked out when he had given her his recommendations. Tine imagined the ensemble complete with her black body-stocking and was pleased to think Red saw her in the tempting outfit. It was an indication of how he viewed her and was reassuringly sexy.

Red's bag contained his video, a book called *Wetting your Whistle* and the vibrator with which he had teased her. She peered at the cover of the tape, the tousled, red curls and slim thighs feeling remote, as her mind went back to the afternoon's exploits. She let herself be drawn into the memory but rewrote the ending, slipping the buzzing shaft into her as she snuggled down. Soon Red's face was joined by that of Rupe and her imagination generously allowed her pampering by the ministering pair. She came with Rupe's fingers teasing at her nipples, his mouth warm and seeking on hers; and Red beneath her, his hand manoeuvring the vibrator tip against her clitoris.

Chapter Fourteen

*T*ine woke with a feeling of apprehension. The house still had the empty feeling of the previous night although the clock on her bedside table showed seven o'clock. Daylight was creeping underneath the hem of the curtains, seeking to shed warmth over her ominous feelings. It seemed strangely reassuring, despite the early hour, when the front doorbell broke the silence. She leapt from bed and raced downstairs.

A policeman was just raising his hand to knock as she swung the door open. He looked serious and Sharon, who stood beside him, looked embarrassed. Her hair was unbrushed and her white dress was smudged and wrinkled. Her sandals dangled from one hand, their straps broken. An older policewoman stood to the rear. In response to Tine's querying and concerned look, Sharon shrugged apologetically and gestured for the policeman to explain.

They followed Tine to the kitchen where the young man accepted a cup of coffee before he told her the story. It transpired that Sharon had left Silky Lizzie's at two o'clock that morning and made her way into the centre of town where she had met with a man. They had shed their clothes in the deserted shopping precinct and were engaging in sexual congress when a security guard called the police. The man had run off and the policeman had not given chase. Sharon, however, had simply begged to be handcuffed, fought while the policewoman attempted to dress her, and laughed throughout the whole incident. She had been taken to the police station, and was only released when the security guard decided not to make a formal complaint.

Tine, for all her concern, found it extremely difficult not to snigger. Aware of Sharon's penchant for exposure, she could not take the incident seriously and the blonde woman seemed more irritated than penitent. The police-woman kept glancing around the kitchen as if she thought she might find more incriminating clues. Tine wondered, as she moved around in her short T-shirt, if the arbiter of the law thought she had discovered a house of ill-repute. The temptation to act accordingly was almost overwhelming except that Tine still held a grudging respect for the law.

Once Sharon had been safely handed over to her, the police left and the true story emerged. Sharon and Jerry had provided a show for the security guard on previous occasions. He had been a willing audience. That evening he had demanded to participate, which contradicted the rules Sharon laid down for voyeurs, and on being spurned he had called the police. Jerry had run off and Sharon doubted whether he would ever return.

Despite her bravado, Sharon was shaken. She had spent four hours at the police station, on the wrong side of the law, and had found it extremely unpleasant. She had refused to say anything, and when the guard withdrew his complaint she was relieved. Her incarceration had given her time to think and her meeting with Richard the previous day had provided plenty to think about. To cap it, there had been a reporter at the station nosing around. He had followed them back to the house, then drove off when the policeman had approached his car.

As Tine listened she tried to read between the words. Sharon's attitude had so far been defiant; she had exhib-ited a freedom which denied any control or conscience.

215

Since her meeting with her father it seemed that she had developed other concerns. Her preoccupation with the reporter seemed to imply that she did not want her misdemeanour reaching her father's ears.

'Although my father is involved in the sex industry, he does have a good reputation. It would be humiliating to be the daughter who brought disgrace on him.'

'There is no reason why he should know.' Tine was reassuring.

'Yes there is. I shall tell him.' Sharon looked at Tine. 'It's only fair, because I've decided to take him up on an offer he made me.'

Tine stayed silent, inviting Sharon to continue.

'He said I could open a shop here and he would provide the start-up capital. It does not have to be part of his chain if I prefer not.'

'However, you are his heir,' Tine encouraged.

'Yes.' Sharon laughed suddenly. 'I am, and it's about time I proved I can handle the business.'

'Well, if there's anything I can do to help, I shall. After all, I have plenty of time on my hands.'

'You bet. I need a partner.' Sharon looked vulnerable, aware of the commitment she was making and what she was asking of Tine.

'I would love to!'

They sat drinking coffee, exploring the venture, loud with ideas. Their excitement grew as possibilities were examined, until Tine eventually pointed out that Sharon was late for work and if she wished to resign she should do so without blotting her copybook. As the blonde woman sped upstairs, Tine smiled to herself. It seemed that more adventures were in the offing; yet still she could not shake the feeling of foreboding which had woken her.

She perched on a stool at the counter, promising herself breakfast and then ablutions. The view through the kitchen window revealed a swiftly moving bank of cloud, bearing more rain. Tine was thankful for the cooler weather. She heard Sharon hurtle down the stairs and slam the front door and a moment later the Porsche hummed to life, the wheels screaming on the gravel as she sped to work.

Tine relaxed with a bowl of muesli until her tranquillity was disturbed by raised voices, followed by the slam of the front door. A moment later Stevie propelled Demmy into the kitchen, her hand gripping hard on the pale girl's wrist. In the other hand she held a folded tabloid newspaper, which she threw onto the breakfast bar.

The first thing Tine noticed was the photograph. It was grainy, but the sweet features of Demmy were unmistakable. Her hair had been carefully combed to cover the shaven side of her head and caught back in a tidy ponytail. Gone were the earrings, nose stud and make-up. She looked young and vulnerable, her eyes wide, her mouth a small pout. The headline shouted: 'Corrupted for Art'. Tine slowly unfolded the newspaper to reveal more pictures. The first was a full-colour reproduction of the demmy.jpg image, the young woman at work between John's thighs. A black bar, strategically placed, made the picture seem more repulsive than had the fellatio been fully revealed. Next to it was John's painting, the one Tine had recently offered for sale. Tine wondered how she had missed the resemblance but then she had not, until recently, found John's private directory containing the original pictures.

She lifted her eyes to peer at Demmy. The young girl stared back with defiant, turquoise-eyed venom. She was still firmly gripped, her wrist flushed around Stevie's vice-like grasp. Stevie waited silently, her expression unreadable. Only her chest rose and fell swiftly to betray her anger. Demmy remained quiet as Tine returned to the paper to read the article.

The journalist had done his homework well. His story covered John's success, his death and carefully described the way the artwork in the picture had been created. His style was objective until he described Demmy, and then it became emotive. She was portrayed as the only child

217

of a divorced mother, protected and innocent. An aspiring artist, she had apprenticed herself to John because she worshipped his work. During their association John had seduced the young girl and forced money on her which, because she was a struggling student, she had accepted.

Tine was described as 'unavailable for comment'; although it was noted that she had recently opened her home to the daughter of a porn baron. John's agent had been quoted, protesting that any art undertaken by John in such a manner formed part of his private collection, and that he had never used models in his work without their full knowledge and consent.

Tine finished reading and sat staring blindly at the newspaper. She was not aware when her tears started, only when the small, wet stains blotted the porous sheet and smeared some words. When she next looked up it was to gaze at Demmy, her eyes awash.

'You must have hated John very much to do this,' she said quietly.

Demmy looked startled, recoiling from the hurt in Tine's eyes. She lost her angry stance and her face crumpled with bewilderment. Whatever she had expected, it was not Tine's painfully soft observation, nor the grief in the older woman's expression.

'I loved him! He didn't need to pay me. I would have done it anyway, for him.' Demmy's voice broke as she tried to recover her anger and failed. She slumped against Stevie who, refusing to loosen her grip, forced Demmy harshly onto a stool.

'It's you. I hated you, you were always in the way. You flounced about the place like an angel, always kind and so stupid. You never understood that you should have just shoved off and left him for me.' The girl's voice was bitter. 'Then he died and I had nothing. You had no time for me. You had it all. You stupid, stupid old hag.' She wailed loudly, almost drowning out the strident and unwelcome demand of the front doorbell.

Tine jerked, as if waking suddenly from a dream, and

gazed with horrid fascination at the howling girl, then slipped from the stool. She nodded to Stevie who changed her hold to grip Demmy's shoulders, the closest that Demmy would get to proffered comfort.

It seemed clear to Tine that Stevie did not trust the display of grief and suspected another trick. Tine, however, realised that Demmy at least believed in her own words, but she amazed herself by feeling no concern. She was sad for John, believing he did not deserve this shoddy, posthumous exposure, no matter how ill-judged his actions might have been.

Tine made her way slowly to the door and opened it to reveal a tall young woman. Slim and tanned, her hair hung in a straight, glossy black fall to her buttocks. She wore faded blue jeans, a chequered shirt and scuffed Doc Martins. A khaki, ex-army knapsack bulged at her feet. Her plain, square face betrayed an American-Indian bloodline, her eyes jet beneath heavy eyebrows. Her expression was calm and serious as she looked at Tine.

There was a moment as they studied each other, and neither spoke. Then the visitor said, 'Hello Astyr.'

The woman's voice was a deep, soft burr made musical with stretched vowels. Tine, startled by the use of her IRC name, was unable to speak.

'I am Dickens.'

Tine blinked once, her eyes drawn by the gentle mounds of Dickens' unfettered breasts and the flat area where masculinity should have bulged in her jeans. She was flabbergasted.

'Actually,' the stranger continued, 'my name is Sky. I am sorry if I've surprised you. I should not have let you continue to believe that I was a man.'

'My name is Tine.' The whisper, even to Tine's ears, sounded remarkably stupid. She was recovering from her bewilderment, delight slowly overtaking her astonishment. 'I – I wasn't expecting you. You've caught me in strange times. Come in!'

She was tempted to divert Sky to the lounge and avoid the kitchen, where the sobs of Demmy were still audible.

But it was Sky who took the initiative. She overtook Tine and entered the kitchen, stood for a moment staring at the scene and demanded, 'Shut up, girl. Your crying is not fooling anyone.'

Demmy stared up into Sky's unyielding glare and subsided into a sulk, her face red and unattractive. Sky sat opposite her and studied Demmy carefully, until the girl squirmed under the scrutiny.

'I am a true-blood Indian, and I can tell you have the jackal in you,' the newcomer said at last, 'I figure you are in the wrong place, and you have done the wrong thing.'

Stevie was peering at Sky with wonder, clearly enjoying the unexpected confrontation. She had softened her grip unwittingly and Demmy chose that moment to slip swiftly out of her grasp in an attempt to scuttle away. Unfortunately her rush propelled her into Tine, knocking her to the floor. Demmy lost her footing and staggered sideways, catching herself painfully on the corner of the breakfast bar. Sky's hand shot out to restrain her.

'This is different.' Sky sounded thoughtful. She gave Demmy a severe look. 'Sit tight, huh?'

Surprisingly the girl did as she was told and slipped alongside Sky, her expression bemused and watchful, as Stevie helped Tine to her feet. Tine bustled around preparing breakfast, glad of the domestic chore, while Sky read the newspaper article. Stevie contented herself with alternately glaring at Demmy and covertly studying Sky. When the American girl finished reading she carefully folded the newspaper and slid it aside. She tucked into toast and fresh orange juice, then announced she was jet-lagged and needed to sleep for at least five hours.

'You be around when I wake up. I need to talk to you.' She peered at Demmy, who nodded silently.

Tine showed Sky to her bedroom. The tall girl surveyed the crumpled satin-clad duvet still scattered with the garments from Richard's boutique. She plucked the video from the clutter and studied the cover.

'Tine, or Astyr, you are one interesting lady!' She bent

and kissed her softly on the cheek, then gathered her in a swift, hard hug. 'I'm exhausted. I'll explain what I'm doing here later – it will make more sense after sleep. But I am real pleased to see you.'

Tine smiled. Sky had walked into her life only half an hour earlier but she seemed a part of the house already. Tine needed time to herself and was reluctant to face Demmy, but she felt she needed to establish some control. As she returned to the kitchen she realised that the telephone calls the previous day must have been attempts by the journalist or John's agent to reach her. She resolved not to answer the telephone if it rang. The damage was done and she felt no need to fight it.

'However, it has got to stop,' she muttered to herself, feeling a little uncertain of what she meant. She entered the kitchen and repeated herself loudly, glaring at Demmy.

'It has got to stop!' The young woman seemed about to respond, but Tine swung towards her. 'Do you hear me Demmy? It will stop now, or you will regret the day you ever set foot in this house; before John's death or after it.' She paused a moment, feeling the anger build in her, a boiling, cleansing flow followed by a cold, determined calm.

'If you seek to hurt me, or John's memory, ever again, I will make sure that nobody, nobody at all, will ever deal with you kindly; no one will protect you, and no one will care if you fall. You are a stupid little girl who has not the first clue about life, and I will crucify you. Do I make myself clear?'

Demmy was shocked into silence. There could be no doubt that the older woman was deadly serious. At that moment she looked more lethal than a furious Stevie. The girl was mesmerised, afraid under the unblinking, brown glare.

'I do not hear you, Demmy,' Tine hissed. 'Do I make myself clear?'

'Yes.'

'Now get the hell out of my house. I will call you

when Sky wants to talk with you and I then expect you to return at a run. Oh, and you bring that back-up tape with you, or I'll have you charged with theft.'

Tine did not stay to argue. She strode into the lounge and threw herself down on the sofa. She breathed carefully through her mouth until she felt her fury ease. Her neck felt stiff, her shoulders tense and her head hurt. She heard the front door close softly and relief seeped over her. She had been very much afraid that, if Demmy had chosen to argue with her, she would have physically attacked the young woman despite the odds stacked against her. She felt angry, tears fighting to escape. She wondered if she could have avoided the problems with the press had she lost her temper with the girl earlier. The thought made her feel guilty.

After Tine had left the kitchen Demmy had sat for a moment, pale and shaken, then risen and softly left the house. She would not reappear until Tine allowed it and Stevie was sure that she would return the tape. Tine's anger and loss of control had clearly left her feeling distressed and Stevie longed to comfort her.

When Stevie heard the telephone ring she ignored it, expecting Tine to answer, but after five rings she answered it herself. After a hurried conversation with a caller who refused to be deflected, she entered into the lounge where Tine was lying.

'It is John's agent. He says the offer on the painting has doubled, and would you consider selling more of the private collection? He's not going to go away until he speaks to you.' There was an apologetic tone in her voice. Stevie had been awed by Tine's anger, and had even experienced a pang of sympathy for Demmy. There had been no doubt in her mind that Tine would ensure every threat would come true if Demmy continued her vendetta. Stevie had been prepared to stand in front of Demmy to shield her if necessary, but also to protect Tine from the likely consequence of the violence of her anger. However, unlike Tine, she suspected that Demmy would have been the loser.

Tine lay on the sofa, her eyes closed and her face drawn.

'Thank you,' she said softly. 'Please will you tell him that none of the private collection will now be sold, and the one he has must be returned immediately. The set will never be broken.'

Stevie padded out and relayed the message. She replaced the receiver softly on the frantic protests pouring down the line, then returned to the lounge and sat on the end of the sofa. She lifted Tine's feet and slowly started a reflexology massage.

'Only you,' Stevie muttered as she pressed her thumbs into the arch of Tine's foot, 'could look ferocious in a T-shirt and no knickers!' She was rewarded with a giggle, followed by a sigh of pleasure as she pinched along Tine's heels.

She took her time, concentrating hard as she worked around Tine's toes, taking each one in turn and pinching along them, then rolling the toe-tips firmly. Eventually resistance ebbed and Tine's small feet could be manipulated freely, Stevie's soothing ministrations seeping into her muscles via the pressure points.

'You need a proper Shiatsu massage.'

Tine rallied reluctantly. 'You must be tired, Stevie. I suspect you had very little sleep.' She described Sharon's return, accompanied by the police.

Stevie felt shocked. She had left the club after a couple of hours, tired out, although Sharon had seemed still energised. The blonde woman had been a huge success and there was no reason to chaperone her. Stevie had been sure she would have received many interesting offers but had not been aware of the proposed tryst with Jerry, nor would she have intervened if she had known.

Tine shuffled to lean against the arm of the chair, her knees drawn up. She appeared unaware that, without undergarments, her pubis peeped temptingly through the diamond-shaped window created by her ankles. She told Stevie all about her agreement to partner Sharon in the opening of her shop, her face alight with anticipation, and the words tumbled out untidily in her effort to relay her excitement at being involved.

Stevie watched her with pleasure. The lounge was dim, the curtains drawn. In the mute light Tine seemed to be childlike, all soft contours and pale flesh. She wriggled her toes as she spoke. Unable to stop herself, Stevie reached across and stroked Tine's calf, as if to still her. She simply wanted to touch her. The limit of her endurance had been reached. She wished to trail her hands over the nearly naked woman and explore Tine's textures and scents. Her yearning felt illicit, but she was aroused. The offer of a massage was an innocent way to get what she wanted. She knew that she was good with her hands and simply prayed that she could control herself and would not take things too far.

'The massage?' she prompted.

Tine hesitated for a moment, during which she rolled her shoulders, grimacing. 'Actually,' she smiled, 'I would love a massage.' She leapt from the sofa and yanked her T-shirt over her head. Naked, she grabbed cushions from the sofa and threw them to the floor, adding herself to the pile, tummy down. She shuffled to achieve a comfortable position and lay waiting.

Stevie stared in surprise and delight. She had grown accustomed to shy clients who awaited instruction. Tine lay prepared, already suggesting the relaxed state which usually took a few minutes of reassuring contact to achieve. Her breathing deepened, the response to conscious effort, and her legs were relaxed, falling slightly apart. She seemed to sink deeper into her mattress of cushions. Tine's willingness confirmed the suspicion that had been buried in Stevie's mind since the previous night; that the older woman was only now admitting to herself that she found her attractive, and maybe even sexually desirable.

Stevie was a thoughtful physical therapist. Despite her arousal, she concentrated hard on untangling the knotted

224

muscles she found in Tine's neck. She worked slowly and methodically to encourage the flow of energy through the starved pressure points, centring the warmth of her healing. As she pressed softly into Tine's lower back, she felt the natural resistance beneath her palms give way to the choreography between practitioner and client, a surrendering to the cure; compliance. Now Tine was truly in her hands and Stevie felt her strength flow into the small form, the flesh becoming warm and responsive under her fingers. As she stroked her hands firmly down Tine's thighs, manipulating along the calves and ankles, Stevie felt extraordinarily powerful and found reserves of energy to pour into her work.

It was only when Tine turned to lie on her back that Stevie's resolution faltered. Before her lay the person she desired most, naked and supine, under her control. She gazed along Tine's body with hungry eyes, resting on the small, areola-tipped mounds. Tine's nipples, moved from the cosy warmth of the cushions, had become pinched. Her tummy with its soft contours rose and fell with her easy breathing. Her thighs were slightly parted and her mound was a shy clam sloping down to pale lobes, closed coyly to shield the pearl within.

If Tine felt the slight tremble of Stevie's hands as they rested on her ribcage, she did not react. Perhaps her breath caught for a moment but the movement was so slight it could have been imagined. Stevie drew her palms firmly to cross each other and worked her way over Tine's hips and stomach. The woman's breasts bounced a little as her body swayed to the rhythm, her flesh elastic and yielding. The sight was distracting and demanding on the second pass and, on the third, Stevie succumbed.

Tine's nipples had eased a little but they were still puckered, betraying that it was no longer the cold which affected them. Stevie empathised, her own breasts hard-tipped and chafing under the material of her tracksuit. She cupped her hands higher, so that when she next drew them together she captured Tine's soft breasts, the nipples firm protuberances which nudged under her palms. Tine's breathing deepened and she lifted her body towards the warm traps, relaxing only when Stevie caressed over, around and between her beasts, her fingers skilfully travelling around, then settling to roll the peaks. Her patience was rewarded when Tine's stomach muscles trembled, and shivers drew her delight to below her waist.

Stevie followed, kneading gently downwards until her hands spanned Tine's hips, fingers teasing above her mound. Tine flexed her buttocks, moaned and shivered in demand. The fleshy clam had opened, the lobes swelling to reveal soft pink underlips, and her pearl peeked shyly from its hood. Stevie slid her hands between Tine's thighs and they parted in anticipation even before she applied pressure. She circled her thumbs softly over her desire's mound, close to her jewel, then drew along each side of the vulva, rubbing inwards so the delicate inner tissues thrilled to the friction of the outer, fleshier lobes. With one hand Stevie continued the massage, while with the other she unzipped the top of her tracksuit. Underneath, her beasts were unrestrained.

She rose to her knees and hooked her thumb under the elastic of her waistband, drawing it downwards until the fabric slid past her hips. She wriggled until her ankles were trapped and gave up, unwilling to attempt the obstacle of her trainers. Then she shuffled forward until she kneeled between Tine's calves, slid her tracksuit top from one shoulder and shook it from her arm, before changing hands and releasing her other arm. Now she reared naked between Tine's legs, both her hands intent on their task.

Her fingers rippled softly, not penetrating the cleft but racing over it, then slowing and tracing around and down, stroking closely along the inner thigh and pressing gently on Tine's mound, urging the flesh down to cloak the pearl with thick pleasure. Stevie edged higher, then bent to Tine, her mouth replacing her hands, working her tongue the same way, over and around; but

226

not until she heard the woman's sharp demand and felt an urgent rise towards her did she penetrate. She slipped her tongue inside Tine's cleft, drawing along the slick, warm canyon with deep satisfaction. She scooped the sweet juices with her tongue, lapping them into her mouth to savour, and inhaled deeply to saturate her senses. The control she had maintained so far was lost and her mouth was feverish and hungry, sliding around the now wide-open maw in frenzied feasting.

Her own cleft was hungry with demand, aching for the pleasure of the meeting of flesh. She wanted to blend with Tine, share her juices and bring her wet, hot pressings to completion. Stevie crawled up a little and edged one thigh closer so she trapped Tine's leg between hers, then swung her weight upwards on her powerful arms, rearing over the prone woman in a frozen press-up. She dropped her head, bent her arms until the muscles bulged, and slowly worked a nipple into her mouth. Her tongue slid and swept, as if she wished to capture the whole mound. She nursed one breast and then the other, until the perspiration slicked over her and her salty sweat dripped on Tine.

Eventually she looked up, her eyes wet and glowing. Below her Tine quaked for release. Stevie lowered herself until she rested on her elbows and covered Tine; their breasts pressed together. When she relaxed her hips, their mounds meshed. Tine shifted instinctively, her thighs clenching the dark, muscular one which lay between. Stevie twisted her weight inwards and Tine rose, shifting to ride her hip into Stevie. They circled, muscles tensing and relaxing, rolling their weight, the flesh of their groins riding.

It was Tine who gently urged Stevie onto her side, lifting her leg until it lay under Stevie's waist and urged her to relax. The weight of the muscular woman settled easily and they rocked slowly, pelvises locked, at arm's length. Tine stroked Stevie's breasts, her small fingers nimble and sure as they rolled and pinched the dark nipples. The anxiety of pre-orgasm had eased to a dreamlike, holistic glow which held no pressure of time; so much so that Tine curved to suckle at Stevie's breasts, the anticipation between her thighs a sweet, postponed pleasure.

They explored each other, never parting their hips, their hands and tongues wandering. Tine leaned away to allow Stevie access, then eased forward to bury her face in the dusky neck. She breathed deeply to inhale the perfume of exertion and lick the sweat and effort from Stevie's still-damp jawline.

When their mouths met, all their senses seemed to focus on the soft teasing of lips and tongues. A curious finger slipped to dance between them, entering their damp mouths and duelling with the writhing tongue-tips. Tine stilled Stevie with small bites along her lips, her sharp teeth grazing along the tender inner flesh. Stevie sucked in Tine's lower lip, holding it taut then releasing and kissing it softly.

Without conscious volition, the rocking resumed. Dark hips worked against the pale as the rocking became a rhythmic bucking which crushed the two together. They stilled, frozen, as the echoes of each movement pulsed back through them. Stevie stared fiercely, her eyes narrowed, to witness Tine's unleashing. The small woman was lost in sensation, her eyes tight-closed, her mouth a gash of ecstasy. She mewled to climax, then growled as the passion rode through her.

For some moments they still rocked, prolonging the throb, then rested to enjoy the wet sharing. They touched and stroked each other, clinging tenderly and kissing softly. Neither wished to leave the warm, moist clench of their thighs, even when a small knock on the lounge door broke their trance.

When Stevie shouted her permission to enter, Sky crept in to press steaming mugs of coffee into their hands. She left for a moment, to return with her own mug, then wound herself into a yoga position alongside the now seated pair. She had swapped her denim jeans

228

for cotton shorts and vest, and her long legs seemed impossibly sleek as her heels rested easily on her thighs.

'So, Astyr . . . ' She smiled softly at Tine, then at Stevie. 'Bring me up to date!' Her eyes wandered with pleasure over the naked and sated pair. Neither would have guessed the situation to be new to Sky, and she was herself amazed at how comfortable she felt. The house carried an aura of peace and acceptance. Love, she reasoned, in all its forms, seeped through the rooms to embrace all comers.

Chapter Fifteen

'*I* can tell you one thing, Dickens. Rupe is going to get a major surprise when he sees you!' Tine eased back on her elbows, wriggling her toes thoughtfully.

She explained the IRC friendship to Stevie, who was fascinated and managed to elicit a promise that she would be introduced to the medium. The conversation ranged between the three of them, mostly discussing the house and its tenants. Sky eventually remembered her appointment with Demmy.

Tine pulled on her T-shirt and went to the office, located Demmy's telephone number and dialled. The hand-set was lifted after the first ring.

'Hello.' Demmy's little-girl lisp was hesitant.

'Come.' Tine's command was soft, and she replaced the receiver gently. She knew Demmy would be on her way. She hoped she would bring the tape.

The telephone rang as she re-entered the lounge. At that moment Sharon burst through the front door and raced to answer it. She looked jubilant, already loosening her hair from its neat pleat and shrugging her suit jacket from one shoulder at a time, swapping the telephone receiver from ear to ear. She tucked it between shoulder and chin and shed her skirt, kicked off her shoes and wriggled with pleasure at the release.

Tine leant against the doorpost, watching the woman strip and remembering the first time that Sharon had discarded her garments in the kitchen. It seemed so familiar now. She was delighted with the thought that their friendship already boasted a history, and that their future was joined and seemed bright. The phrase 'best friends' came to her mind and a sense of well-being flooded through her. They would be business colleagues, companions and partners in adventure, and she believed the contrasts between them would keep the friendship strong. They already knew that no man would come between them; unless it was for consensual sex.

Sharon waved to Tine, whispering, 'I did it!' then paid attention to the receiver. She pointed to the mouthpiece and mouthed, 'Richard.' Tine smiled and continued into the lounge. As she drew the door closed she heard Sharon say, 'Oh, I was telling Tine I'd resigned.' Then, after a pause, 'Yes. Yes, let's do it!'

The scene in the lounge looked much as Tine had left it. Stevie had drawn on her tracksuit bottoms, leaving her firm breasts free to be admired, a task Sky seemed happy to undertake. Sharon soon joined them. She had discarded her blouse and wore a peach-coloured satin bodice, a tiny matching thong and suspenders. She slumped to the carpet, lay on her back and stretched her legs in the air, unclipping and rolling the fine denier stockings. She kicked them from her feet and gave the interested watchers a cheeky look.

'Behold, the porn baron's daughter. Next stop, the naughty shop!'

She had seen the newspaper, she told them, and had alerted her father. He had been furious at the cavalier way that Tine had been treated, the innuendo implicit in the mention of his daughter, and the bloody-mindedness of Demmy. He was taking steps to quell the situation before the bad publicity got out of hand.

Richard was also travelling up to discuss business with them, Sharon informed Tine. She laid her finger

231

against her nose and managed a salacious expression as her eyes told Tine that she expected that her older friend could expect to enjoy far more than a cordial meeting. Only then did she seem to notice Sky, her eyes widening.

'You have longer legs than me!' She demanded a comparison and Sky laughingly stretched out her legs while Sharon nestled beside her. It was true.

When the knock came, Tine went to answer the front door. It was Demmy. She had been reluctant to ring the bell, not wishing to alert the whole house to her presence. When she was ushered into the lounge she realised her caution was futile. Compared to the assembly, she was overdressed in a short black shift dress. Her jewellery and her hairstyle had been restored to their normal state. She was subdued as she quietly handed the stolen tape to Tine, her eyes downcast. Sky patted the floor next to her and the young woman sunk gracefully to sit cross-legged beside the tall American.

Sharon's elation, Stevie's happiness after her love-making with Tine, and Sky's calm curiosity all refused to permit misery. It was not long before Demmy perked up, exhibiting a clever, caustic wit and a laugh so dirty it provoked responding chuckles. In spite of her transgression, she recognised that she was not to be punished and, if she behaved, this company would be good to her.

Tine did not sit down again. Instead she went to the kitchen and threw together a ploughman's lunch, raiding all the shelves of the fridge until platefuls of mixed salad, French bread and cheeses covered the butcher's block. She added pickles and carefully carried the plates through to the lounge, finally returning with a tray laden with small bottles of French beer, chilled Chablis and glasses. Stevie leapt to her feet to help her, her hand brushing Tine's fingers in an intimacy not missed by Sharon. The dark woman was still only half-clad and seemed extremely comfortable.

Sharon recognised the passion shining in Stevie's eyes.

She feared Rupe's reaction but did not think that jealousy was likely. Richard was also clearly interested in Tine. Above all else, she reasoned, Tine's reawakening did not lack enthusiastic participants. If things went well a multi-sided relationship could be on the cards, if all the players were amenable. She just hoped it would be Richard who triumphed in the end. While Sharon had not really become estranged from her father, they had experienced difficult times since her mother's death. She had wanted his full attention, and when new women invaded his bed she had reacted badly and rejected his lifestyle. Her defiant involvement in office work had been useful, a discipline, but now it had served its worth and she could relax into her love of clothes, especially those which celebrated the sexual woman.

She gazed around her. All those scattered on the lounge carpet were highly sexual women. There was Stevie, her dark eyes glistening with satisfaction, her breasts proud and bare. Sky lay comfortable and lanky, her gaze chasing between Tine and Stevie. Tine, now on her hands and knees, was stretching for a jar of pickles as her T-shirt rode up to expose her bare bottom. She seemed so natural, aware of the scents of sex that she and Stevie had generated, yet satisfied the group would find them nothing except pleasing.

Sharon did find them so. She loved the smells of sex, the odours of musk and sweat souring in the aftermath of passion. There was the damp patch on the cushion where Tine had sat after her lovemaking with Stevie, her juices seeping over the dark velvet. Sharon stretched out her leg and felt the small token wet her calf. It was not about Tine's sweet leavings, Sharon thought, it is about sex, the shared fluids. Now she could boast she was involved – they all were.

She looked at Demmy. The young woman was eating enthusiastically. Her fingers dug into the salad and discovered an olive, which she brought to her lips with a gleam of pleasure. She did not pop it into her mouth but pushed it, her lips a moue – she kissed it into her mouth. She licked her fingers, her tongue swirling around her fingertip before she sucked. She would be a greedy lover, Sharon thought, unrefined in her enthusiasm and always willing.

Then there was Sky. Sharon could only see her profile. The American was long, her lines elegant, and reserved. Beneath the calm surface she sensed a deep passion. The beetling brows and wide mouth denied any hint of primness.

'We are a motley bunch,' she stated enigmatically.

As the words left her lips the door opened and Rupe walked in with a stranger. There had been no sounds from the front door. He stood in the doorway surveying the dim room, his astonishment evident, but as he made to leave, Tine noticed his confusion, and leapt to her feet with a protest. She grabbed his hand and drew him to the carpet, beckoning for the stranger to join them in the shared meal. The two men obliged, and swift introductions were made.

Juan, the newcomer, was clearly a programmer. He was older than Rupe, but wore almost the same uniform: cut-off jeans with a loose T-shirt which had obviously visited the laundromat too often. He was fairer than his companion; his hair straight and light brown, scooped untidily into a pink scrunchy which Tine presumed he had acquired from a girlfriend. His face was all straight planes and piercing brown eyes. He had lean, long fingers which caressed his food rather than simply plucking it from the plate, as if testing that the contours pleased him before his mouth accepted the offering. Tine judged him to be in his early thirties.

If Juan was bewildered or embarrassed by the surfeit of female flesh surrounding him then he failed to show it. He glanced around the group with approval, his gaze lingering on Stevie's breasts, Sharon's thighs and then travelling the length of Sky's legs. He peered at Demmy with interest, but his concentration was reserved for Tine, watching her touch Rupe, then Stevie, her eyes fill

234

with laughter as they caught those of Sharon and cloud slightly when she watched Demmy.

Sharon's pose was provocative. One thigh was resting against Sky and she had bent her free leg. The triangle of her thong barely contained her mound. She bulged over the top of the bodice. Some salad dressing had escaped from a piece of lettuce and dripped onto her breast. She carefully drew a finger over the soft flesh, but not until the dressing had run and seeped into the peach satin which barely covered her nipple. She licked her finger and then ran the damp tip over the stained fabric. Her nipple hardened and she looked straight into Juan's eyes, her violet gaze unmistakably predatory.

Juan drew his plate over his lap, where his hardening was obvious, and looked around surreptitiously to see if anyone else was watching. When it became obvious that both Sky and Demmy were, his excitement rose. Demmy licked her lips, her attention fixed on his crotch and Sky looked down at Sharon's breast with a bemused expression.

Rupe had told him a lot, and he had been warned that the house he was visiting had a very liberal atmosphere. Juan felt he had landed in paradise. He was aware enough, given Rupe's words, to recognise that Stevie and Sky preferred women, that Demmy was not fussy and Sharon was a free spirit. Tine was charming; her sexuality seemed to bubble, threatening to explode at the least provocation. It was also clear she and Stevie were intimate.

Surrendering to the inevitable, Juan eased his plate to one side, took a deep breath, and allowed the bulge in his jeans to grow. There was an air of slight suspense, broken only by the low conversation between Tine and Stevie. Soon that, too, ceased.

Rupe was tired. He had been unhappy driving home. As he had feared, he had been promoted, which meant he would have to return to London to manage the project. Juan would take his place at this site. He let the flow of chatter in the lounge wash over him without really listening. From the words he caught he realised they were discussing the Internet, London and a shop in Soho. An occasional burst of laughter caused him to look up.

He was surprised to see Demmy so relaxed and happy, especially as he had seen the newspaper story about John, and he wondered about the tall American woman who had simply been introduced as 'Sky'. As she was seated next to Sharon, who was as underdressed as ever, he assumed they were friends. There seemed to be an undercurrent between Stevie and Tine. The dark girl touched her a lot, the small intimacies made larger by the absence of Stevie's top. Once, as she leaned to reach her beer, her breast brushed against Tine's arm, earning her a smile from the older woman.

Rupe guessed they had become lovers. He did not feel jealous, just hoped that he could share as much time with Tine as possible before his departure on Sunday. He allowed himself to imagine the women coupling; Tine's pale skin against the mahogany of Stevie. His thoughts conjured the clear picture of Stevie suckling between Tine's spread thighs, and he became aware of his erection, and of Sharon's eyes fixed on him.

Rupe could not quiet his thoughts, as images moved in his mind's eye. The remembrance of Tine kneeling before Sharon at the barbecue, her mouth buried in the blonde woman's swollen folds. Then the scene in the garden, Jerry erect as he carried Sharon from view. Tine, on her hands and knees under his desk, her bottom trapped while he fucked her. And Tine on top, riding him as her hand sought her clitoris, her face screwed up in the fierce scowl which preceded orgasm.

Later, Tine would wonder exactly when the atmosphere in the lounge became charged. She was delighted to see Rupe again, and she felt comforted by the familiar man nestling next to her to one side and the loving closeness of Stevie on the other. Then the room seemed to still, the conversation dwindle and then die. When she looked up and sought the reason it seemed all around her.

Rupe and Juan were both clearly excited. Neither made an effort to conceal their manhoods which bulged under their flies; in fact it seemed the opposite. While Juan had laid the view open, Rupe seemed unconcerned, dreamy and unaware. Sharon had focused her hot gaze on Juan and was now slowly circling her nipple with a sharp, polished fingernail. There was a small smile on the blonde woman's beautiful face.

Sky had closed her eyes, her breath quickening. As Tine watched, she opened them again, staring in hypnotic wonder at Sharon. The American's hands were restless, and it seemed that Sky was having difficulty avoiding letting herself touch Sharon. Her thigh pressed outward for greater contact, and eventually Sharon snaked a pale limb over Sky, bending her knee and tucking her foot high so it lodged softly against the American woman's crotch.

Sharon's legs were now wide apart. The thong failed to provide sufficient cover and the string crept loosely along her crevasse, emphasising her vulva. The vee of the triangular peach satin was wet. The view was wide open to Juan, Rupe, Tine and Stevie. Demmy, conscious she was missing out, was the one to break the stillness. She crawled beside Stevie, leaned against the dark woman and stared at Sharon in fascination. Her lips parted.

Demmy had first laid eyes on Sharon at the barbecue and she had been stunned by the woman's beauty. Night after night she had fantasised about her, dreamed of caressing her pale thighs and slipping her fingers in the damp pinkness between. Sharon's quim was as beautiful as she had imagined and she longed to tear away the scant panties and feed voraciously on what lay underneath. She imagined the sharp rake of Sharon's bright nails tearing along her back as she bucked to orgasm. Demmy assumed that it would be Juan who infiltrated

237

that interior and she seethed quietly, determined that she would get her taste of Sharon somehow.

Her anger with Tine had quietened since the small woman had raged at her. In its place had come a dawning admiration. Demmy liked anger, especially when directed at her; it made her thrill with fear but she yearned the physical welts threatened by the bristling energy of confrontation. Sky had said there was a jackal in her and the image felt right. The strong-shouldered beast, scouting for its opportunities, reviled and beaten, appealed to her. She felt her skin tingle, longing for the burn and cut of the strap.

Stevie understood her needs. She had tamed her once with a belt, grimacing as the girl rolled with pleasure when the buckle tore her flesh. After her initial repulsion though, she had been aroused, Demmy's fierce passion making her own blood rise. They had rolled, tearing at each other until the dark girl mounted Demmy's face. She had forced down hard, then buried her face in Demmy's bejewelled quim. When Demmy bit Stevie's swollen vulva, Stevie twisted the clitoral bar sharply and a bolt of agony had lanced through the girl. She came, the wave of orgasm riding hard along the shafts of pain. It was the best experience she had ever had and she longed for a repeat.

Her glance slid to Stevie's naked breast. Again it was she who broke the stillness. She nudged until the dark woman slid her arm around her and then she turned her face slightly, her tongue whipping at the brown skin. When Stevie's nipple hardened she caught it with her teeth and held it firmly. She could suckle on Stevie and still watch Sharon.

Demmy's keen slurps drew Rupe's attention. He watched her for a moment and then groaned softly. Between the feeding girl and him, Tine sat in helpless arousal. Her face wore an expression which he already knew; a slightly lost, unfocused desire. She was watching Sharon and Sky, but her stare strayed to the firm, hard bulge beneath Rupe's jeans and she gazed into his face, wide-eyed, her lips slightly parted. It was as if the sight of him, his green eyes blazing down at her, had cleared her vision, and he knew that her desire for him at that moment was stronger than her awareness of the activity around her.

Rupe gathered Tine into his arms, narrowing his world to her need. His embrace made her T-shirt ride high on her back and bared her to Sky's view. The American tore her gaze from Sharon and examined Tine's small rear. This was the scene which she had imagined during long hours seated at her computer. Rupe and Tine, his firm hands moving over her to cup her breasts, her long chestnut hair falling as she bent to kiss him. For a moment Sky felt distraught at not being the man Tine had presumed and expected; then she acted, easing from Sharon's side gently and slipping away from the pressure of the blonde beauty's foot. It was not a rejection. She had realised that Juan had captured that quarry for now, but she would return and claim her booty at some later date.

Sharon shifted forward onto her knees and beckoned to Juan, who met her half-way. Both were facing each other so that they could still be viewed by Demmy and Stevie. Juan leaned over and placed his mouth over the stain Sharon had tended earlier. When he pulled away his wet mark had enlarged the blot and the nipple pointed harshly at his departure. He slipped his fingers over the top of the bodice so he had a firm grip of each side, then ripped it away. Pearly buttons popped and flew as the fabric tore open.

Demmy gasped, losing her hold on Stevie's nipple, but forced her hand harshly between the dark girl's thighs. The suggestion of violence in Juan's action had tipped her over the edge of control, and clearly had an effect on Stevie, who parted her legs for Demmy, rising to the rough handling. Her own hand rose to cup and pinch her breast, flicking her nipple to hard arousal. Next to her, Tine had stripped Rupe and herself of their

T-shirts, and Sky was enthusiastically assisting in divesting Rupe of his jeans.

It was not the proud arch of Rupe's cock which had increased Stevie's fervour but Sky, who swiftly moved behind Tine, lifting her and almost slamming her down onto Rupe's ready shaft. The woman brought her hands around to cup Tine's breasts and spoke roughly into her neck:

'Oh yes, girl, like we said!'

Stevie recognised that as a reference to their IRC play, and concentrated. She watched the entry as Rupe's rod slid into Tine's moist interior. Sky grasped Tine firmly, one arm crossed and flattening her left breast. She thrust her free hand between her torso and Tine's back, then edged until her captive leaned back towards her. Her fingers sought lubrication, edging around Rupe's slowly thrusting member to drench her fingers, then forcefully penetrated Tine's tight anus. It drew a moan of pleasure from the pinioned woman and she ground down hungrily on the intruding digit.

The bent-back angle of Rupe's shaft was not comfortable, and he moved carefully. He could see Sky's arm imprisoning Tine and, from the pressure on the wall between her cave and arse, he realised that the tall girl had entered her. The knuckles of her bent fingers created a ridge along which his cock travelled with every thrust. When Stevie bowed her head down over Tine's neglected clitoris, he shuddered, watching as the fantasy he had created became a reality. The girl's dark head bobbed at the point of their union, and now and then her thrusting tongue and sucking lips travelled his shaft, as if in benediction.

Demmy forced her head between Stevie's legs. She wriggled onto her back and started to lap in long sweeps, noisy at her task.

'Fuck Demmy,' Sharon commanded Juan. He stopped for a moment, unsure of whether such an action would be welcome, but Demmy merely wriggled out of her pants without pausing at her feed. Soon Juan mounted

240

her and forced his penis in tightly. He carried his weight on straight arms and twisted his head so his cheek nestled on Stevie's bottom. Sharon watched him critically through narrowed eyes, judging his performance. Eventually she smiled her approval. He seemed very fit, moving smoothly from the hip, pistoning rhythmically between Demmy's wobbling thighs.

Sharon stood and walked calmly around to face Tine. She straddled Rupe, so when he looked up he viewed her vivid pudenda. She slipped the string of the thong to one side and lowered herself to Rupe's mouth. With a sigh of pleasure she leaned forward, rubbed her cheek past Tine's, and planted her open mouth over Sky's parted lips. They supped in Tine's ear, their gasps mingling and tongues twining. Tine, frustrated that she could not see Rupe's mouth at work, eventually broke the kiss by grasping Sharon's breasts and forcing her back.

She watched, fascinated, as Rupe's tongue edged and wriggled, tucking in and around Sharon's clitoris. The blonde woman parted her labia with scarlet nails to oblige Tine's view. Rupe's chin was sticky with Sharon's juices. Tine leaned forward, oblivious of Stevie's trapped head, and slipped her fingers around until she encountered Rupe's tongue, which she joined in Sharon's hot canyon. Her touch was not gentle, but Sharon responded to the harsh play by grabbing Tine's wrist and forcing her harder inside her, while she hissed her approval.

'Release me,' Tine murmured breathlessly to Sky, who obliged reluctantly. Tine eased herself from Rupe's penis in spite of his muffled protests, then cupped Sharon's chin and drew her blonde head level with the tip of the naked shaft. The beautiful woman's ruby lips obligingly swallowed the head and stretched wide to take in half his length. Sharon's throat worked smoothly around the shaft and Rupe's groan emanating from her groin betrayed his pleasure.

Tine stroked Sharon's back and watched. The gold blonde waves of Sharon's hair mingled with Rupe's jet curls. It pleased her to watch her best friend suckle her lover. She wanted to see it continue, but that warred with her desire to see Rupe's penis enter and bury itself inside Sharon. She smiled at Sky, who had twisted her fingers in Sharon's hair and was guiding her plunging mouth.

Stevie, deprived of her task, was following Sharon's exertions with fascination, but her imagination was caught up with Sky. She abandoned Demmy's mouth and crept behind the American. She caught the band of Sky's shorts, fingered her way around her hips and slipped the zip down, then eased the scant garment partly from the long thighs before cupping Sky's mound and tugging her backwards. Once the American's bottom was bent and swaying before her, Stevie plunged her face between Sky's bum-cheeks and buried her tongue hard in the tight-ringed anal orifice. Sky's small gasp of pleasure and surprise grew to a rhythmic moan which heightened as Stevie pushed her thumb into Sky's pulsing cave and worked her clitoris with probing, rolling fingers.

Tine left them and knelt beside Demmy and Juan. He pounded himself into the stocky girl, moving faster as she begged him. With each thrust she shook, her breasts bouncing madly. Tine watched Juan's muscles bunch, the sweat running over his back, and realised he could last for a long time. His ponytail had come undone and his hair flew wildly. When he lifted his head to stare at Tine, his eyes brilliant, she suddenly wanted him badly. Unlike Rupe and Red, she perceived a streak in Juan which was truly feral. It repulsed and enthralled her and she wanted to possess it, or for it to possess her.

Juan did not stop pumping into Demmy. He stared into Tine's eyes and seemed to recognise her greed. One of Tine's hands strayed to squeeze Demmy's breast harshly, while her other was clapped to her own mound, clenching rhythmically.

'Ask,' Juan hissed at Tine.

'Please.' Her voice was lost in moans around her. Sky's

whimpers and Demmy's grunts almost drowned the tiny plea.

'Please what?' Juan had almost stilled. His expression was calculating.

Tine felt her lips move silently. She cleared her throat and heard her voice with a strange calm: 'Please screw me, so that Rupe can see.'

Demmy growled in frustration as Juan slid from her and she tried to grab his hips but, slick with sweat, he evaded her and rose to rear over Tine. His penis was heavy, hanging scant inches above her mouth as she gazed up at him. His bulbous tip, huge on its shaft, shone with the wet musk of Demmy. Tine wondered how he could have plunged that massive dome into the short girl. He was too big. His scrotum, purpling and heavy, hung low with the weight of his balls. In wonder, she cupped her hand and hefted his pouch. It was a warm burden, heavy and alive, and she pushed her face into it, feeling the soft balls slide dully over her nose.

Juan's penis quivered. It hung downwards under its own load, rolling heavily to one side as Tine's head shifted in his groin. She raised her head and took the weight of his shaft between her hands. Unable to stop her desire to surround the bulb with her lips, she ran her tongue to his foreskin and tucked around it spiritedly. Her cheeks were coated with Demmy's dew.

Juan was amazed. Rupe's lover wanted him to bury his prick in her, in front of his colleague. One part argued for morality, the other heard Rupe's muffled voice, broken but clear:

'Juan, screw her till she begs to come.'

He lifted his face to the ceiling and wiped the sweat from his eyes. He cast a glance at Rupe. His boss's head was still buried in Sharon's crotch. Sky had released her hold on the girl's blonde head and was now absorbed with Stevie's ministrations. Sharon was sucking and blowing energetically on the head of Rupe's cock, and it seemed that he could not hold out much longer.

Juan helped Tine rise to her feet, and she immediately

turned and whispered in Sharon's ear. The blonde woman swiftly turned to straddle Rupe's weaving rod, waiting until Tine had knelt over Rupe's chest, then lowered herself to take him in. Tine sighed as Rupe's cock slid between the blonde curls and disappeared from view.

As Juan placed his bulb at her entrance Tine knew that Rupe, staring up, could see the intrusion in explicit detail; the hang of Juan's scrotum pendulous above the watchful jade gaze. She could not be sure if he had known of Juan's size. Was he concerned? she wondered, and would he regret his instruction to Juan? It was too late, the man was nudging at her, rocking his hips to aid his entry. Each time he forced a little more, a little harder, and it thrilled Tine although she still feared he would not succeed. Soon he stilled and applied pressure, his hands firm, digging into the flesh of her hips.

Sharon saw the small alarm in Tine's eyes. Inside her, Rupe was satisfying and filling; he was well hung, but the stranger nudging at Tine was exceptionally large. Sharon had glimpsed his heavy organ when he entered Demmy. She placed her hands on Tine's shoulders and held her firmly as Juan forced his entry. He paused and circled his hips lightly, then angled forward again.

He knew from past experience that once his tip was in, it was easy; all he needed to do was wet his bulb thoroughly and stretch that deliciously tight ring. He was surprised at Tine's tightness, although he had no doubt that she was ready. He could see thick fluid gathering in her folds, a drenching he would have anticipated after her orgasm, not before he had entered her. If she showed any resistance he would withdraw: some women balked at this stage and he never, despite his own rampant need, forced his way.

'Okay, baby,' he muttered to Tine, 'if you tell me to stop, I won't mind.' He took his rod in one hand and drew it along her crease, edging it up the cleft between her bum-cheeks and back again. The friction was delicious; if she refused him entry he would merely continue stroking himself along her and jerk himself to release. He almost wished she would refuse; then he would pour himself over her, his jetting stream perhaps reaching the downy, blonde cheeks of the beauty opposite. They could lick each other clean. As he immersed himself in thought he tucked himself within Tine's folds, pressing softly against her ring once more.

Tine thrust back, hard. She moaned loudly as he pushed past her entryway and slid hard into her. To Rupe's astonished gaze, it was as if she had suddenly thrust herself onto a pole. He had been amazed at the size of Juan and would have been happy if she had refused him, but he knew it was her choice. His dark side cried out to see her pinioned on that enormous baton. He had watched the glans, wet with her juices, pressing at her hole and had thrilled. Now his dear, small Tine was filled with foreign flesh, stretched to her maximum with the monstrous impalement. He knew it was she who had fought past the massive head, and felt a swell of pride and naked lust.

He moved his concentration from her to his own succoured member. While he could not see Sharon he could imagine her blonde beauty and violet gaze, and his softening erection burgeoned back into life. As he watched Juan thrusting into Tine, she was viewing Rupe's prick moving in Sharon's wet clench. He groaned and bucked for her eyes and greedily watched Juan move above him, his incredible girth sucking and forging in Tine.

Juan experimented until he felt Tine ease around him, and he then increased his thrust. Tine shuddered, picking up the rhythm. Juan's girth tugged her ring hard and his plunges forced her surrounding skin inwards until she felt the pull on her clitoris and the tight hug of her vulva. No man had been able to produce that heavy tide in her before and her pearl thrilled with sensation, without her intervention. She could feel him deep within her and imagined his fat cock-head fisting into her womb. There was a dull tide of feeling inside her, which she had never experienced before, and she suspected he had done it; broaching the area which no former lover had pierced. Her mind was overwhelmed by the image and she suddenly yearned to be possessed more fully. The increasing demand of her backward thrusts were rewarded and she felt Juan deepen his stroke. He plundered her, the heavy pouch of his scrotum slapping against her trapped clitoris.

Sharon rose in excitement as she watched Tine's face. Her friend was lost in huge sensations, her eyes wide and mouth rounded with surprise as her breath was expelled forcefully in rhythmic moans. Behind her, Sharon heard the eager, quickening cries denoting Sky's imminent coming.

Demmy had crept behind Stevie and was working her orifices roughly with both hands, to encourage the dark girl's wild tonguing of Sky. The stocky young woman was enraptured, hoping that Stevie would exercise the same anal ministry on her at some time. Better still she would seduce Tine. Demmy could see the older woman, wild with the large cock in her. Sharon was riding steadily on Rupe with fierce pre-orgasmic concentration. Her smooth back was damp with perspiration, her nape wet, tendrilled with sticky, gold curls.

It was Tine who came first, keening as a massive tide of ecstasy shuddered through her. Juan rode hard into her spasming body and gouted, flooding her until she felt his fluids would bloat and drown her. It was a delicious, hot pouring which boiled around his waning penis, and he continued to thrust until he was too soft. His penis slipped heavily from her, dragged by its own weight, and his last drops covered Rupe's chest, followed by the flow from Tine's crevice. Juan staggered back, exhausted and empty, and collapsed on his back. He was breathing harshly, as though his heart might erupt. Tine merely fell sideways, her leg strewn over Rupe, sliding in Juan's residue. She felt the rich ooze still seeping from her and drenching her thighs.

Driven by Tine's primeval cry, Sharon arched,

expelled a sharp breath and growled as she ground against Rupe's pelvis. He was torn by her clenching muscles and surrendered his wet offering with a low grunt. Now Tine had fallen from him he could see Sharon, taut and absorbed in the world of her orgasm. She looked majestic, muscles quivering. His rod was purple, still pulsing as she rose swiftly from him then trapped it with her mouth, gulping greedily at his thick, pearly flow.

The cries of Stevie and Sky seemed far away, drowned for Tine by the blood singing in her ears; and for Rupe by his own rough breathing. He felt blindly for Tine and pulled her to his side, cradling her as she nestled in the crook of his arm.

Sharon leaned back against the sofa, surprised when Juan slid to her side and Demmy crawled beside her, to rest her head in her lap. She laid a hand on Demmy's dark hair and sighed. Stevie stretched on her tummy on the carpet and Sky nestled beside her.

The room remained silent for some time while blood settled and breathing eased. Eventually Sharon gazed around.

'It looks like a refugee camp!' she stated, rose, and returned shortly with bottled water for everyone. 'I vote,' she continued, as if she had never left the room, 'that we send out for a take-away. Chinese.' Her suggestion was met with enthusiasm from the weary group. The menu was fetched from the kitchen, and the order telephoned through. Delivery would take half an hour. Nobody had the energy to do more than merely lie around for that interval, although Tine foraged for more wine and triumphantly returned with four bottles of a chilled white.

When the doorbell rang, Juan dragged on his cut-off jeans, produced his wallet and exited to a chorus of protests. He popped his head around the door, beaming.

'Look, it's the least I can do after that!' He punctuated his comment with raised eyebrows and left to a chorus of laughter.

As Tine poured wine and handed out glasses, she felt

thoughts start creeping into her head, beginning to analyse the situation, but she stamped firmly on the intrusion. She was determined to mindlessly enjoy the evening. As she poured the golden fluid into Rupe's glass she smiled, gestured towards Sky and said, 'Oh, Rupe, meet Dickens.' His eyes widened and he stared at Sky's obviously female form, as Tine had done. Sky grinned.

Tine crouched before Sharon, then leant over and kissed her cheek. Demmy had busied herself, helping Juan find chopsticks and plates in the kitchen. They bustled into the room, dispensing aromatic cartons and packets. Before joining in the hubbub to identify their choices, Sharon and Tine clinked glasses in a silent toast.

Tine ate Peking duck, wrapping the shredded skin and plum sauce carefully in the wafer-thin pancakes. She shared her meal with Rupe, who offered her beef with chilli and black bean sauce in return, scattering egg-fried rice across the floor when he attempted to feed her. Demmy chose to eat with a fork, snorting at the wooden chopsticks with contempt. She finished first and wandered through the group, to settle by the video library where she scanned the titles with interest.

'Oh wow! You have *Pulp Fiction*.' Her voice rose with excitement. 'Can we watch it?' Her large eyes pleaded with Tine.

'Yes, but after we've digested, okay?' Tine recalled that some scenes were a little harsh for a full stomach. She stood up, announcing that she was going to have a bath.

'Not before you've digested, okay?' Demmy parried.

Rupe automatically joined Tine. Settled, facing each other in pine-scented suds, he broke the news of his departure. He watched her carefully and was rewarded with her disappointed sigh.

'I hoped it would not be so soon,' Tine admitted, 'but

248

to be honest I didn't think you'd stay the full six months.' She paused. 'I'll miss you.'

Rupe was surprised by the strength of his own sadness. It did seem too soon. So many fantasies were left unfulfilled; fantasies which involved Tine and for which he could not imagine anyone else. He was about to speak, but she leaned forward and placed a finger over his lips.

'Let's not make plans. The future's wide open and I'm sure we'll see each other again.' She smiled. 'This is good, what we have right now. So, no future fears!'

They soaped each other then rinsed with the handshower. Tentatively Rupe proposed Juan as his replacement in the house. A part of him resented the idea that the smooth usurper would almost certainly bed Tine in his attic room, but he recognised his jealousy as puerile. Nonetheless, the memory of the man's rod moving in and out of her, inches from his watchful gaze, caused him to harden. He turned Tine to the wall of amber mirrors, stretching her arms out and imprisoning her hands with his. Wriggling for position, while she shifted to accommodate him, he entered and took her tenderly, watching their gold reflection. When he hesitated, Tine encouraged him. She sighed with pleasure and when Rupe recommenced his stroke, responded with renewed enthusiasm. After the large invasion of Juan, she felt slightly raw. Rupe's increasing pressure burned a little and the feeling was somehow reassuring. She recognised how important he was to her, and the bond they had forged was friendship, close and tender.

'You were the first,' she whispered, not knowing or caring if her words explained her rebirth.

When she came, it was with silent thanks. Juan was an interlude and Red had been a bizarre chance encounter. Stevie was loving and sincere and Sharon was her sister in all things. Now with the sweet ripple subsiding in her, Rupe replete and his cream moist on her thighs, she slipped around to face him. She kissed Rupe softly and, with a sweet, sad smile let him go.

She left him in the bathroom and entered the mess of her bedroom, pulling on jeans and a loose blouse. As she came out she encountered Sharon on the landing. The blonde woman was wearing purple satin leggings and a lacy white sweater which bared her shoulders, and threatened to dislodge and fall away altogether. Her breasts were barely hidden by the fine fleece, her nipples visible. They hooked arms companionably and went in search of a bottle of wine, making their way to the patio with full glasses. It was clear that Sharon had something on her mind.

Chapter Sixteen

*I*t was cool, the evening sky clear, dark and starry. Sharon sat facing Tine, cross-legged on the hard flag-stones of the terrace. They poured the wine and sipped, Tine sensing that Sharon needed time to gather herself. It was obvious that she had questions, and for the first time seemed embarrassed. Finally she evaded Tine's direct approach, and instead said: 'Richard will be here tomorrow afternoon.'

'I look forward to meeting him again.'

'Do you?' Sharon's eagerness was sweet. 'He said he was looking forward to seeing you too.'

There was a silence which Tine broke: 'He can have my room. Stevie can share with Demmy. I can go with Rupe, and Sky can have the pull-out bed in the study. Juan will be in the lounge for the moment.'

'No, you share with me.' Sharon looked embarrassed again.

'You don't want your father to think I am with Rupe?' Tine decided to be direct.

'No.'

'He's leaving on Sunday night, you know. Juan will be here.'

'Are you going to take up with Juan?'

'No, I don't think so – are you?' Tine imagined Juan,

his largeness and the heat of his breath on the nape of her neck. He seemed, like Red, to be a single, rampant experience. In spite of her rational decision she felt herself becoming aroused.

'It is not about Juan,' she appended. 'It's just sex.'

Sharon nodded, and Tine sensed that she understood too well. Her next question was phrased carefully.

'Perhaps Richard could be about sex too?'

'No!' Tine stared at her in surprise.

'You don't fancy him.' It was a statement.

'Oh, but I do. I just think he will matter.'

It seemed that, with Sharon's smile, the evening lit up.

'It already matters, you know.'

'Ye gods, Sharon! I only met him for a second.'

'I know his look, and the way he smiled at you. It's only a matter of time. And you already matter ... ' She paused. 'To me.'

Tine was amazed to see the gleam of unshed tears forming in Sharon's eyes. She reached across and they hugged awkwardly.

'You soppy article.' She grinned happily at the blonde. 'I love you too!'

'And we're going to be rich and wicked together!'

Tine nodded in agreement, although she feared that her wickedness was going to be carefully curtailed by the team of father and daughter. Far from resenting the imposition, she felt herself turn a corner.

'So much in life,' she mused out loud, 'is happen stance. It's about knowing when to stop before the price becomes too high.' She closed her eyes and mentally consigned her fate to time and chance.

She could tell that Sharon did not really understand but the girl nodded sagely all the same, her eyes resting affectionately on her new partner.

'Well.' Sharon tossed back the dregs of her glass, and stood up. 'You have to know when to start as well. seem to have landed on "Go" ... ' she intoned, 'so collect Juan and throw the dice again.'

'Oh yeah? What do you think Richard will make of him?' Tine demanded.

'Probably a movie.'

Tine thought that apt. She eased to her feet and stretched. 'Talking about movies, shall we put Demmy out of her misery?'

'What are we going to do about her?'

'I suppose we've adopted her now. I'll fix up the cellar. If she can't pay rent then she can do the housework and create art on the computer – John did say she had some talent.' Tine was faintly amazed at her own decision, and earned a sideways look from Sharon.

'And Stevie?'

'I don't know.'

'It's "Steve" by the way. They call her that at the club.' Tine, surprised, studied Sharon's profile for a moment. Seeing nothing obvious there, she decided to let it go.

'Okay.'

'Sky?'

'Sharon! You said that office had taught you to organise things, but I didn't expect this! She is here until she is no longer here.' Tine grinned at Sharon's attempt to commandeer her space. She was going to be a pain to work with.

Neither woman moved for a moment. They stood together, breathing in the rain-washed air and looking out over the silvered garden. The lawn had taken advantage of two days of light deluge and was already needing a trim. Tine suspected that daylight would reveal an enthusiastic carpet of weeds amongst the grass.

'Of course,' Sharon sounded thoughtful, 'we do need a new gardener.'

THE GIFT OF SHAME – Sarah Hope-Walker
ISBN 0 352 32935 1

SUMMER OF ENLIGHTENMENT – Cheryl Mildenhall
ISBN 0 352 32937 8

A BOUQUET OF BLACK ORCHIDS – Roxanne Carr
ISBN 0 352 32939 4

JULIET RISING – Cleo Cordell
ISBN 0 352 32938 6

DEBORAH'S DISCOVERY – Fredrica Alleyn
ISBN 0 352 32945 9

THE TUTOR – Portia Da Costa
ISBN 0 352 32946 7

THE HOUSE IN NEW ORLEANS – Fleur Reynolds
ISBN 0 352 32951 3

ELENA'S CONQUEST – Lisette Allen
ISBN 0 352 32950 5

CASSANDRA'S CHATEAU – Fredrica Alleyn
ISBN 0 352 32955 6

WICKED WORK – Pamela Kyle
ISBN 0 352 32958 0

DREAM LOVER – Katrina Vincenzi
ISBN 0 352 32956 4

PATH OF THE TIGER – Cleo Cordell
ISBN 0 352 32959 9

BELLA'S BLADE – Georgia Angelis
ISBN 0 352 32965 3

THE DEVIL AND THE DEEP BLUE SEA – Cheryl
Mildenhall
ISBN 0 352 32966 1

Published in July

LORD WRAXALL'S FANCY
Anna Lieff Saxby

1720, the Caribbean. Lady Celine Fortescue has fallen in love with Liam, a young ship's officer, unaware that her father has another man in mind for her – the handsome but cruel Lord Odo Wraxall. When Liam's life is threatened, Wraxall takes advantage of the situation to dupe Celine into marrying him. He does not, however, take into account her determination to see justice done, nor Liam's unlikely new alliance with some of the lustiest pirates – male and female – to sail the Spanish Main.

ISBN 0 352 33080 5

FORBIDDEN CRUSADE
Juliet Hastings

1186, the Holy Land. Forbidden to marry beneath her rank, Melisende, a beautiful young noblewoman, uses her cunning – and natural sensuality – to seduce Robert, the chivalrous, honourable but poor young castellan she loves. Capture, exposure, shame and betrayal follow, however, and, in her brother's castle and the harem of the Emir, she has to exert her resourcefulness and appetite for pleasure to secure the prize of her forbidden crusade.

ISBN 0 352 33079 1

Published in August

THE HOUSESHARE
Pat O'Brien

When Rupe reveals his most intimate desires over the Internet, he does not know that his electronic confidante is Tine, his landlady. With anonymity guaranteed, steamy encounters in cyberspace are limited only by the bounds of the imagination, but what will happen when Tine attempts to make the virtual real?

ISBN 0 352 33094 5

THE KING'S GIRL
Sylvie Ouellette

The early 1600s. Under the care of the decadent Monsieur and Madame Lampron, Laure, a spirited and sensual young Frenchwoman, is taught much about the darker pleasures of the flesh. Sent to the newly established colony in North America, she tries in vain to behave as a young Catholic girl should, and is soon embarking on a mission of seduction and adventure.

ISBN 0 352 33095

To be published in September

TO TAKE A QUEEN
Jan Smith

Winter 1314. Lady Blanche McNaghten, the young widow of a High-land chieftain, is rediscovering her taste for sexual pleasures with a variety of new and exciting lovers, when she encounters the Black MacGregor. Proud and dominant, the MacGregror is also a sworn enemy of Blanche's clan. Their lust is instantaneous and mutual, but does nothing to diminish their natural antagonism. In the ensuing struggle for power, neither hesitates to use sex as their primary strategic weapon. Can the conflict ever be resolved?

ISBN 0 352 33098 8

DANCE OF OBSESSION
Olivia Christie

Paris, 1935. Grief-stricken by the sudden death of her husband, Georgia d'Essange wants to be left alone. However, Georgia's stepson, Dominic, has inherited Fleur's – an exclusive club where women of means can indulge their sexual fantasies – and demands her help in running it. Dominic is also eager to take his father's place in Georgia's bed, and further complications arise when Georgia's first lover – now a rich and successful artist – appears on the scene. In an atmosphere of increasing sexual tensions, can everyone's desires be satisfied?

ISBN 0 352 33101 1

If you would like a complete list of plot summaries of Black Lace titles, please fill out the questionnaire overleaf or send a stamped addressed envelope to:-

Black Lace
332 Ladbroke Grove
London W10 5AH

WE NEED YOUR HELP . . .
to plan the future of women's erotic fiction –

– and no stamp required!

Yours are the only opinions that matter.

Black Lace is the first series of books devoted to erotic fiction by women for women.

We intend to keep providing the best-written, sexiest books you can buy. And we'd appreciate your help and valued opinion of the books so far. Tell us what you want to read.

THE BLACK LACE QUESTIONNAIRE

SECTION ONE: ABOUT YOU

1.1 Sex (*we presume you are female, but so as not to discriminate*)
Are you?

Male	☐
Female	☐

1.2 Age

under 21	☐	21–30	☐
31–40	☐	41–50	☐
51–60	☐	over 60	☐

1.3 At what age did you leave full-time education?

still in education	☐	16 or younger	☐
17–19	☐	20 or older	☐

1.4 Occupation _____

1.5 Annual household income
       under £10,000 ☐   £10–£20,000 ☐
       £20–£30,000 ☐   £30–£40,000 ☐
       over £40,000 ☐

1.6 We are perfectly happy for you to remain anonymous;
but if you would like to receive information on other
publications available, please insert your name and
address

_____

_____

_____

_____

SECTION TWO: ABOUT BUYING BLACK LACE BOOKS

2.1 How did you acquire this copy of *The Houseshare*?
       I bought it myself ☐   My partner bought it ☐
       I borrowed / found it ☐

2.2 How did you find out about Black Lace books?
       I saw them in a shop ☐
       I saw them advertised in a magazine ☐
       I saw the London Underground posters ☐
       I read about them in _____
       Other _____

2.3 Please tick the following statements you agree with:
       I would be less embarrassed about buying Black
       Lace books if the cover pictures were less explicit ☐
       I think that in general the pictures on Black
       Lace books are about right ☐
       I think Black Lace cover pictures should be as
       explicit as possible

2.4 Would you read a Black Lace book in a public place – on
a train for instance?
       Yes ☐   No

SECTION THREE: ABOUT THIS BLACK LACE BOOK

3.1 Do you think the sex content in this book is:
Too much ☐ About right ☐
Not enough ☐

3.2 Do you think the writing style in this book is:
Too unreal/escapist ☐ About right ☐
Too down to earth ☐

3.3 Do you think the story in this book is:
Too complicated ☐ About right ☐
Too boring/simple ☐

3.4 Do you think the cover of this book is:
Too explicit ☐ About right ☐
Not explicit enough ☐

Here's a space for any other comments:

SECTION FOUR: ABOUT OTHER BLACK LACE BOOKS

4.1 How many Black Lace books have you read? ☐

4.2 If more than one, which one did you prefer?

4.3 Why?

SECTION FIVE: ABOUT YOUR IDEAL EROTIC NOVEL

We want to publish the books you want to read – so this is your chance to tell us exactly what your ideal erotic novel would be like.

5.1 Using a scale of 1 to 5 (1 = no interest at all, 5 = your ideal), please rate the following possible settings for an erotic novel:

Medieval/barbarian/sword 'n' sorcery ☐
Renaissance/Elizabethan/Restoration ☐
Victorian/Edwardian ☐
1920s & 1930s – the Jazz Age ☐
Present day ☐
Future/Science Fiction ☐

5.2 Using the same scale of 1 to 5, please rate the following themes you may find in an erotic novel:

Submissive male/dominant female ☐
Submissive female/dominant male ☐
Lesbianism ☐
Bondage/fetishism ☐
Romantic love ☐
Experimental sex e.g. anal/watersports/sex toys ☐
Gay male sex ☐
Group sex ☐

Using the same scale of 1 to 5, please rate the following styles in which an erotic novel could be written:

Realistic, down to earth, set in real life ☐
Escapist fantasy, but just about believable ☐
Completely unreal, impressionistic, dreamlike ☐

5.3 Would you prefer your ideal erotic novel to be written from the viewpoint of the main male characters or the main female characters?

Male ☐   Female ☐
Both ☐

5.4 What would your ideal Black Lace heroine be like? Tick as many as you like:

Dominant	☐	Glamorous	☐
Extroverted	☐	Contemporary	☐
Independent	☐	Bisexual	☐
Adventurous	☐	Naive	☐
Intellectual	☐	Introverted	☐
Professional	☐	Kinky	☐
Submissive	☐	Anything else?	☐
Ordinary	☐	_____	

5.5 What would your ideal male lead character be like? Again, tick as many as you like:

Rugged	☐		
Athletic	☐	Caring	☐
Sophisticated	☐	Cruel	☐
Retiring	☐	Debonair	☐
Outdoor-type	☐	Naive	☐
Executive-type	☐	Intellectual	☐
Ordinary	☐	Professional	☐
Kinky	☐	Romantic	☐
Hunky	☐		
Sexually dominant	☐	Anything else?	☐
Sexually submissive	☐	_____	

5.6 Is there one particular setting or subject matter that your ideal erotic novel would contain?

_____

SECTION SIX: LAST WORDS

6.1 What do you like best about Black Lace books?

_____

6.2 What do you most dislike about Black Lace books?

_____

6.3 In what way, if any, would you like to change Black Lace covers?

_____

6.4   Here's a space for any other comments:

_____

_____

_____

_____

_____

Thank you for completing this questionnaire. Now tear it out of the book – carefully! – put it in an envelope and send it to:

Black Lace
FREEPOST
London
W10 5BR

No stamp is required if you are resident in the U.K.